"Stop where you are,
where the strawberries grow."
Frank Ricapito, age three

Table of Contents

Prologue

Dovie moved restlessly around her stateroom as she dressed for dinner. She jumped when the whistle of a paddle wheeler sounded as it approached the dock. Her nerves were on edge after her latest quarrel with Grover. On the wharf, she saw a miner in dirty, worn clothing leading two pack mules, a group of Union soldiers in their blue uniforms, Chinese in coolie hats and pajamas, and a great many men in bowler hats and collarless shirts.

In her mind she composed a letter to her sister describing the busy scene. *Dear Shelagh, from my window, I look through white satin curtains*, she touched the blue cord that tied them back, *and see the port of St. Louis.*

She started over: *Dear Shelagh, I am married to a man named Grover Ames.*

It would be nice to make Shelagh a bit jealous. *We live on the riverboats and dine out every night.* Shelagh must never know the truth about Grover. Dovie's face burned at the very thought of the words Shelagh would use: *card cheat, crook.*

Dovie opened the box on her dressing table. Inside was gold dust, taken by Grover to settle a gambling debt. Some of it was coarse like cereal, some fine powder. She sifted some of the gold powder into her palm. Holding her breath so as not to blow it away, she put a small amount into each hand. She lifted her curved hands and brushed gold dust on the waves of her red hair. *If only you could see me now*, she said to her sister. She turned her head this way and that to see the gold gleam in the mirror.

Her face pink with excitement, she stood up and looked at her splendid reflection wearing her pale dress with white lace. It was useless to think of telling Shelagh about Grover's fine-looking ruffled shirt, brocade waistcoat, and white gloves because she didn't know where her sister was, only that she was somewhere in Colorado Territory.

She draped a shawl around her shoulders and turned out the lamp before she left her room. Grover was already upstairs with the other gentlemen.

Entering the salon, she paused at the top of the stairs until every eye was on her. She removed one glove, pulling each finger off. Looking down, she could see admiration shining in Grover's eyes. Moments like this were the only shred of life left in their marriage. She swept down on him and his companion, a young man with a mop of hair, who watched her, dazzled.

Grover had already chosen his victim for the evening and introduced Mr. Tolliver to her. She took notice of his black silk waistcoat, white under-waistcoat, and frilled cuffs. She announced that she was too warm. He bent his round, white neck that curved swanlike to hear her. She removed her shawl. Up close, his cheeks were plump and smooth above his stiff collar points and seemed fresh from a mother's pecks and kisses. She smiled on him, noticing how his hair feathered below his ears.

He saw that he was seated next to her at the table. She repeated, "Oh, Mr. Tolliver!" so many times at dinner that she thought herself ridiculous, but alas, Mr. Tolliver did not. His eyes followed her every move over his wine glass, and his honking laugh greeted any pleasantry. After dinner, he was all too easily led to the card table where she left him with a sugary smile. He would be thoroughly plucked by Grover, but she did not have to stay to watch.

As she left the room, Grover was cutting the deck of cards, but his eyes met Dovie's. Her look was full of contempt for Mr. Tolliver, so easily led on; for Grover, a heartless crook; and for herself, smirking and displaying herself.

As she walked through the salon, she heard music and saw a young girl seated at the piano. The first notes brought her back to her mother on the piano bench with Dovie seated close beside her. Her mother, with a crown of braids wound around her head, hummed and picked out the tune by placing Dovie's small fingers on the keys. The girl in the salon began to sing, and the sound of her pure, young voice drove Dovie from the room.

VIII

Wales

Five years before, Dovie was in the mountain village in Wales where she was born and had lived the first ten years of her life.

She walked behind her mother, who was huddled in a thick gray cloak and rode the only horse. Her sister, Shelagh, came next, and two dogs that had followed from home. Gussie, the maid, followed at a distance on the narrow path. The small procession emerged onto the cliffs where a cold wind sent their long skirts flying. The sea below turned and glittered in the sun.

Dovie saw that her mother, Muriel, had to make an effort to stay seated on the shifting back of the horse as it picked its way over the rocks. Once on level ground, the horse tossed its head and trotted forward. The dogs chased each other underfoot, barely missing the horse's hooves. Dovie turned and kicked a pebble off the cliff. Gussie hung back, swaddled in a cast-off cloak of her employer.

"Gussie is following, Mother," Dovie tattled.

They continued along the road.

"Let her come then. I don't want her and she knows it." Muriel spoke without turning. Dovie said no more out loud. It was a game she and Gussie played at. Gussie would pinch her in the morning if she dawdled about dressing, and Dovie would tattle on Gussie in the afternoon. "Mother, Gussie dropped the whole tray of tea biscuits and then…"

1

"No more, child, haven't I told you I don't want to hear tales..."

"But, Mother, then she just brushed them on her apron and fed them to..."

"Hush or you'll be in trouble."

Dovie looked down at her new dress, warm, dark blue, linsey-woolsey. Her gold medal was around her neck on a shiny chain. She had worn it every day since it had been presented to her by the headmistress for excellence in arithmetic and literature. She had never been prouder of anything in her life and looked down frequently to see the engraving of a hand lifting wisdom's flaming torch.

Her leather shoes Dad brought all the way from Cardiff. For Shelagh, he had brought new boots that buttoned with a hook. Her sister moved a little ahead, humming to herself. The sun shone on her red hair that waved in curly tendrils. Shelagh said to stay out of Gussie's reach if she seemed angry. As the older sister, Shelagh was fond of giving advice.

They wound uphill. There was the Reeses' place. Dovie had never been inside this isolated house but Shelagh had told her that the Rees family was so poor that they ground the yellow gorse that grew on the hillside and boiled it to eat. The house was made of rocks piled between boulders with lichen growing up the walls.

The commotion of their passage brought children to the door where they clustered, looking out. Mrs. Rees came out. Dovie sighed; now she would stand in the road saying, "Mrs. Lloyd, how is this and how is that." Muriel stopped. Mrs. Rees blocked the path waving a paper. Dovie pretended to pet the dogs so she could get a closer look at the Rees children with their dirty faces and layers of faded clothes. A girl Dovie's own age had rags tied around her feet instead of shoes. The girl saw Dovie staring at her feet and stepped back into the gloom of the house. Dovie knew the oldest son had left for America, tired of rags and hunger. She parked herself on a corner of the house, which was a large stone cracked by frost.

"A letter from Clwyd. He's gone to America, to a place called Ohio. I never did hear of it, did you?" Mrs. Rees handed the letter to Muriel. "I'll hear it again if you'll read it out to me. I am not but a little lettered."

"'Dear Father, Mother, and Brother Owen, and sisters,'" Muriel read. I was on the ship a long time and hungry and…'" "His hand is hard to read," Muriel complained. She squinted her eyes and held the paper farther away. "Here, Dovie, you have young eyes. You try it."

Preening a bit, Dovie stepped over the dogs lying at her feet and took the letter in hand. She moved her lips over the paper and then commenced, "Hungry and stomach bad." Dovie frowned and said, "That ought to be 'stomach felt badly." She continued to read, "'I thought I would never get here. When we saw the harbor of New York, most people cried. I come here in Ohio two days on the train and am pretty far into the land. I have a job and everyone here has work not like at home. There is free land and I aim to get some. Your son, Clyde, which you call Clwyd." Dovie paused and then announced to all, "I'm ten years old and best at school in reading, penmanship, and French language."

"She's got a good opinion of herself, this one," Mrs. Rees said. She slapped her hands together indicating what she thought this opinion deserved. "My Clwyd, he was good at school. I can say that without bragging a bit. You better from your condition, Mrs. Lloyd?"

"No, but I'm bound to see the preacher, this Preacher Jones. I want him to put my mind at ease."

"And what is it that bothers your mind, missus?"

"If I must go, it's the afterlife I want to be sure of."

"Has it come to that? Ah, the poor child here! And her sister." Mrs. Rees turned to Dovie and patted her head.

Dovie frowned and flipped her hair away from the woman's hand. "Well, it's red and it's curly her mother had told her. "With every advantage, Gwendolyn, comes a disadvantage." Her mother only called her by her given name when she was being serious and preaching. "If you have something pretty, people want to get their hands on it," she said.

"I'm not a poor child," Dovie said.

This was ignored and Muriel went on. "They'll have their dad, and he's promised to take care of them as though I were still here. I made him swear it on his Bible."

3

"I know we've missed the preacher." Though a toothless, old servant, Gussie had learned how to get her way. "I know he's come and gone and we stand here in the road."

Without ceremony Muriel kicked the horse's sides and it lurched forward. "This preacher, he's one-eyed, but they say he's eloquent."

The party brushed past Mrs. Rees, who hurled her last bit of conversation after them. "It didn't do him no good though. For all his learning, my Clwyd found no living here in Wales." She shivered and returned to her lonely house folding the letter back into its envelope.

The procession went on in silence. At the top of the next rise, Dovie, still smarting, blurted out, "My dad owns his own store. I should have told her that."

Shelagh gave Dovie an annoyed look. "Don't you think she knows that? Everyone hereabouts trades at the store."

"Look!" Gussie said. She pointed to the crossroads below. There, people were converging, some on foot or in wagons, some on horseback. "See, a grown man in a wheelbarrow!" Gussie's face had lost its habitual scowl and looked alive with interest.

The girls looked and laughed. "The boy who is pushing him is so small. The man is smoking a pipe. I bet he's lame," Shelagh said.

"And I bet he's just lazy," Dovie replied.

They hurried down the hill and joined the throng streaming toward Preacher Jones who sat on a mule at the crossroads.

"Come one, come all! We have here with us a girl of sixteen who's walked barefoot over the hills. How many miles?" The preacher bent to listen to a girl with dark curls. "Over the Dee, she's crossed over the River Dee. And why have you crossed over the River Dee?" he shouted. He bowed his head to listen, then threw his head and arms open wide to the sky. "She's walked barefoot, barefoot over the Dee to get a Bible from Preacher Jones!" The crowd had drawn near and turned their faces toward the girl.

Dovie hurried ahead to look at the girl, who now carried a brand-new Bible and clutched it to her heart with both hands. Dovie looked at her feet and saw dark mud on feet red with

4

cold. "What's your name?" Dovie would have liked to ask her, but the crowd pushed her on.

A man leaning heavily on his cane called out, "How far? How far to go?"

"You are near, brother, near to salvation! Walk on this road!" Preacher Jones led them and they followed.

Dovie came up next to her mother, who was saying, "My husband's people are great believers, but they don't hold with these Methodists. They will preach in a barn or your neighbor's house as soon as in a church."

The skinny woman riding next to her shook her head. "They say he gets the lame to dance, this Preacher Jones."

"Here's my daughter, Dovie," Muriel said.

"Oh, the poor child. It's lucky they don't know what's ahead of them. The poor thing."

Dovie retied the bow on her new, lace-trimmed, velvet hat to draw attention to it and show that they were rich. She couldn't hide her annoyance at being called "poor thing" again.

But the woman, astride a big horse, was busy talking about herself. "Now me, I like a good, rousing sermon. I, myself, have never sinned. Most of them here want forgiveness. When the preacher says, 'All you sinners repent...'"

Muriel snorted in her face. "What about the sin of pride, missus? Some don't recognize a sin even if it's staring at them out of their own mirror." Muriel rode on. "Dovie, come along," she called.

Dovie walked forward but twisted her head around to get a good look at a sinner as she followed her mother.

On a hillock, the preacher sat in the saddle of his sturdy mule. Preacher Jones had a black patch over one eye, but the other eye glowed. In a high-pitched voice he harangued the people gathered below. He shouted, he singsonged. He made them laugh and cry and believe his warnings.

"Flames will forever burn in the stomach of the glutton. The eyes of the envious will be sewn closed with hot needles and thread of rusted wire."

When he seemed to stop, the people cried, "Go on, go on." His helpers came through the crowd carrying sacks and people tossed in coins.

A song was started, and on the words, "As David danced before the ark," a man and woman began to jump and leap, shouting praise to God. Others joined in clapping and singing. The shuffling sound of heavy shoes seemed to intoxicate the swirling mass of people. Few noticed the preacher slip away in the dusk.

Dovie's mother called herself a free thinker, so when Dovie came upon her kneeling before the shrine the preacher had set up, she stopped, surprised.

"He's weak, and without me to tell him what to do in the morning, I don't know how he'll get through the day," Dovie heard Muriel say. "He's that dependent. More like my child than my husband. I have to wind him up like a clock every morning and set him ticking. 'What about the big, gray hog? Shall it be slaughtered?' he asked me the other day. 'Keep it, of course, for siring,' I told him.

"Lord, if you could see your way to sparing me, I'd be so happy. If I am spared I'll sew you a robe." She rubbed her cold fingers together. "Let these hands be strong again, and I'll make you a beautiful, blue robe for the Easter service."

Dovie turned away. It seemed wrong to spy on her mother and overhear her prayers. Something else bothered her. *Weak.* She didn't want to think about it. And *spared*, what did mother mean? Dovie walked away.

Two girls who had called to her earlier grabbed Dovie on the path. The one with braids took her arm and smiled into her face. The other laughed and pulled her along. They hurried toward the sound of shouting and music from fiddles and a horn. Out of the woods they came and burst into a scene of leaping dancers who called and sang.

Dovie was pulled into the circle. Faces and bodies went by in a whirl. She felt a tug on her hair as the girl next to her pulled the lace cap off Dovie's head. The girl ran, her braids flying out behind her.

Dovie opened her mouth and shouted, "My cap! You thief!"

No one heard her. She looked around; the other girl was gone, too.

Gussie pranced past, her face transformed by a loose smile. She had looped her skirts over her arm and showed thin shanks as she clogged.

6

Dovie yelled again, "Thief!"

The woman without sin was in front of Dovie. She had her mouth wide open shouting, "Glory, glory!"

Dovie tried to run past, but the woman's foot came out and tripped her and she fell to the ground. With her face in the dirt, big tears squeezed out of her eyes as the dancers stepped over and around her.

Everyone clapped and dropped back as a girl stepped to the center of the circle. She danced, shimmying and tossing her black hair. People in fine clothes held the hands of grimy workers and chanted, "Holy, holy." Couples drew away into the shadows where the tussle of bodies carried on the frantic pace of the dance.

Dovie pushed herself to her feet and stumbled to the edge of the clearing. Her shoe was coming loose. She wiped sweat off her forehead and leaned her shoulder against the rough bark of a tree. In the light of the flames, she could see the slobber hanging on a man's jaw and watch as a child, slyly wielding a knife, cut the purse off his belt. He noticed nothing as he pawed the mother and tried to land a kiss on her lips.

She turned away from the sight and went into the darkening woods. She walked a few seconds. It was quiet, and she put her foot up on a rock to tie her shoe. Beyond her, back in the trees, she heard something, the boom and gurgle of a river rushing down its twisted course. She listened to the familiar sound but heard something more, low moans. Cautiously, she moved in that direction.

She heard the sound of thrashing, and then around a large rock saw the sprigged and flowered skirt of the Bible girl and a tangle of muddy boots and bare legs in the air. As Dovie moved forward, her foot struck something. She bent down; it was the girl's Bible thrown to the ground. Two figures pressed together in front of Dovie. Head tossing, the Bible girl seemed to meet Dovie's eyes but without recognition. Dovie turned and ran, her hair falling in her face with no cap to hold it back.

She went toward the light of the campfire. She searched the crowd. "Mother!" she screamed, but no one answered.

She came upon a pale figure collapsed against a tree, uttering bits of prayer. She had found Gussie. Dovie called her name.

When the maid looked up, her face was sour again. Dovie felt a jolt of gladness; Gussie's pursed lips and beady eyes were familiar in the midst of strangeness.

"Where have you been?" Gussie asked her accusingly.

Dovie didn't mention the dancing.

"Your mother is past ready to go."

A few shouts rang out in the cold. The first stars had appeared in the sky. Mother sat quietly at the edge of a group that sang hymns around the campfire. Dovie would recognize her anywhere with her braided hair wound high around her head. She looked frail in the flickering light as Shelagh sat beside her and held her hand. They helped her up and onto the horse's back.

They joined the line of people leaving the valley. The procession toiled a long way up to the top of the hill. In the dark, Dovie's group diverged from the rest.

Next to them, a bearded man pointed to the sky and called, "We'll all meet again up there."

His bony finger was outlined by the vast sea of stars above. Dovie looked up and felt small and insignificant. Even the earth under her seemed tiny below the immensity of twinkling stars and velvety darkness. The larger group went on, chanting as they went. The sound receded into the distance. The three plodded in silence following Muriel on the horse.

After a long while Dovie said, "Is your mind set at ease, Mother?"

There was no answer for so long that Dovie felt the heat of embarrassment warm her face.

Then, her mother's angry voice came out of the dark. "I hoped too much. He was only a man. When he rode away, I knew the trip had been misguided." There was a pause. "I leave my two girls in the world. My time is running out. The thought of that drives me wild."

"What do you mean, Mother? Time is running out?" Shelagh asked.

"If only spring would come. Warm weather and you'll feel fine. You'll plant your garden again," Dovie said, beseeching her mother.

As she turned, she saw Gussie's face, her mouth twisted in a skeptical grimace just as when the peddler tried to sell her fish with sunken eyes. A chill came over Dovie. Muriel was still strong in her mind and opinions, but her body had all the signs of weakness that could lead to death. Dovie saw that this was what death was, the body wearing out.

The rest of the long trudge home passed in a trance for Dovie. She felt the sharp rocks underfoot on the hilltops and heard her boots squelch water in the valleys, but her mind was numb.

☆ ☆ ☆

Dovie awoke hearing the sound of a ship's horn down below in the harbor. It was a sound she had heard all her life. The ship would be leaving the harbor, sliding away into morning fog. It was nice to lie in her warm bed and hear the distant sounds. This would be the newly built packet boat going to Ireland.

The whole town would be listening; those who had bought shares would listen with special interest. The ship would go with the good wishes of most of the town. Her Dad bought shares whenever Gruffydd's had a venture. Gruffydd, the shipwright, was among the best of them, Dad said. Dovie liked the thought that her ship was out on the ocean, that now she, too, had her venture. She had begged to join in.

"Even Gussie buys her penny's worth! Why can't I?" she said.

Muriel let her put money on the packet boat, *Delight*, sailing to ports in Europe.

"He's a savvy captain who trades well, and if no storms get his ship you'll see profits," her mother said. "But if it's lost, well, you had better be prepared for that, too."

Gussie came into the girls' room to light the fire, grumbling to herself.

"Up since five o'clock. I work while they sleep. Lumbago in my back and the weather damp."

Gussie laid Dovie's petticoat and gray, everyday dress out on the bench in front of the fire to warm.

9

Dovie gave a big yawn and stretch. Gussie had uttered this or similar complaints so often she hardly heard them anymore. She pulled the goose down comforter up around her shoulders. She liked to wait until the fire had taken the chill off the room before she put her feet on the cold floor.

"A headache like a thorn in my head. Will you be going out or staying in, Miss Shelagh?"

"In."

"The brown wool then." Gussie continued grumbling, "No one will remember me when I'm gone. I'll not even have a stone over my grave. Mark my words, I'll not be here come next Christmas."

Silence. Then Shelagh said in a cajoling tone, "Oh, Gussie, of course you will. It wouldn't be Christmas without you, and besides, Dad needs you to make his tea every morning."

They all knew Gussie was loyal only to Dad. She had come to the household long ages ago from his family.

Dovie, sitting up in bed, said thoughtfully, "Mrs. Rowlands used to complain a lot, too, and look, she outlived her own daughter." Ignoring a look from Shelagh, Dovie went on, "Seems like the complainers live longer somehow."

"Dovie!" Shelagh said.

"Dovie, the last one out of bed or dressed. Same as every morning!" Gussie complained.

"Miss Dovie! When do I get to be called Miss Dovie? You always call her Miss Shelagh."

"When you are twelve years old and not before. I've known you in nappies!"

Later that Saturday, Dovie sat basking before the fire as she read a book. The new maid, a girl from the country, came in bringing hot tea and a lap robe.

"Your mother sent this, Miss. Said to tuck it around yourself and stay warm, miss."

"I don't want it. Take it away, Sallie. No, wait, I'll take it after all. There, tuck it around my feet."

As Sallie handed her a cup of tea, Dovie recoiled. "Your hands are dirty," she said.

The maid's face turned red; she continued to hold out the teacup.

"Go and wash before serving tea," Dovie ordered her.

"Sorry, Miss," the girl whispered and left the room.

Dovie heard the jangle of a harness and bells outside. She knew what she would see but got up and went to the window anyway. The sky was full of clouds. She had just finished reading that Wales was the rainiest place in Britain. She looked down on a wagon that was only some wide planks with sides nailed on. It was pulled by a horse of a gray color like ice when it had cold, dark water underneath. This equipage was driven by Miz Emrys, whose thin body was clothed in layers of skirts and sweaters. Dovie had tried to count the hems of different colors but still wasn't sure how many the woman wore.

"Rags, metal, paper!" At the sound of the cry, Muriel put on a shawl and went outdoors. It was rare nowadays for her to feel strong enough to go out.

Mother actually seemed to like that old creature, Dovie thought. She stared out the window at her mother. Muriel's hair was hanging down unbraided. She held on to the stair rail to have her usual little chat.

"You're alone today. You had a man riding with you last time," Muriel said.

Miz Emrys puffed on the pipe in her mouth. Her hands were filthy as she reined in the knobby-kneed horse.

"Yep," Miz Emrys answered and went on sorting the bags Muriel always saved for her. "All he'd do is take my money and try to sleep in my bed—I got rid of him." Then she grinned, showing teeth stained brown where she gripped the pipe.

Dovie's mother laughed but then gasped and broke off, coughing. The two women began to converse in low tones.

Dovie went back to her book. She remembered one day, when Mother was feeling particularly bad, she had sent her out to deal with Miz Emrys. Dovie stood up on the steps and threw the bags down, not wanting to get any crawly bugs from the peddler. She never thought Miz Emrys would notice that she was keeping her distance.

Her head bent over her work, Miz Emrys had said, "This is how dirty life gets you. But you can wash clean. You can wash clean and live a good life."

11

Miz Emrys looked up then. Her tanned face and young, green eyes were a surprise under the battered fedora.

"This is how dirty life gets you," Dovie repeated to herself. "Not me, never me. I have Mother to take care of me—and Dad too, of course."

Dovie heard Mother's racking cough down below. She put aside her book and went to the lavatory. The water in the pitcher was still a little warm. She poured the basin full. She took special pleasure in washing her hands that were so soft and pink under the soapsuds. She dried them on a clean linen towel, went back to her chair by the fire. She tried to concentrate on her history book and not listen for Mother's cough, which sounded lately like her chest would rip open.

✵ ✵ ✵

Dovie saw the first green of spring like a haze over the trees. She opened the gate, and Shelagh led the way toward the cemetery. She walked head down, buttoning her thick coat.

Mrs. Murray passed them and, not to be ignored, said sharply, "Good morning, Dovie. Good morning, Shelagh."

Dovie nodded and mumbled. When she got to the grave, she stood with her eyes closed, letting the pale sun shine on her face, hoping for some warmth. She felt for the cord around her neck and drew it out. She closed her eyes and kissed the pearl and ruby ring that hung there. It was something of her mother's that she had kept with her constantly in the months since Mother died. She only removed it when she bathed. When she opened her eyes, they were clouded with tears that made wavy lines of the budding trees. Spring had come, but her mother was gone.

Dovie had never told anyone, not even Shelagh, how she had gone to see her mother in the parlor where Muriel was laid out. Dovie wasn't allowed to enter since she was only a child. She sneaked in and was looking in the coffin. Her eyes took in a form, white and still. *That's not my mother*, she thought. *It looks like her but something is missing.* She heard steps in the hall. Dovie looked around for escape and at the last moment hid behind the green velvet drapes that covered the window. Someone came in and there was silence.

She heard a voice whisper, "Goodbye, Muriel," and peeped out just in time to see her father's back as he left the room.

Now, in the middle of the cemetery, Shelagh began to weep.

"I can't believe I'll never see Mother again," Dovie said.

The two girls held on to each other, and Dovie felt Shelagh's tears running down inside her collar as she mopped her own eyes with a hanky.

When the sisters stood on the walk leading up to their house, Shelagh said, "I wonder if Dad will be home tonight."

"He'll be with that widow, again, I bet," Dovie said.

"Ever since mother died, ever since he met her, we hardly see him. She says she's a widow. Maybe she isn't, I heard Aunt Olivia say so." Shelagh pushed open the heavy wood door.

"Dad says we have to meet her."

Ada

A week later when Dovie came home from school, she took the slate steps two at a time and pushed open the front door. She dropped her books in the hall and then heard laughter. Was it a woman's laughter in this mournful house, the very floorboards of which creaked like complaints as she trod upon them? She sniffed and smelled a trace of flowers, of perfume. She opened the door of the parlor and saw a woman seated with Dad. Shelagh and Aunt Olivia shared the sofa.

Dovie ran to her dad and sat on his knee.

He lifted her up to face the woman. "To show what a great, big baby I have," he said. "This is Dovie, eleven years old."

He kissed Dovie's cheek, and she felt the woman's eyes glitter as they rested on her. The next moment, the stranger smiled at Dad and a glance passed between them.

Dad blurted out, "Ada is to be my wife. I've asked her and she has accepted."

A crash—Gussie had dropped the tea tray on the sideboard. Her wrinkled face stretched almost smooth as her jaw dropped open. She was not supposed to "hear" what the masters said, but she turned around and gaped at the newcomer.

Aunt Olivia spoke to her brother. "You've surprised us all, Evan. Now, we must hear more. Your plans, how you met—and of course, offer our best wishes. Girls..." Aunt saw that the sisters were incapable of speech and filled in. "Miss Ada—may we

15

know your full name? Even though this, it seems, is about to change."

"It is Mrs. Ada Powell. And the lovely lady," as Evan said this, Ada smiled and smoothed her sleek bun of black hair, "has come to us from Cardiff, widow of a ship's captain. Soon you will know her son, Miles..."

Dovie made a strangled sound, and her dad turned to her. "Yes, missy, a brother for you. I know you'll be great friends."

Shelagh gave a weak smile. "How old, ma'am, is your son?"

Ignoring her question, Ada gushed, "Two motherless girls! My poor boy, his father lost at sea! One of my joys in this," she turned to Evan, "is that I know both situations are soon to be repaired. Yes, on our wedding day, Evan, two families are to be made whole again! Imagine my joy when I realized that my pleasure to know a fine, strong man to spend my life with also meant a better life for Miles and these two unfortunates. My happiness is unbounded!"

She turned wide eyes on Evan, who fairly melted. He came to her and took her hand. He placed it on his raised arm and escorted her a few steps to the tea table.

Dovie witnessed this with something approaching horror. She tried to catch her sister's eye, but Shelagh had gripped her hands together and was staring down at them.

Evan announced to them all, "Here you have two of the happiest mortals in all of Wales." He laughed and said, "And one of them now invites the other to serve you tea." Evan led Ada to the blue, high-backed chair.

"That's Mother's chair!" Dovie cried out.

Evan scowled at Dovie and said, "This will be your place, my dear Ada, as my hostess and helpmeet." He continued with extra emphasis, "And the sooner all adjust themselves, the better."

"Now, Evan," Aunt Olivia murmured, "the little ones may need time. Here, Dovie, have a seat by me," she called out.

Pale and biting her lip, Dovie let Aunt Olivia put an arm around her.

"I do believe you owe Mrs. Powell an apology for your outburst, Dovie," Evan insisted.

"Oh, I'm sure she's very sorry," Shelagh hurried to say when she saw Dovie getting her stubborn look.

Aunt Olivia chimed in, "Dovie's near tears, Evan, let her be."

Shelagh sat beside Dovie, who put her arms around her sister's waist and clung to her.

Ada allowed a small frown to cross her countenance. "Too much temper in a girl is unpleasant. But, Evan, you're longing to enjoy your tea. Miss Olivia, cream, sugar?"

"Sugar, one lump. I'm sure Miss Ada will be a delightful addition to the social scene here. When is the wedding date?"

"Saturday, week. We wanted you to be the first to know."

"Oh my! That is hasty!" Aunt Olivia clapped her hand over her mouth the moment the words were out of her mouth.

"We are two who have been buffeted by the storms of life." Ada spoke, and Evan nodded at her words. "And we will waste no time in claiming happiness when it is offered us," Ada said, displaying her fine profile as she lifted her face to heaven, "by benign providence."

"My dear, I could not have said it better myself," Evan said. "You continually astonish me with your abilities. Do you not see, Olivia, why I am so eager to wed this lady? She represents all that has been missing in my life!"

With an incredulous face, Shelagh looked from one to the other as they spoke. Dovie buried her face in her sister's puffed sleeve.

"Oh, yes indeed, in the months that have passed you must have been a lonely man. Six months must seem an age to you. Well," Aunt Olivia said and set down her teacup, "I must go. There's a meeting of the literary society that I suddenly feel I don't want to miss."

When she had gone, Ada stood before the mantel. "It will be all over town in an hour. Literary society, indeed!"

"Good," Evan said, stretching his legs out to the fire. "Save me the trouble of telling one and all. Girls, please excuse yourselves to Miss Ada and go on. I'm sure you have lessons to do. I'll show you the house, Ada."

The two sisters left the room holding hands. Once in the hall with the door shut behind them, Dovie whispered, "I feel..."

She rubbed her chest, at a loss to explain the tumult contained there.

"It's terrible, just terrible," Shelagh hissed. "A half hour ago I didn't even know this woman. Now she's to be our new mother in a week. Well, I don't want a new mother."

"Did you see how Dad acted? I couldn't believe it. He said 'a brother for you.'" Dovie's cheeks flamed with resentment.

✳ ✳ ✳

"Gussie doesn't have time to wait on you; you're a big girl and lazy," Ada said.

Dovie gasped at the injustice of it. Miles got his breakfast on a tray that Gussie carried to him. Home on a brief visit from school, he ate breakfast in bed every morning. She herself had been up since six that morning to gather the eggs from the henhouse. Ada had a new rule that Dovie was to do this three times a week while Gussie prepared for Ada's afternoon teas with guests.

"Lazy donkey, so hardheaded," Ada went on. "Stay out of the parlor, that's not for children. Making messes, leaving cloth and pins everywhere. The parlor is for a lady to entertain her callers. It needs to be ready at all times for my visitors."

"But where will I sew and do my lessons?" Dovie asked, astonished.

"The kitchen or your room. You've that great, big room—too much for two little girls, anyway."

Dad came home that evening from market trips to four cities. Dovie was waiting but restrained herself from bursting out with grievances when she saw his tired face. After dinner, she lurked in the passageway looking for the right moment when she could speak to him alone. She told herself, *I won't cry, it only annoys him. Squabbles, he'd say, don't come to me with your household squabbles. You've a mother to settle those now.*

In the dark hall, Dovie breathed deeply trying to quiet her thumping heart. He must be told that she had been forbidden to enter rooms in her own house. *He'll help, he'll see to it,* she

18

thought with a hand on her chest. Through the crack of the door she saw Dad enter his office. She had to know if he was alone. If Ada was there it would spoil her chance of being heard. Ada had a way of turning all Dovie said against her.

Dovie slipped out the back door and around the side of the house. Ashamed, she looked around to make sure no one would see her spying at the window. The yard was empty so she pulled up a bucket, balanced on it, and held a crossbeam to peer into the office. She saw the lamp on the corner of the desk and some movement. She shifted her position and two figures came into view, closely entwined. The woman had her buttons open down the front and her bosom quite bare. It was Ada; she bent backwards as a hand caressed her flesh. Dovie's mouth dropped open.

In the lamplight, the scene looked warm and indistinct. Dovie could see that the man covered her with kisses as she twisted in his embrace. The next minute Dovie felt sick in her stomach; she couldn't look anymore. That was Dad! Acting so strange and hurried in the shadowy room. She dropped to the ground and lay there. Her dad and Ada—she felt hot and cold at once. She pushed herself up off the ground and ran. She fled but could not outrun the awful feeling.

She scrambled over a low wall and ran into the barn. The odor of hay and leather was familiar and comforting. She reached out to touch the horse, and her hand grazed the cottony thread of a spider web. Dovie saw the spider clenched in one corner of its web as the horse whinnied and butted her hand looking for sugar. She caressed the horse's muzzle, angry tears spurting from her eyes as she muttered, "Benign providence," and "two unfortunates."

Ada seemed to have spun a web and caught Evan in it. They two were together inside this web while she and Shelagh were outside. Dovie stopped petting the horse. Only moments ago, she had thought she could tell Dad what was happening and get help. Now she knew there was no use. It was a long time before she crept back inside the house and up to her room.

✳ ✳ ✳

"Now she has taken Mother's pearl ring! It isn't fair! While I was bathing, I put it on the dresser. Gussie must have told her. Ada pretended to come in by accident. 'I must put this away for safekeeping,' she said." Dovie was almost breathless with indignation.

"From the moment she entered our house, I could see how it would all go," Shelagh told Dovie. "She intended—her eyes ransacked the parlor. Was anything worth money? And us! We were in her way. Oh, she said she believed in doing exactly the same for her son and Dad's daughters. 'What is good for one, exactly that is good for the other,' she said."

"Lies. I am so sick of lies. By her second day as his wife, it was 'Goats, she-goats, out of *my* parlor.' When she stamped her foot, Dad went and hid in his office," Dovie said. "He told us, his own daughters, we had to ask her permission—in our own house—before taking any food from the pantry. He gave in to her every time."

"He tries to keep the peace. But, remember when she was going to feed us porridge when the others had meat? He got so mad. Remember his face, so red? The veins in his forehead were standing out!"

"When he's home, we eat all right, but she slips a lot past him. Just bread for our lunches, no cheese," Dovie said. "No, in our own kitchen we go hungry. Oh, Mother would never have let this happen."

"He doesn't dare do anything. She'll make him pay, if he does, with her pouting and screaming. She belittled him to her precious son. She said, 'Your father was a captain in the navy. You'll have a military career. No shopkeeper's life for you.'"

"When I know she is in the house," Dovie said, "I'm afraid. It's as though there is a..." Dovie struggled to describe her feelings, "a snake in the house with us. In the hallway I circle far around her or run past. She smiles, then strikes."

✲ ✲ ✲

It was six o'clock, getting dark, when Ada handed Dovie a parcel. "They've given me the wrong order. This must be exchanged before the party tonight. With your dad called out of town at the last minute and people coming in, I'm half mad. The mayor and his wife are expected. You just make sure you're back in time."

When Dovie returned she found the door locked. Grumbling, for she was tired after running most of the way home, she went around to the back. It was locked also. No one answered her knocking or calling. It was dark and getting chilly.

Again, Dovie knocked loudly on the door. No one came. Shelagh was still away at her new job. Dovie felt a cold shiver and pulled her sleeves down to cover her elbows. She walked out into the yard and looked up at the windows on the second floor. She could see lights and hear music. She called out. No one came.

A surge of anger came over her, and with superhuman energy she grabbed some vines and climbed to the pantry window. It was high and small and always left unlocked. She cut her arm pulling herself in over the sill, and rubbed the blood off on her dress. Climbing in and dropping to the floor, she felt her skirt rip but hurried on. In the hall she saw that the doors had all been shut leading upstairs. Whoever had done this had made it more difficult for anyone upstairs to hear her calls.

She climbed the stairs at a furious pace, leaping at them. Her heel caught in the torn hem, but she disentangled it. In the upstairs passageway, she encountered the hired girl carrying a pitcher. Dovie swept past as the girl pressed herself against the wall. Dovie's ripped hem dragged behind her down the hall.

She threw open the door to the parlor. The guests turned, the fiddler held his bow suspended. All stared at the girl in her bloodstained, torn dress.

Dovie paused a moment hardly knowing what she would do. She saw Ada across the room. Dovie walked swiftly toward her. The crowd parted. Dovie was in a towering rage as she faced Ada, who stepped back with an alarmed look.

Mrs. Murray breathed, "Oh, Dovie, dear, your arm is bleeding."

Dovie turned to look at her. "The doors were locked. I had to climb in a window." A red spot burned in each of Dovie's cheeks.

The mayor's wife said, "I saw Dovie hurrying to the market. I was already on my way home. She had to change Ada's purchase, she said. 'I must hurry or she'll be mad.'"

"See, the poor girl's exhausted and overexcited," Mrs. Murray said as she brought out her handkerchief and dabbed at Dovie's cut arm. "Trying not to anger her stepmother," she muttered.

Dovie stared into Ada's face. "You locked me out of the house," she accused her. A murmur went around the room.

Ada pulled herself away from Dovie's gaze. She drew up her skirts angrily. "The child is a liar. I've spoken to her father about it."

Dovie took a deep, sobbing breath and threw the bloody handkerchief on the floor. She looked suddenly small and defeated.

Mrs. Murray, who had been Muriel's close friend, rushed forward. "I'll take Dovie to her room, now. Dear, let's go and wash that cut."

Mayor Emerson stepped forward frowning and said, "I really think Mrs. Emerson and I must go."

The others began to say hasty good-byes and hurry away. Ada stepped grandly over the stained handkerchief to bid them good-bye. She was soon alone with the ruins of her party. On the table sat the untouched cake, the dish of candied fruits, and the punchbowl still half full.

✳ ✳ ✳

"Shelagh, go to the minister, tell him," Dovie spoke urgently.

"I've done that, I've gone to Mister Doctor Reverend Coe," Shelagh said mincingly in a high, refined voice.

Dovie looked up surprised; this was the first glimpse in a long time that she had of the old Shelagh. Her sister used to make her laugh mimicking their teachers or the boys from mountain

22

villages who had to wear the Welsh Not, the piece of wood the schoolmaster hung around their necks when he caught them speaking Welsh.

"Dr. Reverend said, 'You should never have been sent to work in that man's house. He'll have to marry you. I'll speak to him about it. You understand, don't you? It's that or worse.' Then he tried to be kind. 'In the meantime—well, you mustn't allow any, um, favors that only married men receive.'"

"What did you say then?" Dovie asked.

"I told him, 'I don't know how to stop him.' And then he said, 'I'll speak to him very soon.'"

"Oh, Shelagh! When Ada said, 'I won't have her here, this is my house,' I never thought you'd have to give up school and go out to work. No one can stop her, it seems."

"I don't want to marry, and I certainly don't want to marry Mr. Hughes."

"You're only fourteen. Mother wanted you to go to boarding school in England. If only she were here!"

"I've got to get out of this place! I'd like to go to the States. But I'm afraid. I'm afraid to leave here." Shelagh, who was usually so certain, slumped, and her voice fell to a whisper. "It's all I know."

Dovie could hardly hear her sister, but what she heard next made her uneasy.

Shelagh said, "I hate my life. Life seems too hard."

☆ ☆ ☆

Dovie threw grain to the chickens. The clucking of the flock was a soothing sound. They crowded around, the stronger ones pushing the others aside, getting in first. The rooster pecked at the neck of a white hen, and she backed off. Dovie filled her hand with grain from the sack and tossed it in an arc over their heads. As they rushed to get it, she threw some feed to the white chicken on the side.

"Daughter," a voice hissed. She turned. Dad was around a corner of the building beckoning to her. With a surprised look, she went to him. Evan took her arm and moved them out of sight of the windows. He looked over his shoulder before speaking.

"I know life has been hard for you and your sister since your mother died." Evan bit his lip then reached inside his coat. He brought out a small packet wrapped in the brown, speckled paper they used in the shop. He put it into Dovie's hand and said, "They were your mother's. I wish I had kept more to give you. My life doesn't seem to be my own anymore." He rubbed his forehead. "Ada..." His voice trailed off.

"It's all right," Dovie found herself saying just as Muriel used to when he came in tired or discouraged. "Shelagh and I will be all right."

"I never thought it would come to this. I can't get a peaceful moment." With an effort, he straightened his back and pressed her hand between his own. "When you were born, your mother said, 'I am so happy today.'" He kissed her forehead and walked quickly toward the shop.

Dovie felt discouraged by the sight of her dad slinking around, afraid. She felt the package but didn't open it. Instead she put it in her pocket to show Shelagh later. Through the paper she could feel the rounded shapes of Mother's two matching bracelets of etched gold.

That night Dovie woke herself with a scream. Her heart was pumping and her throat working as her eyes popped open. She said in the dark, "You can never go fast enough." Then, the dream was gone, fallen back into some dark place. Her heart slowed down and she had just a memory of creatures with wild eyes and writhing snakes for hair.

"Ada—she'll get on your back and ride you if you let her. She'll whip you but you can never go fast enough," Dovie murmured, beginning to doze off.

The next night when the house was dark, the two sisters lay on Shelagh's bed talking in low voices.

"We're in her way. This is to the death, this struggle," Dovie said. "I'm tired of struggling. Things will never be as they were when Mother was alive."

Shelagh's eyes were dark and pained as she spoke. "Dad is no help."

"It's not our home anymore."

"I've thought about leaving. I can go down in the port and talk to Mrs. Murdock about it. She finds places for girls. In America there's work, she says, though we may start out low."

"Well, how much lower can we be?"

"We would be far away, probably no coming back," Shelagh warned.

Dovie gave a shrug. "I never want to see her face again. Do it soon."

"Tomorrow I'll speak to Mrs. Murdock. You work as a servant for a year or two. However long it takes to pay for your passage or save something."

"We're servants here. Let's face it, we're servants or worse. Besides, I have money, my money from the packet boat, from the *Delight*. Hidden."

"Maybe we should go to Dad after all."

"That's no good. I've watched them together. It's like she's put a spell on him. She means to take everything and drive us away."

"Then she will have won if we go!"

Dovie frowned when she heard this. "But we'll save ourselves. We'll be on our own—free of her. And he'll be sorry."

"Tomorrow, I'll find out more," Shelagh said drowsily.

Dovie's eyes closed and her ragged breath came through her mouth.

"Tomorrow," Shelagh whispered as she put the blanket over Dovie and crawled under the covers.

The next day, Gussie and Dovie were folding sheets at the linen closet when the maid looked over her shoulder and then whispered to Dovie, "There'll be a baby. I would guess in about five months. Don't you see the mistress's stomach growing?"

"No," Dovie said, "no."

"I've known for months," Gussie went on. "I was the one who had to help her with the morning sickness. As if I didn't have enough to do waiting on everyone in the household from morning to night. I brewed a special tea for her. I could see you didn't guess. Or Shelagh neither. Ignorant girls."

Dovie stared at the maid.

"I know other things, too. I don't tell all I know." Gussie waited for Dovie to respond, but the girl just stood there.

The maid shrugged and went on, "Mr. Evan is pleased. The men always are—they don't have to carry the thing nine months, heat and cold, whether or no. He thinks only of having a son. 'We'll name him Elliott after my granddad,' he says. 'He started the business.'"

"That's the end of us. Everything will be for the new baby," Shelagh said when Dovie told her.

✵ ✵ ✵

The two sisters waited almost a week; the inaction made them anxious and yet they were frightened of making their next move. Then suddenly on a Thursday, Shelagh told her employer she was sick, nauseated and throwing up. She deliberately used what she knew were the symptoms of pregnancy. He gave her money to go to the doctor in the port so no one in the village would know and gossip.

Shelagh went to Mrs. Murdock, made her inquiries, and set their plan in motion. She came home bursting with news but had to wait until night when she and Dovie were alone to tell her that one of their mother's former music pupils was in touch with Mrs. Murdock.

"This woman, Mrs. Llewellyn, married and went to America and is asking for girls from the home place, Welsh girls to work for her in New York City. She went and married a hatter, now become a rich man, and wants to hear sounds of home around her. That is her whim and he is for indulging her, and we have places if we get there." Shelagh was laughing and hugging Dovie as she told her.

Dovie's face looked serious. "It's good news. Isn't it?"

"Mrs. Murdock'll send a letter on the next ship—we have to pay her a fee. But we won't wait, just go and they'll know we're coming. That's how to handle it, Mrs. Murdock says so."

"What if they find out here at home?"

"Don't worry. I'm going to fix it so they'll think we've gone to visit relatives. We leave from Liverpool in six days. Start thinking what we need to do."

26

The two sisters grasped hands and danced behind the closed doors of their room. Their voices rose and they had to bury their faces in the pillows to keep from shouting.

Finally, the last morning arrived. Dovie stiffened her back as Ada brushed past her. *You've won*, Dovie thought. *My mother's home is now yours. We leave in defeat. We lost the fight.* Dovie could hardly stand to look at her dad; his weakness shamed her, his capture by Ada was complete.

Ada smiled as she filled his cup and handed it to him, but it was a brisk, empty smile as her mind moved on to other matters. "The minister's wife is paying her first call. And later, a lesson with my new music teacher. Dovie, it's time to wash up these dishes," Ada said. "Your lessons can begin a little late today. I need your help around the house."

Dovie stared at her dad, but he looked away. She felt anger burn in her chest as he avoided her eyes. Mother had always valued learning above all. *Coward*, she thought turning her back on him. *You'll be sorry when you find our beds empty in the morning.*

You may never see him again, a voice inside Dovie said. She looked at her father. Firelight outlined Evan's hair and shoulder. He was a large, pudgy man sipping from his teacup, a sight she had seen almost every morning of her life. She turned quickly away and began to wash the dishes.

When Ada called her to clear her plate, Dovie looked at her knowing she would soon be free of her intolerable presence. Ada's feet were up on a footstool, her stomach rounded slightly under her clothes. Dovie hummed under her breath trying not to think.

It didn't seem real that this was to be her last breakfast in this room with the fire in the hearth and the round, oak table.

That night, Dovie's mind was full of their faces, Evan, Gussie, and Ada, fearful, angry, and mean. She dozed a little but was disturbed by dreams that jolted her awake. She crept out of her bed and went to Shelagh.

"I can't sleep," she whispered as Shelagh raised her head from the pillow. "I only want to get away from here." She grabbed Shelagh's hands. "I'm glad we're going."

Shelagh sat up. Dovie saw that she was fully dressed.

"Wear several layers. I am. It's easier than carrying them and warmer, too," Shelagh told her.

Dovie left the room. She had one more thing to take care of while it was still night and the household asleep. Then she dressed in her warmest clothes and was waiting long before it was time to move silently through the house and out, closing the door behind them.

Shelagh and Dovie looked at each other in the dim light before dawn. They sat in the back of Mr. Murdock's swaying wagon as it jolted downhill towards the port. Dovie looked back at the village and heard the stream rushing down to the sea. She longed to run over there, cup her hands, and drink the cold, clear water. Then the horse plodded around the hill and the village was gone. Around them lay gray fields, wet and dark. Sheep huddled next to a stone wall.

Shelagh crouched with her head hanging down. Dovie touched her shoulder, and Shelagh raised eyes that had the light of pure panic shining in them.

"I'm glad to leave," Dovie said but heard her voice quaver as she spoke.

She turned herself around and refused to look back though tears ran down her cheeks. Jostled about on the rough boards of the wagon, the two girls leaned together as the stone cliffs merged into the rain slick and were no longer visible.

Providence, The Ship

Dovie dozed as the wagon traveled overland. When they changed to a coach at Caernarvon, they left behind Mr. Murdock, the last person who could have identified them. The trip had been hurried and dark; they wanted to leave no trace.

Once seated in the coach, Dovie had to kick Shelagh when she began to smile and greet the other passengers. Shelagh had been just about to answer a query as to what town they were from.

"She gets terrible headaches from the travel," Dovie explained to the woman next to them. She leaned over her scowling sister and said sweetly, "Here, Jane, dear, I'll put this handkerchief over your eyes so you can rest. Mother will be so upset if you arrive home ill."

With Shelagh taken care of, Dovie opened the bag of cheese, apples, and bread that Shelagh had brought and ate hungrily.

At the northern coast, they boarded a small boat that took them over choppy waters to Liverpool, where they followed the crowd along the docks. The noise and confusion made it difficult to move. Dovie was afraid of losing Shelagh and gripped her cloak and hung on regardless of the crowds.

At last they saw the *Providence* among the large ships. Up the gangplank they went, tickets in hand and hearts in their throats, fearing someone would stop them. To be caught and taken back was the thing they feared most. Shelagh had thought to leave hidden in her bureau drawer a flyer about jobs in London.

They stepped on deck, walked on the boards, and stared at the mass of ropes, boxes, and baskets piled on the deck with more being lifted aboard every moment.

A few steps more and they faced the desk of the purser, who stopped them. Surprised, the two girls stammered out their answers to his questions. He wrote in a large book, recording their names, ages, last place of residence. "Occupation?" he demanded. Shelagh answered, "Maidservants."

Dovie said, "No, we're not. I'm not going to America just to scrub floors."

The man's dark, unshaven face flushed angrily. "I'll tolerate no smart talk from a chit like you."

Shelagh gripped Dovie's arm, warning her.

"So what is it?" he demanded.

When Shelagh answered, "Maidservants, sir," in a meek tone, he glared at Dovie and waited with the pen suspended above the paper. She kept her eyes downcast and held her breath. Finally, she heard him scribble on the page and breathed with relief. When he waved them away to take care of the next passengers, the two sisters hurried out of his sight.

Now aboard the *Providence*, Dovie went below decks to find her allotted space. Number fifty-eight was a bed slot in a wall, four beds high. She climbed up a crude ladder made of wooden crosspieces nailed to a support post. Her bed was just under the ceiling and was made of wood slats covered with a thin cloth. In the crowded, dark space she began to feel waves of panic move up her chest. She climbed down, reaching with each foot for the next rickety board.

This place is like death or prison she thought. She took deep breaths and closed her eyes. She remembered the tree outside her window at home and how its leaves glittered in the sunlight. When she woke in the mornings under her fluffy blanket, she smelled cold, fresh air through the window she always kept open. She took more deep breaths, holding on to the wood frame, and was grateful just to breathe in and out. *Seventeen days out of the rest of my life*, she told herself.

While she was down below, the ship began to move. Dovie felt the boards creaking under her feet and heard the ship's horn. She ran to the ladder and climbed out onto the deck where flags were flying overhead. The first mate held a bullhorn and issued commands. Dovie looked over the railing. The harbor was busy with boats of all sizes, small ones with oars, tall sailing ships, and steamers plowing the water. The passengers crowded the rails watching the land recede, their eyes clinging to the shore as the buildings became smaller, then were only a line, fainter and fainter.

Dovie looked for Shelagh. She needed the comfort of seeing her familiar face. The woman next to Dovie spoke, and Dovie turned to look up into a round, pink face. The sounds seemed like words but made no sense. When Dovie only stared and made no reply, the woman said, "*Dummkopf!*" and turned away.

Dovie burrowed into the crowd calling, "Shelagh!"

She encountered locked gates. She rattled them but they wouldn't open. She turned and went back into the maze of corridors and doors. Outside on deck, she rounded a corner and a sweep of wind almost lifted her off her feet. She breathed in big gulps and ran with her hair streaming after her.

She was calling, "Shelagh!" when a boy in a brown cap grabbed her arm, pointed to her red hair, and pointed toward the railing. Dovie ran there. Beyond the rail there was only water, seagulls wheeling, and the setting sun casting a strange yellow light on the sky and water. Shelagh was there, her red hair blowing in the breeze. She was talking to a family of thin, dark people.

"Dovie!" Shelagh called when she saw her sister and put out her hand. Dovie ran to her and held on. "This is my sister. I have told the Muellers about us. They are from Germany, but Mr. Mueller speaks English."

"Only a little," he said. "Two sisters, I see it," he said, pointing to their red hair.

31

"Where were you? I couldn't find you," Dovie broke in.

Shelagh laughed. "None of us is going anywhere. We'll be right here on this ship, on this deck for weeks. Say hello, please, this is Mrs. Mueller and Katrine...and Karl?"

The boy set down the suitcase he was holding to shake Dovie's hand.

They stood together on the deck, reluctant to go below into their cramped quarters. "The wind and spray is better than being below," Shelagh said.

Intent and serious, Mr. Mueller turned to his wife and children. "We must learn English. Talk English. In America, English." But he turned to Shelagh and asked, "*Sprecken Sie Deutsch?*"

"*Sprecken...*" Shelagh repeated.

Karl was a thin, slight boy. When he spoke Dovie saw that he was kind and quiet, and this drew her to him. She sat down by him and began to speak slowly in English.

Later, Dovie wandered away and stood on the front deck. All she saw was gray and black, and their ship like a shell floating in between water and sky. *We got away, they didn't catch us*, she thought.

Dovie would have liked to see if her father was sorry when he saw her empty bed. She pictured him, his head in his hands, crying. "If only I had been nicer to little Dovie." She shed a few tears just thinking about how she might walk in the door and how surprised and glad he would be.

"I beg you, forgive me," he would say.

She would reply, "I just want my real mother back."

Then, in her daydream, a woman came into the room. With a jolt, Dovie saw Ada's face glaring at her, saying, "You little thief, you! Where is the ring you stole?"

She imagined Dad, Gussie, and the minister, even the sheriff, all looking at her with hard eyes.

"Yes, I have the ring, but I have a right to it. Mother wanted us to have it."

The adults turned their heads away, stony faced. Dovie shook herself; better not to think about it. *Dad wouldn't believe I'm a thief...would he?*

That night the two girls carried their tin plates of salt pork and sauerkraut onto the deck. They sat down, smelled the food, and made faces at its strong odor. All around them people speaking many languages sat on the deck eating. The sisters set their plates down and made a circle with their legs and skirts. In the middle they opened their packs. They leaned forward with their shoulders trying to create a private area just for themselves.

Shelagh showed what she had brought, bread and a small wheel of cheese sneaked from the cupboard at home.

"I made four extra parcels, dried apples, nuts, you'll see," she told Dovie.

Dovie had brought a warm shawl and two dresses. The two slender gold bracelets and the remainder of her stash of money were both sewn inside the hem of the blouse she wore. These she told Shelagh about in a whisper. "And of course, my medal." She touched her chest where she could feel the chain hidden under her clothes.

Dovie brought out a photograph of the family. She remembered her mother tying ribbons in her hair and saying, "You must stand very still for the photographer." Dovie laid it on a fold of her skirt and they both looked at it silently.

"Mother would be so sad if she saw what was happening to us," Shelagh said, studying the photograph.

"Sad? She'd be angry. And so am I!" Dovie replied. "And tired. I haven't slept at all!"

She shuddered, remembering her dream. She wandered in dark, empty rooms where once she had worked and studied and been happy and carefree. She woke and fell asleep again only to find water covering her feet as the ship sank. It had felt so real that when she woke and touched her skirt and found dry cloth, she couldn't believe her senses.

Dovie pushed those thoughts to the back of her mind. She pictured Ada's face when she opened her bureau drawer planning to wear Mother's pearl ring. *She has to have found out by now.* She thought of telling Shelagh about the ring but put it off.

"We'll be halfway across the ocean in eight and a half more days," Shelagh said to her. She chewed the salt pork and grinned. "We go west to find riches!"

"We never have to eat sauerkraut again!" Dovie added. They chewed silently, each girl thinking her thoughts.

That night when Dovie climbed up into her bed, she waited a few minutes until the woman across from her turned on her side to sleep. With the woman's back to her, Dovie felt at last that no one could see her. She took out the chain she wore under her dress. On it was not only her medal but also her mother's pearl ring. As she turned the ring in her hand, she felt guilt instead of comfort. Ada would say Dovie stole it, probably was already saying this. She would not be there to defend herself. Ada would call her a thief, and Evan would not take up for her, nor would Gussie. Dovie began to twist and turn, hearing their voices in her mind. Her thoughts tormented her.

When daylight came, Dovie prowled the ship from one end to the other. When she came to a locked gate, she looked through the bars to see all that she could see. Once she saw the purser. He was berating a cabin boy. The boy hung his head while big tears plopped out of his eyes and landed on the dirty little paw he was wiping his cheeks with.

Dovie wanted to find a place away from all the people, the congested decks and crowded dormitory. Being small, she was able to climb onto a pipe where it entered the wall between two decks. She slipped into an alcove above. Seated on the pipe with her feet on a ledge, she had found her place. Chin resting on her hands, elbows on her knees, she became absorbed in watching the people below on the open deck. They hardly noticed her, and she was free to observe their daily lives lived in this small space. She passed many hours in her perch where she could crane around and look up to the topmost deck or down into the water.

She soon noticed a man who looked splendid in a uniform of darkest blue with gold buttons in two rows down the front and red piping on the collar and sleeves. He was Captain Frank Briden of the *Providence*, tall and quite slim, with a large nose and chin. He walked with a bounce, and when Dovie came upon him around a curve of the bulkhead, she stared, amazed at his splendid appearance. He spoke to her. She only bobbed her head as the country people did at home in the village when they felt too humble to speak.

Dovie saw that he did calisthenics in front of his quarters each morning and took a brisk walk around the decks each evening. She observed from her perch that when off duty, he went to a worktable where he cut, sanded, glued, and fitted small pieces of wood together. He hummed while he worked; Dovie liked that. It made her realize she had often been happy in small tasks such as kneading dough for bread. She longed for those simple pleasures in life to come to her again. Sometimes after fitting pieces together, the captain held them up and turned them to see all angles. One day watching him hold up his work, Dovie could see that he had made a small bed with four posters on it, fit for a doll.

Days on the ship were occupied with getting food and water and getting oneself clean, as clean as possible in the primitive conditions: buckets of wash water, air for a towel, and no privacy. So many people were constantly bumping up against each other that spats broke out. There was pushing and shoving in the lines for meals. The food, peas for instance, tasted only faintly like what they remembered. Loud insults were exchanged in many languages. Sneers and raised fists told the message even if the tongue was foreign.

People were smelly and ugly, Dovie thought, and rude. She longed to be alone or at least above them in her perch with quiet and her own thoughts. But Shelagh knew everybody's story and could soon say phrases in German or imitate the English accents in a way that made Dovie laugh, even over a plate of gray beans.

During another night of tortured sleep, Dovie found a chopped-off stump where once had been a branching birch tree in the yard at home. She dreaded night and lying down. The demons came out once she closed her eyes.

The next day she ate part of her dinner, put the bread in her pocket, and went to walk briskly around the ship hoping to tire herself out before bedtime. She saw Karl Mueller seated on a coil of rope. He had a way of sitting, forehead resting on one hand, elbow on his leg, which she recognized. She stopped to avoid talking to him. His dark hair was slicked back behind his large, pink ears. He was hunched forward holding a slab of bread and cheese. He took a bite and chewed rapidly.

"Hello," he said without looking around. Dovie came forward then and found herself telling him about sneaking away from home, wanting to go back, wishing her mother was alive, wanting to get away from her stepmother, feeling afraid of what was ahead. Karl hunched forward and ate. At the end, her story told, his sandwich demolished, he looked around as if still hungry. She hesitated and then brought out the piece of bread and offered it to him. He looked at her with alert eyes.

"You and sister, this is good. Alone, no good." He wolfed down the crust of bread.

A ball came bouncing their way. With a smile that looked almost painful on his gaunt face, he caught the ball and sent it rolling back to a little boy who had come looking for it.

He has his mother, father and sister, Dovie thought. *Even if he's hungry, he still has a family.*

When they had not seen land in six days, a storm came. The first inklings of bad weather were when sailors began to tie the heavy doors, one open, one closed in each doorway. Then they lashed ropes along the passageways. Frequent orders were shouted to the crew with bullhorns. Then the engines stopped. The noise ceased. The vibrations that Dovie had felt through her feet, through the boards, in her arms and hands when she touched the rails, even her back when she sat, were gone. It was like waking in a strange land.

"What's happened?" the passengers asked each other. No one knew. A wave of apprehension washed over them. Rumors flew. One man said there was a hole in the ship. The picture of water rushing in sent some into hysterics. To quiet a yelling man, another passenger threw the bucket of wastewater right in his face. After that, Dovie tried not to look at him as he lay on the floor sobbing quietly.

Finally, an officer was sent to announce that they would ride the storm out here until it passed. A dark morning came and went. Then the waves and the wind both began to rise. The ship rocked at first, then pounded as waves lifted it and then dropped it down in the trough. The passengers held the ropes to steady themselves as they made their way down to their dormitories where they huddled in their beds.

The boards groaned with every wave. The body of the ship was like a living thing tossed on the wide water. Dovie felt the flimsy nature of their support with each shudder the ship gave, and she feared the boards would fly apart. This went on through the night. Many people were sick and throwing up from fear or the violent motion. When Dovie and Shelagh went to the open hatch to look up at the sky, it was indistinguishable from the sea. Waves towered above the ship, tall as mountains, and came crashing down. It was impossible to walk out on deck without getting drenched. The one time Dovie tried it, the wind hurled water in her face until she had to climb back down with the others. Her clothes were wet through and wouldn't dry out in the damp. She lay down in rivulets of water. Her skirts squelched when she turned.

She hardly slept until near morning when she had a vivid dream in which she stood on solid earth in a place where a green valley stretched away on all sides of her. She stood on the edge of a creek and called out in a foreign tongue to greet a savage dressed in feathers and pelts. She was surprised to speak and understand perfectly this new language. It was the first good dream she had had since leaving home.

When morning came, Dovie felt tired and her stomach was queasy. She waited until Shelagh woke.

"I can't get up," she told Shelagh. "I'll just stay here."

She felt feverish. There was nothing to be done, no medicine, no doctor. After breakfast, Shelagh returned bringing Dovie some porridge, but she turned her face away and wouldn't eat it.

"Well, you'd better eat this because there's nothing else. We've gone through all my supplies."

Dovie looked around. There was no one nearby. She beckoned Shelagh close and whispered, "I'm not a thief."

"No, and I've not heard anyone say you were," Shelagh replied, smoothing Dovie's hair back as she felt her forehead.

Dovie took the chain she wore under her collar and pulled it over her head. Before Shelagh's eyes she dangled the ring, unbelievably delicate, gold shells curved on each side of a pearl set in rubies.

Shelagh's eyes widened as she recognized her mother's ring. "Here?"

"I took it. The night we left. Why should she have everything— our mother's house, our father? I took it."

37

Shelagh caught hold of the chain and held the ring in her hand.

"I'm not a thief and I don't want them to remember me that way. I'm afraid I'll die and they'll call me a thief."

Shelagh was looking intently at the ring. "To see this, here..." She gestured around them at the dark, crowded quarters that smelled of vomit and had water sloshing in the gutters.

"I'm going to throw it in the ocean," Dovie said. She had red spots burning in her cheeks, and her eyes looked glazed. "In the middle of the ocean, halfway to America."

Now Shelagh knew why Dovie had kept after the old sailor man, asking him, "Are we halfway to America yet? Tomorrow, will we be?"

"Throw it in the ocean?" Shelagh said with her voice rising. "We should keep it!" Dovie just shook her head.

"You'll be sorry later," Shelagh said resentfully. They sat silently for a moment. "Dovie, there are people here who haven't lost their homes—only because they never had one. Listen to me, the Muellers, the child is dying, I think. She is so weak and I went to help. You know the suitcase, the one they carry as though it had something precious in it? I went to look for clean clothes for her. The suitcase is empty. They have nothing but an empty suitcase."

Dovie lay very still but her mind was racing. Finally, she pushed Shelagh's hand that held the ring. "Give it away, then." She closed her eyes and turned to the wall. "I can hear what Ada is saying to Dad about me."

When Dovie was well, she hung around one lady, a seamstress, until she got paper and a pen from her. Ruth Laughton, from Liverpool, had well-organized boxes of supplies for she had planned the trip for many months and brought what she would need to start herself as a dressmaker in New York City. Tearfully, Dovie confessed to Miss Laughton, "I've run away from home and sometimes I feel so bad about it. What I want is to write my dad and explain it all to him."

The lady gave paper and a pen to her but with it told her story. "My mother's people, they were always a jealous lot. They had the nerve to accuse me of taking things that were their share out of my own dead mother's house. I left just ahead of the bailiff. But I got away and I fully intend to put an ocean between myself and them."

Dovie saw that Ada might get the law on them for running away, stealing valuables, she would say. Dovie wrote her letter, shedding tears on the paper, but when it was finished, she decided she couldn't take the chance of sending it. She held the envelope in her hand and looked at it with mixed emotions. They might forget her at home. But she didn't want them to find her either.

Mother died and left us. Father didn't take care of us. His new wife didn't want us. She laid her head down on her arms. There was only one thing she liked to remember; it was the waves crashing on the cliffs below the village making a grand sight and sound.

She looked around the noisy deck. All these people, a whole ship full of them, and every one of them had left something to begin a new life. She went to the rail and lifted her arm. When her fingers let the letter go, it fluttered and then sailed in the wind. She soon lost sight of it against the gray waves. Her family seemed to have been like a rainbow that had vanished with a shift of light.

Dovie gripped the rail, about to cry. Mr. Mueller came up wanting to try English words as usual. She turned her back and bent her head so he thought she was praying and left her alone. *That's one thing prayer is good for*, Dovie thought full of anger for everyone and everything.

Fine weather followed the storm, and the ship seemed to fly along through dry and sparkling air.

Dovie was taking a walk around the deck and came upon a crowd of passengers. She heard a boy's voice yelling and pushed her way toward the center. She recognized the passenger, Jackie was his name. He was usually with his mother, a thin and undernourished woman.

"No! No, she has to get to America! They are waiting for her there," Jackie pleaded and clung to a body as it lay on the deck.

"What happened?" Dovie whispered to a woman next to her.

"The poor woman died. She just dropped and died, right there. Now, the captain said she has to be buried at sea."

Jackie screamed as the sailors loosened his hold on the dead woman. As Dovie watched, it was agony to see the boy's hands pried loose finger by finger from his mother's arm.

A few hours later, passengers gathered to hear the Bible read over the corpse. Dovie thought of her own mother as she looked on the woman's body now wrapped in a piece of canvas and placed on a plank. At the words, "consign her body to the deep" Jackie howled like a wild animal and struggled with the burly sailor who was restraining him. The boy twisted and rose up to look as the body went over the side, swung out on a board and dropped into the swift-moving water.

To prevent him from jumping in after her, Captain Briden ordered him put in restraints. Dovie stood near the young sailor who was given the job of tying him to a railing. "Please, give him a longer rope so he can lie down," she asked. The sailor looked grim as the boy tried to bite him but did lengthen the rope. Jackie struggled until his wrists bled. When he collapsed facedown beside the stairs, weeping, Dovie stayed nearby. She had no comfort to offer but felt a duty to stay beside him.

For fresh air, many passengers stayed out on the deck to sleep. That night after dark, a voice rose singing a strange Slavic song. The plaintive sound made Dovie shiver as it wove up and down above the restless, tossing bodies. When the voice ceased, it was perfectly quiet except for the sound of the water against the hull of the ship. Then from over near the ladder, two women's voices rose and sang. Under the lilting harmony was the sound of crying and a sob here and there. Next a man's voice lit into an Irish melody, and others joined in. This went on far into the night, first over here, then over there; they sang songs, mourning, remembering losses and sadness, the boy's and their own. When sleep overtook them and the voices fell quiet, the full moon overhead gave such a light it made a ghost ship of solid wood and metal.

In the morning, Dovie saw that Jackie had finally laid his head down and was sleeping. The next night and the next the passengers sang for Jackie and for themselves. Dovie listened and felt soothed and comforted.

When the final day arrived, the sea was calm. All the passengers turned out on deck, hugging their parcels and jostling for a place. Down below, a crew worked to clean the privies and dormitory. After the whole voyage accumulating more and more filth, the ship now had to pass inspection at port on arrival.

"Where's America?"

"A bird! We're near land."

Dovie strained to see, standing on her tiptoes to look over the shoulders of those at the railing. There in the pale sky above her a seagull glided, wings spread on an air current. It looked white and fierce with its curved beak. The sight took her breath away, this bird from the shore they had sailed so far to reach. She watched it swoop down and land on the ship's rigging.

"That's America over there. You see? New York coming out of the sea!"

Everyone cheered at the sight. As the ship approached the harbor, a tall spire stood above the city, its gilded cross winking in the sun.

The girls stood with the Mueller family. A man told them excitedly, "I've been to America before. There, you can save money better than at home. There, you have more beer than water."

"When the waves were so high and scary, I wondered if we were ever going to get to America," Dovie said.

"Nineteen days' voyage, longer because of the storm," Shelagh said.

Mr. Mueller turned to their group, gesturing back at the open water behind them, "I ate wind, I tasted waves. I thought I could learn in a few days..."

"What? Learn what?" Shelagh asked him. But he had gathered his wife, son, and wan, thin daughter in his arms, and they clung together around the empty suitcase.

Shelagh had tied the ring up securely in a parcel and given it to Mr. Mueller with instructions not to open it until they were on land in New York. Dovie never wanted to see it again; it reminded her of all the wrong things.

Passengers had been instructed to pin a boldly printed tag on their hats or coats so the people meeting them would recognize them. *Dovie Ellen Lloyd, Shelagh Anne Lloyd*. They pinned the labels onto their hats the better to be seen.

"Will we ever go back?" Dovie asked Shelagh but got no reply.

The ship was docking. Dovie closed her eyes and saw the old village where her mother was buried, the houses close to the ground, damp and gleaming like rocks embedded in the cliff. When she opened her eyes, she looked at New York Harbor with bare, rolling hills beyond. Ships sailed out trailing puffs and long streams of white steam.

Once in port, Captain Briden was one of the first down the gangplank. Leaving the mate in charge, the captain, with his bouncy walk, went past Dovie with the doll bed under his arm. It had a patchwork quilt and two tiny pillows tied to it with ribbon. Dovie watched him go, recalling how her father had often brought her a gift from his travels and imagining how the little girl would greet him.

An official coming aboard stopped him, and Dovie heard him say, "I am so sorry to tell you."

"What?" said the captain, looking astonished.

"Your little daughter died on May twentieth."

A woman all dressed in black emerged from the crowd on the wharf and stood at the end of the gangplank. It was windy on the pier, and she held onto her hat while her mourning veil billowed out. She met the captain, took hold of his arm, and spoke to him. He held out the doll bed tied up with ribbon. They both stared at it. The woman began to cry. He took her arm and escorted her past the barriers to a waiting carriage. The doll bed fell to the ground. Karl, walking with his family, picked it up to give to his sister. Katrine let go her mother's hand to grab such a prize and carry it off.

People streamed off the ship carrying their baggage. The girls followed a woman with a shawl over her head and shoulders. She lugged a bedroll and a box. The man behind them wore a felt hat with the round brim turned up. Through his heavy moustache he urged them, "Hurry, hurry."

They were directed into a large, round building right on the waterfront. It was noisy inside, and long lines moved from the dark edges into the light from a dome. Their line led up to a uniformed man behind a counter. He motioned the girls into the women's line. Inside the washroom a woman handed out soap and a towel. Dovie had to remove her clothes, pile them in a basket, and wash herself standing before a long trough. Each female went about this task with downcast eyes. Next, in their petticoats and carrying the rest of their clothes, the sisters joined a line leading up to several doctors, who scrutinized them quickly, eyes, ears, skin clear, no deformities. In the next room they hastily put their clothes back on and joined the moving line.

"What is your destination?" another uniformed man asked.

"New York City, we have jobs," Shelagh said and got out the letter promising employment.

The man wasn't interested. "Resources?" The sisters looked at each other. "Money," the man said impatiently, "What money do you have with you?"

Dovie showed the money she had, worth forty dollars here, the man said.

"Not a pauper," he said and marked her shoulder with a white chalk mark.

Shelagh had her work paper from the housekeeping job and fifteen dollars in wages. She got a white chalk mark on her shoulder, too.

Dovie showed her school certificate because she was proud of it. The man barely glanced at it. He wrote down their names, place of birth, sex, and occupation, and waved them on. After the chalk mark was put on their shoulders everyone else waved them through.

They walked out into the brilliant sunlight of the Battery, part of a stream of people who then began to scatter in all directions.

New York City

Outside the wind was strong, and the gentlemen and ladies passing by held their hats. The ladies had slim waists, fancy gathered sleeves, and full skirts that swayed as they moved. From a slight rise in the ground, Dovie looked back at the sparkling water. Two big ships were just shadows far out in the bay, and small, quick-moving boats were nearer. Seagulls came flapping in low overhead, and there was the smell of coal smoke.

On the dock a military band of two drummers and a piper played while the stars and stripes of the American flag snapped in the wind. A soldier who stood tall in his blue uniform spoke to a young man just off the boat. He put his hand on the immigrant's shoulder and pointed to the recruiting poster that offered a bounty of three hundred dollars for signing up in the Union Army.

Dovie was watching this when a boy bumped into her quite hard, and she dropped her bundle of belongings. Shelagh was tugging her toward the curb where carriages were parked. A tall girl in a faded dress grabbed the parcel, but Dovie held onto one end of it.

"Mine, mine," she said through gritted teeth.

With their faces only inches apart, the two grimaced and pulled. A policeman towered over them.

"You again?" he said.

The girl's grubby hands let go, and she moved swiftly away in the crowd. The flowered bandanna on her hair was the last thing Dovie saw of her.

Shelagh pulled Dovie toward a carriage in which a girl stood up holding a sign written in Welsh. The two sisters looked at each other with disbelief. Their own names were written there. They approached.

"Hello, you're our two girls," the young woman said, looking down from the carriage. Then a torrent of words followed. "I wonder if the mistress knows you're so young. Mr. Joiner has gone to Shipping. We're also arranging a delivery, the new mantel of Belgian marble. You were on the same ship. Lucky you, that's why you got the carriage meeting you. Otherwise it'd be me bringing you on the public streetcar."

"You're from Mrs. Llewellyn?"

"I'm Nellie, the downstairs maid. We had better wait to see where Mr. Joiner wants you to sit; he's very particular, Mr. Joiner is. And this is Jerome, the footman. He's driving the carriage, today."

A disturbance broke out nearby and they turned to look. There was the girl again, the one with the scarf. With her were a couple of younger boys and a girl or two. A man lifted his fist and shouted at the group. They scattered, and he began to chase them, yelling.

Dovie watched, tightening her hold on her bundle, as he took off after the tall girl who ran across the open square. The girl bent her thin body forward and lifted her feet, legs pumping as she ran with all her might. Dovie saw the dirt on the soles of her bare feet as she outdistanced the man and disappeared into the shadows between buildings. Horse cars rattled past, and a policeman appeared blowing his whistle.

"Had his wallet pinched," the maid said, shaking her head. "And in broad daylight, too."

When Mr. Joiner stepped up on the carriage, he was a dry stick of a man, thin and expressionless. "You're Shelagh Lloyd, the new governess?"

The sisters looked at each other in pleased surprise at the word *governess*.

"Well, I am Mr. Joiner to you, butler of the household. Mrs. Henderson, our housekeeper, will be giving you instruction as

46

far as the house goes. For your tutorial, well, Mrs. Llewellyn will instruct you as to her wishes. Step up and sit here—and you, here."

That was all he said to Dovie: "And you, here." After almost having her belongings stolen, she was now being ignored. Dovie felt angry and upset as she stepped into the carriage.

"Home," Mr. Joiner said to the footman. "They'll send the mantel on this afternoon. I am glad to say it arrived in good shape."

All they care about is their mantel, Dovie thought as the carriage drove through a jumble of streets lined by red brick buildings. When the carriage stopped at a corner, she twisted her neck trying to see to the top of a large stone building, bigger than the biggest barn she had ever seen. She counted; it was four stories high.

With a jerk they moved out onto a wide avenue and the horses pulled on the incline. People were coming and going, dodging horse-drawn trams where passengers hung on at the open doors. Bells rang, wheels rattled, and voices shouted. There were more well-dressed people rushing past on this street than in the whole village at home. The next street had as many again, and so did every street. Dovie, with her face pressed to the window, couldn't take it all in.

It was quiet in the carriage. Neither Shelagh nor Dovie ventured a comment. Mr. Joiner sat very straight with his lips in a stern line. After a few minutes, he took out a notebook and began to go over it. His pencil tapped each line and sometimes hovered, then made a checkmark in the margin. The three females watched in silence.

Nellie took his absorption in his notebook as leave to speak but very quietly and with many sideways glances at the butler to see if he minded.

"When the carriage turns, it will be our neighborhood. See, the trolley car comes near just two blocks away. That is the opera house. Our ladies go there in the season."

The carriage turned. Here all was quiet, and the street was lined with trees and elegant red brick or white marble houses. They stopped before a house that looked like a picture from one of her mother's books, a Greek temple with four tall columns across the front.

When they entered the kitchen, a big-boned, tall woman with a large ring of keys at her waist turned. "You're the new ones, greenhorns or farm girls; it's all the same to me. Let me tell you something," she shook her finger in their faces, "standards, standards is the important thing." The finger shook in Dovie's face again. The woman's eyes had a bright, fixed look like the angry bull in the field at home. "There's a right way to do things and there's a wrong way. You'll have a lot to learn. Governess, Shelagh Lloyd? Young, if you ask me." She glared at Shelagh.

"I have my diploma," Shelagh answered.

The woman stood at a tall desk where she made a notation in a ledger. "You are to go directly upstairs to be instructed by Mrs. Llewellyn. Marge here will take you."

Shelagh disappeared up the stairs. Dovie watched until the last of her skirt disappeared from view. She felt abandoned among strangers. When she looked again, the woman's long, sallow face frowned down at her.

"Nellie, show this one—what's your name?"

"Dovie," she whispered.

"Do I have to teach this one everything? You are to call me Mrs. Henderson or ma'am." The housekeeper gave an exasperated sigh and waited, drumming her fingers on the ledger.

Nellie nudged Dovie, who heard herself saying, "Ma'am, my name is Dovie Lloyd."

She spoke in a low voice and looked at her feet. She couldn't believe this was happening to her. *I'm not supposed to be a servant*, she thought. She wanted to laugh, it was all so strange. It wouldn't do; she bit her lip and stared at the floor.

"Well, I can't believe the help we get nowadays. Nellie, show her everything and try to tell her how we do things here. Then you're to bring her upstairs."

As Nellie took her on a tour of the rooms, she chattered on and on. She began slowly, at first like a trickle of water and then opening up to become a river of words until Dovie felt she was drowning in information.

"Mr. Llewellyn is in business and now is a—a spectator, I think they call it. Mr. Joiner said to say the master is in trade for the war effort, but the truth is he's a speculator, that's it, a speculator."

48

Nellie demonstrated how hidden, pocket doors could slide open or closed.

"Can you believe—they bathe every day. That's how the gentry do. You'll see the tub upstairs. I don't think it can be good for a person, do you?"

They entered a room with a shining table and chairs. "The family gathers here in the dining room. Mrs. Llewellyn likes this room; it's warm in winter and cool in summer. You'll be cleaning here. I'll show just you how Mrs. Henderson likes it done, she's most particular.

"Nine in the family, although Mr. Hugh is away at school, so it's eight now. Then there's the staff: housekeeper; cook; kitchen maid; Mr. Joiner, the butler; one footman, that's Jerome; the coachman Bill, he's out sick now; and John, the groom; and us with Marge, that's three maids." She counted them off on her fingers. "That's ten—oh, I forgot the scullery maid, Mollie." She brushed her apron and straightened it. "And all full-time, not like some houses with slapdash help coming in mornings only.

"Mr. Llewellyn has his office at the South Street Seaport. I've seen the ships come in there from the Erie Canal. I've been all over the city on errands. Sometimes I'm given shopping to do when Mrs. Llewellyn doesn't want to go out." They stepped onto the front porch. "See this front here, four columns and two doors in between. We have to keep this bright and shining. One door isn't real. See, there's only plaster and board behind it, a door that doesn't open. No telling what they'll think of next.

"Sometimes, I am sent to shop on Broadway. I get the money and the list from Mrs. Henderson. When they trust you, you get the morning off from cleaning. I like to get out, talk to people, chat with the clerks, you know," Nellie said as they entered the front hall and stepped into the parlor. "Here is where the marble mantel will go. You wouldn't believe if I told you how much they say it cost, and to ship it over here, even more." She rolled her eyes.

They stood in the center of two grand rooms that opened into each other. At the end of each room were two large windows with a huge pier glass mirror between them. Dovie drew in her breath as she looked up at the ceilings so high above.

"When there are parties it's all open," Nellie told her. "Miss Jane recites poetry and scripture for the guests and Miss Eleanor plays this."

Dovie was drawn to the pianoforte, the first she had seen since she left home. She reached out and touched the shiny wood. Nellie frowned and with a corner of her apron polished the spot. Gas lamps hung with prisms stood on the mantel in front of the mirror to reflect light.

"This carpet is from France. See, woven in strips and sewn together, and you would never even know—except if your face is right down there, cleaning."

The fine furnishings had seemed impressive and beautiful a moment before, but that remark made Dovie look at them with a different eye. All had to be dusted and brushed and swept and polished. She would spend her days toiling over these carpets and tables.

"Be careful dusting these," Nellie warned. "Mrs. Llewellyn sets great store by these." She was pointing out two porcelain candleholders. Nellie proceeded to relate the story of the boy and girl painted on the candlesticks. "Paul is sweet on Virginia, and they're on a ship on the ocean, but a big storm comes. Then the ship is sinking and they need to swim away, but Virginia won't remove her petticoat because everyone would see her knickers." With a solemn face, Nellie said, "She goes down with the ship, she's that modest."

Dovie thought Virginia a fool and the story a fake. She remembered the high waves and the *Providence* shuddering as though it would be swamped, and knew anyone real would fight to take the next breath and the next.

They peeped into Mr. Llewellyn's library. Dovie quickly read some titles of books: *Atlas of the World*, *Philippics of Cicero*, and several grammars for children. She would like to have lingered there, but Nellie had more to show and pulled her along the hall.

The stairs at the front entryway were grandiose; dark, carved wood curved into a sweeping staircase. The stairs were narrower and steeper with each floor Dovie and Nellie traveled upward. The top floor attic with dormer windows and angled ceilings had two rooms for maidservants. Dovie and Shelagh would share one, and Nellie and Marge had the other. Dovie found her bundle and Shelagh's things there.

"Next you are to see Mr. Joiner. He explains the bell call. It's the very newest invention. No other house on the street has anything like our bell call. He won't stand for tardiness, either. Follow me in no more than a few minutes," Nellie said and left abruptly.

The stairs were slippery and dark, and Dovie, hurrying to her appointment with Mr. Joiner, felt her feet shoot out from under her. Her back hit each step while her hands tried to catch on to the banisters. She landed at the bottom of the flight. She felt sore but had no time to think about it. She dusted herself off and hurried on, bracing her hand on the wall.

The servants gathered around and stood in silent admiration as Mr. Joiner began to speak. "No other house, not among the entire acquaintance of Mr. and Mrs. Llewellyn, has this system." He pointed reverently at the black bells, seven of them, mounted on the wall of the kitchen. "This is very important, and you must learn to recognize the differences in tone." He pointed at one.

"Mrs. Llewellyn's bell." He paused. "When the mistress calls, answer that bell first by going to her room on the main floor to see what she requires. If it is morning, you can quickly assemble her hot food on her already prepared tray and go immediately up with it. I pride myself that my staff keeps no one waiting. Speed in service is our motto. There are no names under bells. You may have noticed this."

The clapper of one bell began to shiver and sound long strokes.

"Ah!" Mr. Joiner rubbed his hands together. "Nellie?"

Nellie contorted her face with concentration and ventured, "Miss Eleanor's room, sir?"

He nodded, and she visibly relaxed. "I pride myself that my staff will know the tone of each bell. Well, Nellie, go on, go on." He shooed her toward the stairway. "No member of the family or any of their guests should ever sense a delay in service. Your responsibility is to learn to recognize and answer the correct person or room for each bell tone. Commit these instructions to memory. And, for our new girl in the household, be neither seen nor heard. That is all."

At first the coarse, rough cloth of the dress she was given was a surprise to Dovie. She remembered the fine cloth that used to lie so comfortably against her skin. Her maid's uniform scratched her neck and arms, a constant irritant and reminder of her need to meekly say *yes, ma'am* or *yes, sir* all day, every day.

On the second day, the housekeeper told Dovie, "You are to wear your hair pulled tight in a bun at your neck. No curls to look disorderly, and put this oil on your hair to darken it; it is too red. It won't do, no, it draws too much attention." Mrs. Henderson shook her head.

Dovie mumbled, "Yes ma'am," but she felt furious, and that night she twisted on her bed when she thought of what a little toady she had become. She dressed the next day and took perverse pleasure in looking pale and downtrodden. She hated to put on the cheap shoes that were made from a straight last and would go on either her left or right foot. They pinched her toes and fell off her heel as she went from the top floor where the maids' rooms were to the children's rooms on the third floor and on to the parlor floor where the parents' rooms and public rooms were.

All day she trudged up and down and into the ground floor where the kitchen, storerooms, and pantries were. There was a wine cellar that was locked; only Mr. Joiner had the key. She was learning where everything was, and her head was full of instructions. Out back were the laundry shack, kitchen garden, and storage of the barrels of drinking water brought over from Brooklyn. A huge cistern stood next to one corner of the house with a pipe that brought water right into the kitchen. All you had to do was just turn a tap to have water flowing into a bucket.

When Dovie had been at the Llewellyn's a month, Hugh, the eldest son, came home on holiday from school. When he first arrived, he spoke to her: "Hello. You're new. What's your name?" and handed his coat and hat to her.

Dovie noticed his handsome profile and the lock of hair that swooped down over his forehead.

"I'm Dovie, sir," she said, but he was already bounding up the stairs calling his mother's name.

Dovie watched him go. After that he hardly noticed her, but she was very much aware of his comings and goings and always hurried to try to get a glimpse of him.

When he came down in the morning, Dovie couldn't help smiling as she greeted him. "Good morning, Master Hugh."

He was in his last year of boarding school and would go off to college in the fall. Dovie was replenishing the stack of hot toast as he scornfully answered a younger sister's question, "No, you can't go to Yale someday or ever. Girls aren't allowed."

✳ ✳ ✳

Upstairs in the big room, a boy with a large, rosy face dashed and darted between the sheets and clothes hung on the lines to dry.

"I see you, David," Meredith screamed, chasing him.

The two youngest Llewellyn children, Meredith and David, spent a lot of time with Dovie who was only a few years older.

Dovie crept along the wall, and when David ran out the end of the row, she jumped on him yelling, "Tag! I got you. Meredith, he's out!"

Meredith screamed with laughter as she threw herself on Dovie and David. Their flailing legs kicked over the laundry basket.

"Oh, no!" Dovie said. "The clean clothes. I'll get in trouble."

She looked up from the floor to see Master Hugh in the doorway looking in. Dovie scrambled up off the floor, ashamed of being seen acting like a child by this handsome young man. Master Hugh left but she straightened her apron and refused to play anymore. "I'm too old to play," she told the children and picked up the clothes from the floor, groaning when she saw a smudge on white sheets.

"I'll help you," Meredith said when she saw Dovie's face. "Come on, David, help." But the boy ran behind a flounced petticoat and stuck his head through the waist opening to make faces at them. Dovie brushed the smudge and shook it to get the dirt off.

"Go on—play your games, I have work to do," she told them crossly.

"Play with us, Dovie." The boy came over to beg. "It's no fun unless you play, too."

"Play by yourselves."

Nellie came to summon Dovie. "Mrs. Henderson says you must hull the peas before dinner. You're supposed to have it done by now."

David said, "You told us we could play pickup sticks and now we can't."

Down in the garden, Dovie sat on a bench with the bowl of peas in her lap. The children followed her and sat at her feet.

"You can go first," Meredith said enticingly and let the sticks fall from her fist.

Dovie looked at the kitchen window; someone could be watching.

"No, I am not playing," she said and shook her head.

"My turn, then," Meredith said and lay down on the ground to study the pile of sticks.

"You'll need a steady hand," Dovie cautioned her, interested in spite of herself. "I could show you—but..."

She shelled peas and kept her head down, not wanting to give Mrs. Henderson another chance to twist her ear. It was still sore from the day before when Dovie had moved too slowly to suit her.

The first time Dovie went in to answer Mrs. Llewellyn's bell, she looked around with curiosity. The mistress wore a wrapper, long and loose, and had removed her stays. She wore a floppy cap on her head. A framed picture of Little Goody Two Shoes hung on the wall, and next to the bureau were dried flowers in a frame.

Dovie moved around quietly, picking up and folding the clothes strewn on the bed. When she spoke she didn't hesitate to broaden her Welsh accent to curry favor with the mistress. Dovie would rather work up here in this quiet, spacious room than down in the confusion of the busy kitchen.

"I knew your mother," Mrs. Llewellyn said. "I was one of her first pupils; my sister and I took music for many years. I always remember what a good teacher she was. She was a young lady and we were girls. Our mother thought we should have accomplishments. Miss Muriel Howells, she was called then, would play the pieces for us on the harpsichord and give us three to choose from. 'Do you want to learn this one or this?' she would ask. Then once you had chosen the pretty-sounding thing, you were obliged to work away at it."

As Dovie listened to this story of her mother as a teacher, she felt sharp regret. Her mother had taught Dovie French out of her old books. Dovie remembered how reverently Muriel handled the beloved volumes. Sometimes, when the lesson seemed too long or she had to conjugate a particular verb too many times, Dovie used the wrong tense deliberately, over and over. Then, finally exasperated, Muriel would snap the book shut. Dovie would skip away, freed from the desk for the rest of the afternoon. Dovie sighed, full of shame over the memory.

She opened a cabinet and inside saw a row of wigs with three different hairdos. She closed the door and said nothing. Now she understood the reason for the cap.

"My sister mastered the barcarole but I never did. I wouldn't practice as I should have." Mrs. Llewellyn gave a sigh. "Now I wish I could sit down and play and sing, but I'll leave that for my young ones to do. My Bedo, I've put my hopes on her to be the musician."

Dovie noticed her use of the Welsh nickname but only replied, "Yes, Miss Meredith has a nice voice. She sang along as I gave them a little tune on the way to the park yesterday."

"And Dai?" Mrs. Llewellyn said giving her a look.

"Yes, Mr. David gave every sign of enjoying the old songs as much as his sister."

"It's a look back into the good, old times hearing you speak. Sometimes I miss the ways of home. Mr. Llewellyn doesn't like to hear it. He's all for progress and whatever's new. Not that I don't have the best of everything here. After all, I have given him three sons. Now where is my bottle of eye drops? Has someone moved it?"

Dovie quietly found it and put it in her hand.

"Now, Dovie, I do hope that you say your prayers every night. It is very important to Mr. Llewellyn that his household all be well churched. We have a very fine minister where our servants go.

Mr. Llewellyn has every confidence in Parson Wyatt to keep the staff on the right path. Oh, the parson is a perfect saint with his mission to the poor."

Dovie busied herself with her back to Mrs. Llewellyn. Her mother used to decry religion, saying, "The church, oh, the pious ranting I've had to listen to in my time!" And yet at the end she had gone to hear Pastor Jones. She must have been desperate for a cure or comfort for her illness, Dovie thought.

"Get out the long box," Mrs. Llewellyn ordered. Dovie entered the dressing passage between Mr. and Mrs. Llewellyn's rooms. Dovie was curious about the master, who was spoken of in reverent tones in the house. She had seen him, of course, but he would never acknowledge her presence as a mere maid. If they happened to pass in the hall, she had been instructed to move aside, look at the wall, and never speak. Yet here she went about in his bedroom opening his wardrobe and touching his shirts and handkerchiefs, noticing the framed silhouette of his mother on the wall.

When Dovie accidentally dropped the dress box she was carrying, Mrs. Llewellyn jumped and gave a little scream. Dovie turned to see her with her hand over her heart.

"What dress will you wear, ma'am?" Dovie asked opening the lid on two dresses stored lengthwise.

"I should wear the maroon. But show me the blue; it's new and I haven't even worn it."

Dovie was puzzled. Her mother had hand-fed the geese, kept the household accounts, and seen that the maids were well clothed and shod. This woman was vague and could not decide which dress to wear or whom to invite, even what menu to serve when Mrs. Henderson brought her suggestions. Dovie thought her too helpless for any use but said nothing.

✳ ✳ ✳

"Send Dovie to me," Mrs. Llewellyn requested again that week and many afternoons after that.

Mrs. Llewellyn liked to talk and gradually her great secret came out. She had lost most of her hair. Dovie's most important job became caretaking of the balding head. She massaged Mrs. Llewellyn's scalp with oils and shampooed her thinning locks with special soaps—all in the greatest secrecy.

On one of their afternoons, Dovie pulled back the wispy strands of Mrs. Llewellyn's hair and tied them. Then she opened the cabinet where the three wigs waited. She looked at them for a moment and then brought out the one with the middle part and two shiny wings of hair. She held it out invitingly. Mrs. Llewellyn had taken the framed miniature of her daughter, Eleanor, in her hands and was staring at it.

"I prefer life in the country, but, no, I must be in town to go around with Mr. Llewellyn and entertain for him and his business interests." She tapped Eleanor's picture. "I must see that she takes her place in society. Ungrateful girl! When I think of all we have given her, and she refuses to marry suitably. Says she's in love with a medical student.

"As if that's not bad enough, he's a Roman Catholic. Mr. Llewellyn doesn't even socialize with the Catholics. 'If I can't have this man, I'll have no other,' Eleanor said. She can cry all she wants, but he's an Irish immigrant. It's just not acceptable.

"We have other children to think of, and Eleanor can't be allowed to ruin everything for them. Mr. Llewellyn says I spoiled her too much when she was young. Well, it suits him to blame me."

Mrs. Llewellyn shoved Eleanor's picture away. A perfume bottle fell to the floor. Dovie rushed to pick it up before all the contents spilled out.

"Look there, it's practically empty," Mrs. Llewellyn said and tossed it down again. Behind her, Dovie glared and was slower this time, but bend and retrieve it she did.

Working side by side with Nellie, Dovie had learned many details of the Llewellyns, a topic that Nellie never seemed to lose interest in. An Episcopal bishop was an uncle by marriage and the family attended St Bart's, one street away. The servants had to attend the church the family chose for them.

When the Llewellyn family insisted she go to church, Dovie went. The minister bombarded his congregation with talk of piety and good works between hymn singing and prayers. Mr. Parson Wyatt also ran a mission.

"We must be ever mindful of the poor," he said.

When he smiled, his fat cheeks closed his eyes. Some described his smile as beatific. Dovie listened to his sermons curiously, warily. She thought this might be the pious ranting Mother had disliked.

As they polished tables, Dovie said to Nellie, "Tell me about yourself. I know all about the Llewellyns, what time Mr. Llewellyn takes the carriage to his office, what Mrs. Llewellyn likes on her breakfast tray, but I don't know anything about you, even where you come from. Have you always lived in the city?"

"No, no, I'm a farm girl. I'd like to go back and live in the country some day. But what if I marry a city man?"

"Do you have a boyfriend?"

Nellie put her finger up to her smiling lips and nodded, but she said, "Oh, no, we're not allowed." Quickly changing the subject, she asked, "Guess how many times I've been on the ferry over to New Jersey?"

Dovie shook her head.

"Six times. It's a steam ferry, the *Marianna*. When the family goes to the farm for the summer, I've gone twice. And every time there's measles or scarlet fever or the like, Mrs. Llewellyn has us pack the children up and she takes them to the country."

✼ ✼ ✼

In the kitchen preparing dinner, the cook moved between the brick oven and cast iron stove.

"You have to check the coals, see? Rake them up around the pot to get more heat," she instructed Dovie.

"Yes, ma'am," Dovie said and moved quickly.

She liked working with the cook, who was a pleasant woman. She had already let Dovie taste the custard she was making for dinner.

Dovie filled the two buckets of water Cook Katy asked for each morning.

"Disease and fire are the two dangers," Cook told her. "When I was a girl fourteen or so, there was a terrible fire, right here in the city. My mother was so frightened we left the house and all that was in it and ran for the waterfront. Ready to jump in the water, she was. We saw the flames roaring from house to house. You couldn't breathe, the air was so full of cinders." She shook her head. "Who could forget a thing like that?"

The butler, passing through, stopped. "That was 18—oh, 1835. I lived on the west side. They said seven hundred buildings burned below Canal. There was smoke and flames all the way up to Thomas Street. My father worked in New Haven at the time, and they could see the smoke from there. He worried all the week until he could get home to see how the family had fared."

Dovie watched and listened. If she had opinions she learned to keep them to herself since no one wanted to hear her, lowly as she was in the household.

These buckets of water kept in the corner near the stove in case of fire took on new importance for her. If on bathing day the water hadn't been used, it was heated on the stove and poured into the tin bathtub in the kitchen. First the tutor, Shelagh, bathed the young children in a great flurry of splashed water and towels and took them off upstairs. Then the maids took over the room and bathed themselves in turn. Dovie was the last to use the water, and by then it was gray. She looked down at the water, at the curd of soap at the edges and had to force herself to step in. After a very quick wash, Dovie helped Nellie empty the water in the garden, mop up the kitchen floor, and bathing day was done.

A laundress came in once a week and worked with her daughter as helper in the laundry house out back. This was because the family was rich, Nellie said; most people only hired a laundress once a month.

Dovie and Shelagh each had a peg to keep clothes on. They wore one dress and had one on the peg. Dovie saw her image in the cloudy mirror over the bureau and stuck her tongue out.

"How long before I get out of here?" she asked but had no answer.

She hardly saw Shelagh anymore. Their duties kept them in different parts of the house most of the time. At night when they got to their room, they were both so tired that they fell asleep after exchanging a word or two about their day.

Dovie recounted to Shelagh, "I see Cook have a nice tipple now and then. I also see the privileges the butler and Mrs. Henderson give themselves, he must have his day off, she gets her nap after lunch. I notice that no one upstairs is counting hours or bottles with them." She laughed with Shelagh over knowing the higher-ups' weaknesses and felt a little less powerless. "I am careful of the big boss, Mrs. Henderson. Everyone knows she runs things because Mrs. Llewellyn won't be bothered."

The sisters' attic room had been hot all summer but now became drafty and cold as the night temperatures dipped. There was light from one window and the narrow bed had a scratchy blanket. Some envy went into the family's beds as Dovie made them up and noticed their blankets were fine, soft wool with bindings at top and bottom embroidered with yellow flowers.

One night, as she got into bed, she caught herself thinking of the past as though it were a life in a different universe. *I had a carved, wooden bed with four posters. I had, I had—I think that a lot now. One bedpost unscrewed and I hid things there, six gold coins from birthdays. When Grandfather Howells was alive he gave them to me. They are still there and someday someone will find them and get to keep them*, she thought.

She yawned, tired from long hours of work and trudging up and down stairs to answer the bells that rang day and night. Even in her sleep she heard bells.

Dovie remembered one of her birthdays, the tenth, when a gold necklace was fastened around her neck. She had looked at herself in the mirror and declared, "Now, I am a princess." The grown-ups had laughed, and Shelagh made a face at her. She wondered what happened to the necklace but couldn't remember.

Nellie coughed in the next room. Dovie turned on her narrow, lumpy mattress, and the ropes underneath creaked. She heard the chamber pot being dragged out from under Nellie's bed and pulled the coarse sheet over her ear so as not to hear anymore.

Dovie had only a thin jacket. Mrs. Llewellyn never noticed, and Dovie suspected that Mrs. Henderson kept money meant for servants' clothes. Now in late September, when she took the youngest Llewellyn children to the park, she felt the chilly wind. Once Dovie saw the tall girl, the thief, begging; she had a baby in her arms. The girl had wrapped a long shawl around the baby and over her hair, but Dovie recognized her. Dovie rushed the children past but was disturbed by the sight. Did the girl have a baby or was it rented as she had heard of beggars doing? *At least I have a job and a place to sleep; she has to beg or steal.* On an errand early one morning, Dovie had seen children, "guttersnipes" Mr. Joiner called them, coming out of the alleys and doorways where they slept.

The wind was cold and Dovie thought longingly of the warm jacket with a high fur collar she had left hanging in her ward-robe at home. *They probably gave it to someone who needed a warm coat. What's bad for me may bring good to someone else.* It was a novel thought for her and kept her occupied all afternoon as she polished silver and dusted. She questioned whether it was true or not. The six gold coins forgotten in their hiding place. Her mother's pearl and ruby ring. *The Muellers should get their new start with the ring. Good came to them because I felt bad about taking it and being called a thief,* she thought.

Then she began to think of the clothes she had owned and worn, some in lovely colors, dark blue, shiny gray, brown with stripes. Soft wools and silks they were, new and warm or light as the season dictated. She had come away with only what she could carry. In her regret she lingered over details of the clothes, a buckle, a deep hem, lace trim.

She had always worn leather shoes instead of these cloth ones. Cloth shoes cost four bits and didn't last well at all; one little tear and then the money out of her wages was as good as lost. They could be cleaned off to look fair enough with a damp rag and a brush and a lot of work. As she worked blacking the scuffed spots on the fender in front of the fireplace, Dovie remembered a lovely dress her mother had. It was as vivid as though the cloth were in her hand, smooth and black with a pattern of red roses embroidered on the skirt.

Lace, ribbons. Embroidered or initialed handkerchiefs. Parasols, hats, gloves, bonnets. Warm coats or fingertip-length capes. She remembered boxes and wardrobes full. And all taken for granted; she had always had them and others had not, she now realized.

She tried to remember what Gussie had worn, but she had never noticed. *That's funny*, she thought, and wondered what she *had* noticed. Whether her tea was hot or the fire lit, only things for her own comfort—was everyone this way? Certainly the girls of the Llewellyn house seemed to be. Here, only Cook had ever seemed to notice when Dovie was sad.

Dovie felt a renewed respect for Cook and her own mother, who had noticed and cared how others felt. Maybe it was only something you got when you were older. But there was Shelagh, who was young but cared when she thought about it. Dovie mulled these thoughts over as she climbed the ladder to brush down the velvet drapes in the dining room.

One morning as she dressed in her cold room, Dovie folded newspaper and stuffed it inside her bodice for warmth. Later that afternoon, when serving tea to Mrs. Llewellyn and her guest, she bent to pick up the tray. All heard a loud crackle. The two ladies looked at each other. The guest raised her eyebrows at her hostess.

Mrs. Llewellyn said, "That will be all, Dovie."

Dovie walked to the door, keeping her body stiff and dreading another loud noise in the quiet room. She burned with anger at herself.

Once she was alone, Dovie took the newspaper out of her dress and crumpled it. Mrs. Llewellyn's requests, "Send me Dovie," had become an accepted thing in the household and a source of pride for Dovie. The lady was fond of hearing Dovie's accent and allowed herself to speak Welsh with her maid. Mr. Llewellyn frowned on the use of Welsh before the children or, heaven forbid, in society. Dovie stuffed the newspaper into the trash. *I would rather be cold than out of favor.*

✳ ✳ ✳

Mrs. Llewellyn ordered a lavish birthday celebration for Miss Eleanor's seventeenth birthday. There had been little good war news since the Battle of Bull Run when the northern troops retreated from the field. The mother made the excuse to her family that they all needed cheering up. She told Dovie, "Her father and I hope this party will take Eleanor's mind off this romance which we absolutely forbid." A bouquet of hothouse flowers was delivered in the morning to Miss Eleanor and her mother picked a rose to put in her daughter's hair.

Family and friends were invited, and a magician was hired to perform before dinner. He entered with a flourish of his red cape. Peeping from the edge of the crowd to see, Dovie hid her feet. Her shoes were broken on the side, and she hoped no one would notice them and tell her to buy new ones. She and Shelagh had been dressed up in black dresses and asked to sing French songs and play the piano for the younger children. Dovie was happy to be without her usual white apron and cap. *I feel like a regular person, not somebody's servant.*

Once during the party, Dovie and Shelagh looked at each other over the pile of gifts on a table and then looked away, each remembering better times. *The house in Wales, three generations meeting around the well-filled table. Aunt Olivia and Uncle Hedwig, Grandma and Grandpa Howells, Mother at one end of the table and Dad at the other.* Dovie didn't dare think for long about it.

Mrs. Henderson ordered Dovie, "Take that pitcher and refill it. Also, bring in more punch."

When Miss Eleanor's birthday cake was brought in, Dovie stared. Cook had made Queen Cake; it was three layers tall and had white frosting studded with figs, nuts, and cherries. When it was set down with flowers around the platter, it looked like a pretty lady in ball gown just joining the party. It was her own birthday tomorrow; she hadn't even remembered until that moment looking at the cake. She felt alone in the world. *I am nobody now*, she thought.

When it was time for them to entertain the children, Shelagh sat down at the combination piano and harpsichord. They had not been able to practice together because of other duties. Shelagh looked at Dovie and launched into "Frère Jacques," an old favorite that their mother had taught them. They both sang and received applause. After another song, the sisters stood and started to retire, but Mrs. Llewellyn called out, "Dovie, show what Meredith and David can sing."

Dovie beckoned to the children. They stood beside the piano with nervous smiles. Dovie played and Meredith sang out, "*Sur le pont d'Avignon, l'on y danse, l'on y danse.*" David stared at the audience moving his mouth but with no sound coming out. They received laughter and applause.

Then it was Dovie slipping out to tie on her apron and Shelagh back to the sidelines, watching over the younger children who were allowed to stay up to see their sister open her presents. Dovie noticed the gift of a silky shawl in light blue that Miss Eleanor unwrapped. *That's exactly what I would have chosen to have,* Dovie thought as she stared straight ahead and tried not to see the graceful fall of the fringe on Miss Eleanor's shoulders. "You have a nice voice," a woman told her and Dovie bobbed her head. The two sisters were given a cup of punch and a slice of cake and sent away to eat it in the servants' hall.

Much later, after cleaning up the kitchen with Nellie and Cook, Dovie dragged herself up to her bed. She had a splitting headache as she climbed the back stairs.

She put on her nightgown in the dark because Shelagh was already asleep. The light from the moon fell on her lumpy pillow. There lay a spray of red berries and three hard candies wrapped in a twist of green paper. Shelagh had remembered her birthday. Dovie felt her chest ease, and she breathed out a big gust of air. She went to the window and opened it wide.

Up between the rooftops she saw the moon, icy and silver. She put one of the candies on her tongue and let it slowly melt. She craned her neck to see the stars up in the sky.

"Heaven," her mother used to snort, "is only stars burning up and falling in space."

These were the same stars Dovie had seen when she walked beside her mother the night they heard Preacher Jones. Her mouth fell open in amazement at the thought that the stars and moon were still moving unchanged through the heavens while her life had twisted and turned on dark paths.

The morning after her birthday, Miss Eleanor rang. When Dovie answered her bell, she said, "I want blackberry jam, not this awful stuff. My tea is cold, bring me hot." Dovie trudged down the flights of narrow stairs to get hot water. When she returned Miss Eleanor pointed to a green shawl on the chair.

"That's for you. I noticed that ugly brown one you use."

"Thank you, miss."

On her way down the hall, Dovie stood on tiptoe to look at herself in the hall mirror. She remembered Miz Emrys, the rag merchant, back in Wales. There had always been a dark half-moon of grime under each fingernail as she held the reins of her skinny, old horse. Dovie's blue eyes stared at her own pale face topped by lank hair. "This is how dirty life gets you," she whispered to her reflection.

Down in the servant's hall, Dovie overheard Cook mention Mr. Hugh. He was to be home for a short time before going on an outing with friends. Dovie remembered that he had spoken kindly to her once and she had admired him in his fine, tailored clothes.

That evening when he entered the door, she noticed that he wore his cap at an angle in the most handsome way, and then, that he was escorting a young lady. One glance showed Dovie the girl's delicate, pink face and beribboned bonnet. Dovie felt awkward and common taking their hats and wraps, and she tried to hide her cracked shoes. She had spent one whole evening polishing black into the thin places so they wouldn't show. She was saving her money for the trip west with Shelagh. Worse than Mr. Hugh noticing her shoes, he didn't notice her at all. He handed her his hat and gloves as he spoke to the young lady, who ignored her also.

Dovie felt sad and empty the next day. If her mother hadn't died and she still had her home, she might have been a girl that Mr. Hugh would offer his arm to and exchange smiles with. She donned her petticoat and stockings very slowly, hating the stiff feel of them. They were dingy from many a washing in cold water and harsh yellow soap. *I would like to have clean, new clothes where the color is not faded*, she thought. *And bright, new shoes—shoes with nice, curved heels like Mr. Hugh's friend wore.*

Mrs. Llewellyn entertained guests that afternoon. Dovie was told to watch Meredith, David, and the visiting Penrose children. After rides on the big tricycle turned into a quarrel about whose turn it was, Dovie sat down at the small piano in the playroom and played a few chords to distract the children. As though from another life, another world, a French song came back to her and she sang it to them. Dovie felt genuinely happy for a moment, singing.

The guest, Mrs. Penrose, stopped in the hall to listen, a beatific look on her face. When Dovie finished she turned to Meredith and said, "Now you." Dovie played a few strong notes, and Meredith sang along with her, "*Frère Jacques, Frère Jacques, sonnez les matines.*" Dovie turned, beating time, and saw the doorway filled with powdered faces, curled hair, and lace. She stopped abruptly.

"We have permission..."

"Never mind, Marie," Mrs. Llewellyn said.

"She would just do for my youngest two," Mrs. Penrose declared.

"They can never start French too early," Mrs. Llewellyn remarked.

"She would do nicely with my Francine and Prudy. I am looking for someone for them. She would be helpful around the house, too."

"The little ones love her. No, no, we could not do without her, absolutely not."

"I'm quite taken with that girl...." Mrs. Penrose was not easily deterred from her objective.

Mrs. Llewellyn hurried her friend along the passageway. "Now, I do want to hear about the opera on Saturday."

The next day, Dovie was at the piano with Meredith and David when Mrs. Llewellyn pushed the door open and watched with a smile and narrowed eyes.

Looking up, Meredith said, "*Bonjour, Madame Mère.*"

"I've thought it over. It's what I want," Mrs. Llewellyn declared. "From now on you'll be French tutor to the little ones and ladies' maid to Miss Eleanor when needed. Mrs. Henderson says you will have to have some serving duties when company is in. Oh, and you will be called Marie now." She started to leave the room but turned and said, "Mrs. Penrose is not to have you. Don't you speak to her. If she asks you any questions say simply: I am loyal to my mistress. You are loyal to us aren't you, Marie?"

Dovie looked at her thinking, *There! Out of the kitchen! Can she change my name—just like that? Marie!*

Weeks later, Dovie was tidying Miss Eleanor's room when she noticed the jewelry box left open. Dovie looked at its contents enviously. *I never have anything pretty anymore. Wouldn't Master Hugh notice me if he saw me wearing one of these jewels?* Her hand hovered over the box, lifted out an amethyst pin, and then put it down when she saw the pearl choker. It was a lovely thing centered with a cameo set in gold. Dovie held it up to her throat and turned her head, admiring how she looked.

She heard the click of heels in the hall, someone coming. She hastily dropped the pearls inside, closed the box, and heard it click locked. Then, she saw, to her horror, the amethyst pin left out on the dresser. She panicked; the footsteps came closer. She put the pin in her apron pocket. Her heart was pounding when Miss Eleanor entered the room, but the girl didn't seem to notice.

She wanted, "Hot water and make it quick; I'm tired and want to bathe and lie down before the party tonight."

Dovie hurried up and down the stairs carrying the water from the kitchen to fill the bathtub in the corner of the hall. She set up the screen; all the time the jewel in her pocket weighed as heavily as the pails of hot water on the steep stairs. The thought of her stepmother telling everyone back home about Dovie, the thief, flitted through her mind. On her third trip, Miss Eleanor had gone into the bath. As Dovie picked up her clothes to hang them in her room, she saw the jewel box unclasped. She held her breath at the sight. Dovie waited for splashing sounds to cover any noise she might make as she cautiously opened the lid. Her fingers grasped the amethyst pin and pulled it out just as Miss Eleanor's voice called, "Marie." Dovie caught her breath but slid the jewel into its place.

In her ladies' maid voice, honeyed and sweet, she said, "Yes, miss?"

"The lavender dressing gown. Make sure it's warmed."

"Yes, miss," Dovie said, her heart thumping in her chest. She laid the robe out on a chair by the fire. When she was finally dismissed from the room, Dovie went limp with relief against the stair railing.

Work And Good Works

The next week, Dovie was sent on errands. She took the streetcar by herself for the first time. It was early morning, and the shadows still lay in the side streets as she approached the Bowery. She saw a figure sprawled on the sidewalk. It was a man lying facedown. She wanted to look away but instead stared at the body as she approached. Was he asleep, drunk, or dead? He wore flashy clothes, but his shoes were missing, stolen off his feet when he collapsed. His hands were curled beside his head of oiled and shiny hair. She veered a wide circle away from him in case he should jump up and do some terrifying thing before she could get past.

Dovie turned onto the Bowery and stared at all the posters advertising plays and vaudeville shows. A nickel museum was open. She peered in without entering. *Exotic Animals*, the poster said, and she did want to see the tiger snarl and the gorilla swing from tree to tree as pictured. She had a nickel in her pocket, tied in the corner of her handkerchief, but she couldn't bring herself to spend it when it could go to help her and Shelagh go west.

Next door, Bunnell's Museum advertised a tattooed man, a double-brained child, and most intriguing of all, the human pincushion. The nickel seemed like nothing as she stood on the threshold of actually seeing such wonders. Her fingers in her pocket undid the knot around the nickel. Dovie's eyes glazed over, and her fingers ran over the design on the coin.

She walked on, dragging her feet. The building a few doors down held a freak show, and a little farther on "tableaux vivants" were advertised. Dovie studied the posters from a distance; the emphasis seemed to be on women without any clothes on but carefully concealed behind a fan or a convenient palm tree. What would be on the other side of the door? It seemed dangerous to enter.

The barker, a man in a red striped jacket, rolled his eyes at her and called out, "And what's your name, Miss? Mollie, I bet."

Dovie blushed and hurried on, the nickel safe in her pocket.

She stopped by a low wall to look over the view from the hill. She saw the tall girl from her first day in America and her gang of street children down below. They were lying in wait at a wooded, deserted spot where the path turned. A man and woman came along, and the gang swarmed them. Their hands were all over them, in his pockets and her purse. There was a struggle; they took the man's wallet and ran. He chased them and fiercely grabbed and hit them until a boy handed the wallet back, probably less some money. Dovie watched, unable to look away, as each blow was struck. The gang of kids didn't fight back, only dodged and ran.

Dovie waited until she could walk down the hill in the safety of a group of shoppers. The robbed man and his wife were still quivering when Dovie told them, "I saw it all from up there." They were too upset even to reply, just stared at her.

Later, on her way back to the house with a sack full of purchases, Dovie saw the urchins lined up, hands on each other's shoulders to be marched away by a policeman. She looked at them closely. It was the gang but without the tall girl, the leader, she had heard them call Elsie.

Dovie asked the policeman, "What have they done?"

"Thievery, that's what. Crates broken open, bread stolen, nothing is safe with them in the market, and the merchants are fed up with it."

"What will happen to them?"

"The judge will scold them, scare 'em by throwing them in a cell with the big criminals. They'll be back out running the street like rats; it won't be a fortnight."

Dovie watched them in their march toward punishment. *I recognize them, I wonder if they recognize me? They have grown a little taller, a little thinner since I first saw them on the wharf.* She surreptitiously checked the housekeeper's money she had hidden in her waistband to see that it was still there.

Dovie's mother had taught her that there were good and bad people in the world and she'd better learn to tell the difference. "Judge them good or bad," she had said, "and treat them as they deserve." *Now, life seems more complicated. Who is good and who is bad? Police who put children in jail, are they good? Hungry children who have to steal for food, are they bad?*

Even the sight of the rag merchant passing by didn't make her laugh. He wore a tower of hats he had colected, but she didn't even try to count them this time. Another policeman appeared, and the two marched the ragged children away.

That night when Dovie and Shelagh went up to their attic room, Shelagh was in a nostalgic mood. "We had a feather bed and a goose down comforter that the maid plumped up each day," she said as she turned down the threadbare coverlet on her narrow bed.

"And a fire every morning," Dovie added.

"Our clothes were laid out on a bench to warm before the fire, and," Shelagh's face brightened, "when company came I had a dress with crimson braid and three flounces on the skirt. You had a green bombazine and a frilled pinafore. There was hot punch served on a lace cloth; we were given a cup and plate with bonbons and slices of cake."

"Buttered scones," Dovie added dreamily.

They fell silent.

"Do you feel hungry?" Dovie asked.

"No, not at all." Silence. "Well, maybe a little."

"I'm tired of bread and cabbage, dried beef, and tea for dinner."

"It's best not to think about it."

"Yes, you're right. But I wonder how they are, Dad and the horse and even Gussie. It all seems a long time ago."

"Best—"

"I know."

The next morning, when she served Mr. Hugh breakfast on a tray, she added extra butter and arranged it on a gold-rimmed plate. Pleased with how the crown imprint in each butter pat looked next to crusty rolls enticingly covered in a napkin, she knocked and went in with the tray. He sat in his mother's parlor as they discussed a party to be given in honor of his graduation from boarding school.

Hugh looked at Dovie and then said to his mother, "Now I won't have her wear those shoddy shoes if she's to serve my friends from school. They aren't even leather."

Dovie wanted to turn and run from the room but stood there waiting to be dismissed. Mrs. Llewellyn put down her teacup and looked her over from foot to head.

After a silence during which Dovie's face grew hot from embarrassment, Mrs. Llewellyn said, "That will be all, Marie."

She left the room hating herself for appearing so ugly and poor. She managed to get to the garden and behind a shed before the tears came. But after only a few minutes, she heard Cook calling her. Dovie wiped her eyes, threw some water on her face from the sprinkling can, and went in to peel potatoes.

Nellie was out sick again, and Dovie had to fill in for her. She kept her face bent to the ground to hide her red eyes. She peeled like a demon and gouged the eyes out of the skins with a vengeance until Cook said enough and sent her up to change clothes for helping with the midday dinner.

Dovie was now thirteen and a half. Her hands had grown so thin she saw spaces between her fingers. Sometimes she cried at night, missing her mother and the old life. She kept a sock in the back corner of a drawer. When she counted her little hoard of money hidden there life began to seem as though it might have some possibilities.

Mrs. Henderson resented Dovie's promotion and insisted she needed Dovie for help at a grand dinner that was the talk of the household. Dovie stifled her anger and worked hard, doggedly, doing both jobs for several weeks.

One evening, Mr. Llewellyn spoke to Dovie in the hallway outside his wife's room. He motioned for Dovie to move away from the lady's door.

"Now, Dovie, is it?"

"Marie, sir."

"Mrs. Llewellyn has good things to say about your service. I appreciate it." He took out his watch from his waistcoat pocket and looked at it. "I like to know that I can indulge her whims, that I am in a position to protect her from life's difficulties. In fact, the housekeeper has instructions to—well, Mrs. Llewellyn is a person who benefits from careful treatment, and I am a man who likes to have things go smoothly. At my place of business, I pay to see that things go smoothly." He put his hand in his pocket and drew out two large, silver coins. "This will be a very important dinner. I appreciate a smooth-running operation, and I pay for it."

Dovie recognized this as a favorite phrase of his: a smooth-running business, ship, household, now a smooth-running wife and dinner.

"My father was a hatter and kept a shop, but I got into the trade in beaver pelts at the right time. Now, I can keep up with the best of New York society." He thrust the coins at Dovie. "If all goes well Saturday night, I will remember you."

He walked away. Dovie was dumbfounded. How was she alone to keep Mrs. Llewellyn "smooth running?" She looked at the coins and shrugged as she pocketed them.

It was Wednesday, and in the foyer a great fuss was being made. Mrs. Llewellyn's new, beribboned bonnet quivered at the center of it. In her weak voice she sent Nellie scurrying upstairs for a lap robe in case of drafts and back again for a fan in case of heat. Nellie, out of breath and holding her side, rolled her eyes when only Dovie could see. Mrs. Llewellyn leaned on Dovie's arm in the vestibule and issued contradictory orders to the household. She would return early and would want tea promptly. She might be away till late and would have her tea at Taylor's establishment. Nervous smiles played over the faces of the staff, except for Mrs. Henderson who remained stone-faced. The servants stood on one foot and then the other. They longed to see her go out the door and hear the carriage wheels roll.

Jerome had been instructed to bring the carriage right around to the very doorstep. He had jumped down and unfolded the stair steps, then stood for some time with the door open ready to assist Mrs. Llewellyn into the cab. Dovie, dressed up for the occasion in new dress and shoes, was in attendance. She had done this before. She would ride opposite her mistress and would be told when to jump down and leave Mrs. Llewellyn's calling cards at selected doors or call a merchant out of his shop to show her a bolt of cloth or offer a selection of gloves at her carriage door. *Taylor's is splendid, like a fairy palace. Oh, I hope we go there for tea again.*

Mrs. Llewellyn was handed in, the carriage door closed, sighs of relief issued from the staff. The door popped open again. Her card case had been left in the purse she had decided not to bring after all. The case was produced, the door closed, the horses began to trot, and they were off. The staff went silently but grumpily back to work.

Mrs. Llewellyn sat like an effigy on the carriage seat; she wore gray pleated taffeta with a lace frill at her throat. She held her hanky up to her temple and moaned that Jerome drove too fast and she wouldn't tolerate it. Dovie took the cane and tapped the carriage roof for Jerome to slow down. Mrs. Llewellyn clutched the armrest when the carriage swayed around a curve.

She spoke from behind the handkerchief. "I wonder how that girl can be so selfish." Dovie looked straight ahead. "She does nothing and yet is too busy to accompany her own mother for an afternoon."

Miss Eleanor again. Dovie thought it wise to say nothing.

They traveled up Broadway so far north there were apple trees bending over the roadside and the coach wheels went over a carpet of pale blossoms. At Nineteenth Street, there was an area of mansions.

"This was all farms a few years ago. Why the Goelets are up here among the goats I can't say!" Mrs. Llewellyn said looking out the window.

Dovie hopped down at the marble entryway to leave Mrs. Llewellyn's new visiting card for the lady of the house. The photograph of Mrs. Llewellyn showed her looking very grand with her hair burnished and tightly coiled into a bun and her dress of silk with velvet bands. Through the iron railing of the magnificent place, Dovie saw peacocks and golden and silver pheasants trailing about the lawn.

Then the carriage went all the way down below Spring Street on Broadway with its crowds of people thronging the streets. Dovie stared at the women in fine dresses and large, feathered hats. As they approached Tiffany & Co., "I wonder Ma'am if I can look for Atlas?" Dovie asked. "Yes, yes, go ahead," the mistress replied. Dovie lowered the window and craned her neck. "Oh, I see him, Atlas holding up the clock right over the door. And one foot still about to step off of the building!" Dovie sat back satisfied.

They drove on and the mistress had just said, "I am her own mother, I should be put first," when a thud and a jolt threw her against the side of the carriage. She fell to the floor. Metal scraped on metal as Dovie was jostled to her knees. She pulled herself up and looked around. The footman opened the door and peered in. His expression was of great dismay. Mrs. Llewellyn's dark corkscrew curls still wore her new bonnet, but the hair now adorned her left knee. Her bald head gleamed dully in the light from the open door. Jerome gulped and slammed the carriage door shut. He turned to deal with the driver of the horse-drawn hack.

Dovie could hear their rising voices as she scrambled to right things. She said soothing words, replaced the wig on the uncovered head, the bonnet on top. There was a lurch as the two conveyances were disengaged, and moans from Mrs. Llewellyn. Dovie ministered to her, smoothing her cape.

Hearing her deep, shuddering sigh, Dovie sighed along with her mistress. This could not be described as a smooth-running operation. *Am I going to be blamed? What if Mrs. Llewellyn returns home overtired, or worse, ill? And the grand evening only days away!*

There would be no more tips from Mr. Llewellyn. This might signal the end of afternoons spent reading novels aloud in Mrs. Llewellyn's sunny sitting room. It would be back to toting buckets of hot water up the stairs and dreading Mrs. Henderson's knuckles rapping my skull.

"Now, I'm exhausted," Mrs. Llewellyn said, laying her head back on the cushions. "My handkerchief, Marie."

Dovie listlessly handed it to her as she pictured her privileges coming to an end. As Dovie wilted, Mrs. Llewellyn seemed to perk up. She looked out of the window with interest as Jerome and the other driver examined the vehicles for damage.

"Oh, look, Marie, the driver of the hack! He looks a perfect villain. Jerome is telling him off. Now he's slinking away. Tail between his legs! There's some relief in the worst having happened and it's not too bad," she said cheerfully and sank back in her seat quite relaxed.

Dovie, too enervated to reply, tried to smile agreeably. *The mistress is in good spirits for the moment.*

✵ ✵ ✵

For days, quantities of food and drink had been delivered or hauled in by Cook and Nellie and Jerome in preparation for the dinner party.

Looking over a delivery, Cook wailed, "No pineapples?"

"It's the war. We can't get those; you won't find any in the markets," the deliveryman answered.

"Let me see that menu," Cook said with a frown. "Yes, the menu lists cake and pineapples. It'll have to be changed and then approved. I won't go ahead with anything that hasn't been approved by the mistress. Then I get all the blame."

The servants had not heard the menu except in tantalizing bits and pieces.

Mr. Joiner, bursting with importance, informed the staff at lunch the week before, "A whole pheasant is to be skinned, cooked with spices, deboned, reassembled on a plank of pine wood especially made for the occasion, and then—the great challenge for Cook—decorated with its own tail feathers and beak as though it were alive."

Finally, it was to be borne in by Jerome and a hired helper. It would be paraded around the table, which would be lit by as many as thirty candles.

"Counting the sideboard, forty, sir," Jerome added proudly.

The guest list included a general of the Union army. A famous society beauty was to be there. Mrs. Caroline Van Zandt, Dovie repeated the name. It had an exciting sound. The mayor of the city and his wife would come. The Episcopal bishop, an uncle by marriage, was to be in attendance. It was an honor to the house, Mr. Joiner said.

Dovie was pounding sugar for wafers and listening with all her might. She had coconuts in a pile to break open next, get at the meat, and grate a bowlful for the cakes. She intended to get a hard white chunk of it and put it in her pocket. As the beautiful array of lemons, raisins, and pastry shells passed through her hands and under her nose, she had to know what some of it tasted like. Alone in the kitchen for a few minutes, she carefully pulled the cork from the bottle of apricot brandy and breathed deeply. She threw her head back with her nose full of the intoxicating nutty, sweet aroma. A noise on the stairs made her close up the bottle and pick up her mallet.

"An honor to the house, yes, but we work for two weeks solid and afterwards just sweep up the crumbs," she grumbled to Nellie.

The staff had been cleaning silver for a week, and the front door had been repainted, the brass fittings removed and shined. Everyone in the servants' quarters was constantly busy; there were always floors to be polished when you finished in the kitchen.

The dressmaker had been brought in and stayed a week, busy with lace and ribbon, pins and scissors. The evening of the dinner there were hair curlers to be heated before the fire, ruffles to be ironed. There was no end to it, Dovie thought rushing up and down the stairs between the two ladies' boudoirs. She particularly admired Eleanor's dress of pink silk as she carefully hung it on the wardrobe. When Miss Eleanor dressed for the dinner and twirled before the mirror, Dovie clasped her hands in admiration at the skirt caught up by a bow to show the pleated white silk underskirt.

As time for the guests to arrive came, the three maidservants watched from the hall. In charge in the foyer, was Mr. Joiner. The first carriage rolled up to the door the obligatory fifteen minutes late.

The men wore smooth, fine coats and displayed the gleam of gold watch chains across their waistcoats. They removed top hats and doeskin gloves which were placed on the hall table. Dovie was enjoying the excitement; after all the preparations, the evening was finally here.

The general arrived, splendid in his uniform with a sash and sword. The famous man paid little attention to the admiring ladies who peered at him over the banisters and through the pantry door. He arranged his sash; he removed his sword. Dovie was handed the sword by Mr. Joiner and nearly fainted with delight at the envious stares of the other servants. The general felt the cigar in his pocket but did not remove it as he entered the drawing room.

Mrs. Van Zandt arrived. Jerome straightened his jacket and hurried out to her carriage. Mr. Joiner was the only one authorized to speak to the guests. He was dressed up very fine in a new coat of dark gray. The others were to nod and reply briefly if spoken to—which was unlikely, Nellie said.

With a rush of cool, night air, Mrs. Van Zandt entered. She wore a sweeping velvet cape with an ermine collar; white plumes shimmered against her black hair. She turned and Dovie saw her large and lustrous dark eyes. Dovie stared. She saw slippers with the gleam of pale satin. The lady paused to shrug off her cloak. It fell from her shoulders into Mr. Joiner's gloved hands. There were jewels round her throat, pearls and garnets. She had creamy shoulders, wore pale satin with lace dripping at the sleeves and—she was gone, sweeping through the double doors. The last Dovie saw of her was a deep, red rose twisted up in her waves of hair.

Mr. Llewellyn's chest was quite puffed out as he went about greeting his guests. He wore a black silk coat with a velvet collar, a dark waistcoat and trousers. His white shirt had stiff collar points above a white tie. Mr. Llewellyn's brown hair was drawn back in a tail and reached down below his collar, but the other gentlemen wore their hair loosely waved above the collar line.

"The last man in New York to wear the queue," Dovie heard the mayor remark to another guest.

The general stood among the guests. His remarks showed at one point that he did not fully realize who his hosts were.

He was heard to say to Mr. Llewellyn, "Let's hope this fellow keeps a good cellar." His aide colored and spoke in his ear. The general bumbled into a remark about how fine the horses were here in the capitol, that he had never seen a finer display of horseflesh than this afternoon's parade. The aide looked distressed but persevered.

"Sir, you are in New York!" he whispered, but it only made his superior glare around at the company.

All stood back at a respectful distance.

Dinner was announced by Jerome, whose voice squeaked on "served." He saw the other servants laughing at him behind the hall door. Mrs. Llewellyn twisted her hands together. Pairing people for the procession in to dinner was her most difficult moment. Strict protocol governed it and if mistakes were made people would be offended and the dinner ruined. Dovie watched, hoping she could handle it.

Earlier, the mistress had confided her worries to Dovie. "Pairing Mr. Llewellyn is easy. He should lead the procession in to dinner with the bishop's wife on his arm. I have the general. I am rather afraid of him but will do my duty; precedence demands it. That puts the bishop with the mayor's wife, who is too talkative and will annoy him. These things are so hard to manage."

As Dovie watched from the hall, Mrs. Llewellyn spoke to the mayor, who was delighted with his partner, Mrs. Van Zandt. The rest fell nicely into place, the widow Hancock with Mr. Van Zandt, as was proper, and the two young people together, the aide escorting Miss Eleanor. All arranged, the host and hostess led off and proceeded into the dining room where they found a table gleaming with white damask in candlelight. Relieved, Dovie raced through the back hall to the butler's pantry

Jerome hurried into the pantry to grab his side of the pine plank and hoist the unwieldy pheasant onto his shoulders. The guests turned in their chairs when the serving door was opened with a flourish. Preceded by a blaze of candles,

Jerome and his helper accomplished the great moment of parading the bird with its long, sweeping tail and brilliant feathers around the table one time. The "oohs" and "ahhs" of the party were interrupted somewhat when the general had a coughing fit. His aide got up and pounded him on the back.

"Too many cigars," the aide muttered as he returned to his place.

Conversation turned to the telegraph, the war, and the latest battles. Mrs. Hancock wore black bombazine; she was in mourning for her brother, a colonel fallen at Balls Bluff, Virginia. Dovie watched from the pantry as a solemn toast was drunk to the gallant heroes who had given their lives for the Union. The host bowed toward Mrs. Hancock as he raised his glass.

Seated next to the general, Mrs. Van Zandt, in her paint and jewels and plumes, shone her smile on him; but the oysters, gingerbread, and wine claimed the general's attention. The beauty was unable to engage him in any repartee, though she tried her best. Dovie thought he paid a comical amount of attention to his beef roast and wine. Mrs. Van Zandt watched him consume many glasses. Little conversation issued forth. He decidedly did not want to talk about the war. The campaign was not going well at this point, not for the general but not for the beauty either.

Petulantly, she increased the lisp she affected. "Now, no more serious conversation, I won't sthand for it," she suddenly announced. She turned from the general on her left toward the mayor on her right.

"What has received such strong disapproval from such a lovely lady?" asked the mayor. "I know that all anyone talks of anymore is the income tax; I hear too much of it."

"Why, no one likesth it, it can't lasth beyond its second year. Let usth speak of entertaining thingsth!"

"Well, I attended the exhibition of fine sculpture presently being shown in Schaus's gallery on Broadway. The White Captive is the outstanding thing, though somewhat daring. The pink flesh, they tell me, is gaslight shined through a tinted shield—"

"Daring? What are you sthuggesting, Mr. Mayor?" Mrs. Van Zandt batted her eyelashes. She seemed to like this more than the general's snuffling and grunts, Dovie noticed.

"Oh, I hasten to assure you that many ladies attend there with perfect propriety. The nudity is historical, purely classic. The female captive portrayed is so lifelike as to be astonishing. When a gentleman requested it, the attendant could make her—er, the statue, revolve..."

"You have great apprecthiation for worksth of art, I can sthee, Mr. Mayor."

Dovie remained in the pantry stacking used plates and could see Mrs. Van Zandt as the door opened and closed.

Dovie heard her lisping and lovely voice say, "Misther Lincoln hath said and it'sth true. I would like to meet the 'little woman who causthed the big war' by writing a book."

Mr. Llewellyn, at the head of the table, stood to propose a toast to the general and the Union cause. Everyone raised a glass, some repeated, "To the Union," and then they all drank.

Next they toasted the beauty for her good works in planning a ball to raise funds for troop hospitals. "To Caroline Van Zandt, lovely representative of the Woman's Central Relief Association, for care of our sick and wounded. You have aided a noble cause!"

Dovie stopped her work and, with some forks clutched to her chest, stared. She thought this must be the epitome of fame and renown to be toasted in champagne by all these fine-looking people.

Through a crack in the door she was free to assess what had been wrought by weeks of work and planning. Mrs. Llewellyn at her end of the table had the general and was coping thus far. A frieze of curls sat on her forehead. Dovie had wound the string of pearls around her topknot and they both had admired her handiwork. The dress was a creation of black and gold with a taffeta bodice. Mr. Llewellyn had spared no expense for the occasion. He was the victim of soaring self-regard this evening and smiled regally along the table.

When the last carriage had rolled away and the guests were gone, the rooms were silent. Dovie stacked the good plates and started for the kitchen with them.

"They're boiling mad in the kitchen," Nellie whispered as she pushed the swinging door open.

"Why? I thought everything was so beautiful."

Dovie entered the kitchen after Nellie. Mrs. Henderson turned, fire in her eye.

"Who is responsible for the macaroons being served before the fruit?"

Mrs. Henderson, in a towering rage, grabbed Nellie's hand and twisted. Nellie bent over her painful hand.

"I thought it was time. I told Nellie it was time," Dovie said.

Cook clapped her hand on her forehead. "Uh oh, ye've slit yer throat with yer own tongue!" she said.

"Do you mean you deliberately changed my orders?"

With an almost inward gaze, Mrs. Henderson turned to Dovie. Her eyes grew dark and widened, her face flushed, her mouth moved like a viper ready to strike. She grabbed Dovie's shoulder. The sound of her thick hand was sharp, back and forth as it struck Dovie's face. Dovie reeled backwards, but Mrs. Henderson lifted her up and slapped her again. When she released her, Dovie's face had red marks, and there was blood on her lip. Dovie gasped for breath and stared with her blue eyes wide at Mrs. Henderson, and then dropped slowly, dramatically to the floor, rolled her head at a crooked angle, and lay still. Blood trickled down her chin, and she appeared lifeless.

"What have you done?" Cook yelled as she dropped her pan and ran to the girl.

Mr. Joiner hurried in. "Just what is going on here? Mrs. Henderson?"

Jerome, Nellie, and Cook Katy stared at Mrs. Henderson, on whose face surprise was being chased away by fright. Nellie held her red, twisted wrist out to Mr. Joiner and began to blubber.

"Mrs. Henderson, go to my office and remain there. Jerome— Nellie, quit crying!" Mr. Joiner, down on his knees, leaned over Dovie for a long moment.

"She's breathing," he said in the tense silence.

"It's a good thing," Cook said as she turned away, "other-wise...That woman has a terrible, ungovernable temper."

Mr. Joiner cut in. "I'll take care of this please, Cook. Jerome and Nellie, you two carry her up to her room. Look out, I suppose everyone in the house has retired, but go quietly, mind you. And Nellie, take care of that cut with some alcohol. Say nothing of this and refer any questions to me."

Once in her bed, Dovie moaned and stirred. Nellie reached for her hand. Dovie opened one eye the barest slit and surveyed the room.

"I'll take care of her now, Jerome," Nellie said, and the door closed.

"She looked scared, didn't she?" Dovie said from her pillow.

"Mrs. Henderson? Yes, we all were."

The two girls stared at each other. A slow, comprehending smile came over Nellie's face, and she sat on the edge of the bed. "Mr. Joiner was worried, too."

"And Cook! 'Ye've slit yer throat with yer own tongue!' I could hardly keep from laughing. Now I have to decide whether to have a quick recovery or feel poorly for a while," Dovie said, sitting up in bed and reaching for her hairbrush.

After one day of rest, Dovie was told she was needed and to get back to work. In the kitchen, she saw that Nellie's face was red from crying. When Dovie tried to talk to her, she just shook her head and ran up the stairs. The next morning Nellie was gone.

Dovie watched for Cook to be alone and went to her.

"What happened to Nellie?"

Cook Katy gestured a large stomach on her front. It took a few seconds for Dovie to make the connections.

"Throwed out. They won't keep her here a minute now they can see she's getting big with a baby on the way. Lucky for her, her ferryman says he'll marry her. He needs someone to take care of his other two brats. The story is that his mother's tired of it, and his first wife died in childbirth."

Months later, when Dovie heard that Nellie had her baby, she got her address and found the building. She climbed two flights of stairs and knocked on the door. A dog barked, and she heard children's voices. A little girl opened the door and stood chewing the corner of her apron.

"Hello, there. I want to see Nellie."

The child chewed and said nothing.

"Who are you?" demanded a boy who came to the door holding a tan dog in his arms.

"Nellie," Dovie called.

From the other room came a woman in a dirty apron. Dovie recognized her.

"Nellie, it's me, Dovie."

Nellie kept her face turned sideways.

"I've come to see you and, and your new family. I had a hard time finding you."

Nellie motioned at the door behind her. "Bill's home today."

"I've missed you. We all have. Jerome and Cook both sent you greetings."

Nellie came nearer. She had a bruise on the side of her face.

"Oh," Dovie said. "What happened?"

Nellie shook her head. The dog jumped to the ground, circled the cramped room, and settled on a pile of clothes.

"I brought some sugar cookies. Cook made them for you. Here." Dovie took them out of the sack on her arm, and the boy and girl came forward to accept the cookies she held out.

"Nellie, you're so quiet," Dovie said.

She's just a girl herself, Dovie realized. This could have been Shelagh if something had happened, she wasn't sure quite what, and she had had to marry Mr. Hughes back in Wales.

"Lionel," Nellie said, holding an infant out on her arm. She rubbed his cheek with her finger; he looked at her and smiled, waving his arms.

Dovie watched Nellie play with her baby and then held out her arms for him. She inhaled the baby fragrance from the round head and touched the fine hair. With a shock she realized, *I could create my own family. I could have ten children if I wanted to.* Lionel began to cry and she gave him back to Nellie. *I will have ten children; we'll be like an army and nothing will ever break us apart.* She heard the voice of Bill from the next room and thought, *but then I'll have to have a husband.*

"Nellie," he yelled. "Where's my tea?"

Nellie handed Lionel to Dovie and scurried through the door. The loud voice complained and rose over Nellie's replies. The dog stood up, one ear cocked. They heard the crash of crockery. The dog tucked its tail under and whisked across the room to hide under a table.

An agitated man came through the door. The children sat where they were, very still, and didn't look up.

He turned and snarled, "Nellie ought to be busy with supper. Dodie, is it? Had best be leaving now..."

Dovie listened to his braying voice. *He's the one who gave Nellie that bruise*, she realized.

"...let you get on with your work. This setting and visiting, that's for when your work is done."

Nellie ducked her head and ran to get his tea.

"A fine baby," Dovie said and set the baby down. "I must be going now. Good-bye, Nellie." She forced herself to speak to the man whose angry eyes were fixed on her, "Good-bye, Mister Bill."

As Dovie went down the front steps, the sack on her arm caught on the newel post. She grabbed it savagely and it tore. *Nellie wanted to go back and live in the country someday but her life seems as good as over.* She took the sack, ripped it clear across, and threw it down. She kicked it out of her path and walked away down the street.

✵ ✵ ✵

The Llewellyns required that all their housemaids attend Mr. Parson Wyatt's church. It had not done Nellie much good; nevertheless, they were sure it was the right thing to do. So once a week Dovie sang hymns on the street corner with the rest of Mr. Parson Wyatt's ragtag mission group and rattled her collection can. She always turned in her coins at the end of the day.

Counting the coins, Parson Wyatt told her, "You are helping those less fortunate than yourself."

"I hope so," Dovie said. "This is my half-day off."

"Your sacrifice is for Our Lord," Mr. Parson Wyatt said.

On this cold, November day, a woman paused in front of Dovie. Her face was soft and faded. She took out a purse and counted out three coins.

Dovie knew what to do. She rattled the can and repeated what Parson Wyatt had instructed her to say: "You are helping the Lord's work."

The lady hesitated and then added another coin. Dovie felt a rush of warmth at the woman's generosity. She thought of her own goodness out here in the cold, and that brought tears to her eyes.

Dovie walked around to keep warm. She passed a pushcart and inhaled the smell of hot, spiced gingerbread.

The Irishwoman removed the pipe from her mouth and recited the wares on her cart. "Apples, red or green; George Washington pie; and bolivars, hot and spicy."

Dovie had eaten only a piece of bread and a gulp of tea for breakfast. The smell of spiced gingerbread mingled with pipe smoke was ruining her concentration on good works. She kept moving.

The street girl, Elsie, and her gang of urchins were across the street next to the church, sheltering from the cold wind. Dovie had only a few coins in her can but held them close to her chest and crossed the street. She decided to turn the coins in and hope to get something to eat. One time, the pastor had given her a biscuit and hot tea.

The smell of furniture polish was heavy in the silent vestibule as she entered. Lifting aside a curtain, Dovie saw Mr. Parson Wyatt framed in an alcove. She had hurried up behind him before he heard her. He turned and breathed out the reek of liquor. He had opened the high window and motioned impatiently to her to hand him the bucket at his feet. She lifted it, and he seized it and dumped the water out the window. Yells and squawks came from below. Dovie lifted herself to look out the next window. She saw the beggar children. Two of them were soaked, their hair and clothes dripping as they shivered and cried.

"Ah ha!" Mr. Parson Wyatt crowed. "I got you!"

Dovie saw the alarmed faces looking up.

"There! That'll drive them away. Thieves!" he said.

"They're hungry. Why don't you give them food?" Dovie asked indignantly.

"I don't want them here. Street rats, they infest the city. When we gave them Holy Bibles they tried to sell them."

"I thought we were helping the poor. I collected this and it's nothing but a big cheat." She held out the collection can.

When Mr. Parson Wyatt reached to take the can, Dovie clutched it and ran. She ran through the chapel and out the vestibule, slamming the door on the sanctimonious smell of wood and candle wax. On the street, she emptied the can and threw it in a barrel. Clutching the coins, she went straight up to the vendor and bought herself a bolivar. The gingerbread felt warm in her hand, and her stomach was growling.

She had the flat cake up to her mouth when she said, "Now you're no better than Mr. Parson Wyatt."

The beggar children were watching her. She broke off half the cake and held it out to the youngest boy. She saw his astonished face as his thin claw of a hand closed over the gingerbread. He took it and ran before the big ones could take it from him. He sprinted across the street with Elsie after him.

The ragged children crowded around her making soft begging sounds. Dovie crammed the other half cake into her mouth and chewed with tears running down her face. She tasted the salt of her tears as much as the bolivar but kept on chewing and swallowing until she had eaten it all. Their eyes watched even the crumbs as she licked them off her lips. She promised herself, *When I get out west I'll be a good person, but I've got to get there first.*

At the house, Dovie told Shelagh, "And then I told Mr. Reverend Wyatt it's a big cheat."

Shelagh's face was a study. "Well, now you've done it," she said.

"Will we be kicked out?" Dovie asked.

"No, because we won't wait, we'll quit. I fancy a change, how about you?"

They bundled up their meager belongings. Dovie left a note on Meredith's pillow: *Au revoir, Dovie Lloyd.* Then they went downstairs to face Mr. Joiner.

He stared right through them as though they were not there. "Mrs. Llewellyn never wants to see either of you again after your disrespectful behavior. All that she did for you was a waste. Some people simply cannot be helped and can only be dismissed. I am especially disappointed in you, Shelagh."

Shelagh clicked the fastener on her purse open and shut. She shifted from one foot to the other, but neither girl dared to answer back to him. Dovie never looked up from the place where one of her shoes dug at the floor.

It was January first; the streets were icy as the girls walked away, each carrying a bundle. The lamps were just being lit at dusk.

"I was sorry to leave Cook, but she was the only one. Maybe Meredith, too," Dovie said.

"I got us our wages for half the week." Shelagh jingled the coins in her pocket. She seemed to have come alive once they knew they were leaving. "Just think," she said, "tomorrow morning I won't have to try to teach the classics to those spoiled brats."

The two girls walked along occupied with their thoughts. Shelagh looked up to see lights illuminating a splendid house and people hurrying toward the spectacle. They turned with the crowd and went to see. Once in the courtyard, they saw that every window was draped in red, white, and blue bunting. They climbed up onto a wall to see over the crowd.

"What is it?" Shelagh asked the woman next to her. "What is it for?"

"Don't you know?" the woman said. "It's the Emancipation Proclamation. Lincoln's freed the slaves!"

"These people are happier about it than I am," a man said.

"Yeah," another added, "what jobs are the Negroes going to get now that they're free? Our jobs, that's what."

"No nigger is going to take my job! Who lives in this house anyway?"

"Damned abolitionists, you can be sure of that."

"This is where Horace Greeley, big editor of the *Tribune*, lives."

"No, it ain't."

"Yes, it is."

"They don't look like they have to worry about having a job, whoever they are."

It was dark now. Shelagh signaled Dovie and they started to leave.

"I'm cold, my feet are freezing," Dovie had begun complaining when a group rushed past them into the courtyard. The girls were shoved aside by men whose faces were muffled with scarves and hats pulled low. They pushed a wheelbarrow filled with steaming tar, and their hoarse shouts sent the crowd scattering. Moving swiftly, the men took shovels and threw pitch over the front steps and pavement. Some in the crowd cried, "No!" but most drew to the side and watched or ran away down the alley. One of the men laughed as he took a trowel and smeared the front door with big, black strokes.

Dovie watched in shock. What had been a shining spectacle was now dirty, and the courtyard was filled with the odor of hot tar. Some cheered the men. One man quit shoveling to raise his arms and shake them in the air. They did their job and quickly disappeared as they had come, trundling the wheelbarrow down the street.

The girls turned and walked the other way. Dovie followed Shelagh.

"I don't understand," Dovie said. "It sounds like a good thing to free the slaves."

Shelagh only called, "Hurry!" and they ran for the streetcar and jumped on. They took the car downtown and then walked over several blocks to Orchard Street. They knew a girl named Sharon who had been fired from one of the Llewellyn's neighbors. Sharon had gone to live down on Orchard Street, and they were looking for her place. Dovie could barely see a little slice of sky and stars between buildings as she shifted her bundle to her shoulder. She knew there was a wide world out there somewhere, outside the city. If only she could get to it she would be able to see the whole, immense sky instead of always being crowded between buildings.

They paid the landlady who popped up at the door the minute they knocked. It was a dark, crowded place with the privy and water pump in the alley out in back. There were no lights; they had to feel their way along the hall and up the stairs to a room they would share with six others. Dovie's relief at getting away from the Llewellyn's died with her first breath of the fetid air in their room.

In The Tenement

"Go up to Troy. There's plenty of work there," other tenants told them. They could barely see each other in the gloom of their room.

Sharon said she knew at least two girls who had gone upstate to work in the collar factories.

Dovie said, "Mr. Llewellyn changed his collars as many as four times a day, he was that particular about coal soot dirtying them." She was ignored.

Shelagh said, "I'd never go to work in any factory. I heard the girls were forbidden to talk. Even whisper or sneeze and you're instantly dismissed. Definitely not."

"We'll be moving on pretty soon. Just as soon as our dad gets work," Sharon said. "This is just for a while for us."

It ended up that Dovie found them a job. On the streets near the mission, she had sometimes talked to a woman whose name was Ginger Blue.

The first time Dovie saw her she was fascinated. Ginger wore gray trousers and a white shirt under a short jacket. She had a felt hat jammed down on her forehead with the brim rolled up. She walked with a swagger and paused to light a cigar, striking the match by flicking it with her thumbnail. Dovie had rattled the collection can at her.

"I used to be on the streets myself," Ginger said, "but not with no church." She pointed to her nose, "That's where I got this," she said and laughed. Ginger had a broken nose that had healed with a downward twist and gave her a devilish smile. "Now I have my own business. You seen my signs? Ginger Blue Lunch Wagons, everybody knows them."

Now, Dovie went looking for Ginger.

"What if I need a job, would you hire me?"

"What happened to your place as a maid?"

"Well, I told the pastor I thought it was a big cheat with those collection cans..."

"I could've told you that. Can you drive a horse?"

Dovie nodded. "I drove the wagon at home over fields with no roads."

"One wagon does need a driver. Miss a day and you're fired. People depend on us being there, and they buy their breakfast and maybe their lunch, too, because we're regular."

"I've got my sister; she's doing some work."

"What does she do?"

"She's a letter writer, and she'll read letters for people, too. But she needs more work than that."

"I'll tell you what. You seem like smart girls. I'm too high up now to work anymore on the wagons. You'll be selling sandwiches and you work hard. On the docks, outside the factories, in all weathers. You're young and you're kinda small. You sure you can handle a big horse and wagon? And be sure to show your red hair. You want people to remember you."

It took a trip to the pump, pails of water, and lots of soap but that night Dovie washed her hair clean of the oil Mrs. Henderson made her put on it. When she came upstairs to sleep, her shiny, wet hair hung all around her face and shoulders. She shook her head, pleased that she had a little piece of herself back.

When Monday morning came, Dovie was afraid of not being able to do the job. Penny, the horse, started off. Dovie was shaking and hanging on to the reins. "There is nothing on this job I can't do," she repeated to herself and let the horse shamble forward. After a while she realized that to gather the supplies, sell them, and collect the money was as simple as taking the reins in her hands. After the third day, she forgot that she had ever doubted her ability and was so involved in asking herself, *Are we on time, are the supplies good, does the money tally, are we making money?* that she forgot her worries. By the second week she would have laughed if anyone had questioned her ability. All she had to learn was the streets, and those were beginning to form a pattern in her mind.

Dovie had been driving for weeks when she remembered Miz Emrys. The similarity of her situation to the peddler who came to her mother's house was all too clear to her. *I'm a peddler now, with a horse and wagon*, she thought. She had no time to dwell on it. She only knew she was glad to be making money. Every week, Shelagh went to the bank. It was a grand-looking place, but anyone could go in and put their earnings in an account. The sisters were saving for the trip west that they dreamed of making.

With earnings coming in regularly, Dovie and Shelagh found it exhilarating to be on their own. They went all over Manhattan to the shops and factories and the wharves on the west side. Dovie drove while Shelagh organized the supplies in the back compartment. They exchanged banter with their customers. Shelagh was good at this; Dovie was inclined to lecture.

"You should get up earlier. You've been late to work three times this week. You'll lose your place," Dovie scolded O'Quinn on the wharves.

Shelagh protested, but the man seemed pleased. "She's taken notice of me like no one since my mother, God rest her," the man said.

The sisters loaded up at the bakery, the market, and the house of a woman who made and sold sandwiches. They kept going to docks or shops until they sold everything. Ginger liked that they usually returned with an empty wagon. She paid them once a week. Both sisters knew the money wasn't safe in their room. They each got a miser's purse, as they were called, and carried their money on them. These long purses they tied around their waists and kept hidden under their petticoats.

In the tenement room it was hard to get clean and stay that way. Besides the smell of sweat and grease that hung in the air-less room, Dovie learned to hate the dry, almost burned odor of unwashed people. To pump water, they had to go downstairs and out in the alley. None of these hardships stopped the two sisters from going out to have a good time once they felt their new freedom. There was no one to tell them what to do or when to come in at night.

Not far from the old Bowery and only three blocks away from Orchard Street, a fellow named Tony Pastor had opened a new kind of opera house. Sharon and her friends were regulars there. Often enough in the still of the night, the two sisters had been wakened by giggling laughter followed by a snatch of song and the crash of a bottle flung against the next building as revelers found their way home.

"Oh no, we couldn't go to a place like that," Shelagh said when Sharon first urged the two sisters to go along.

"Oh, come on, you'll see. This is a clean house, no bar and no smoking. And besides, Ruby's brother goes with us. I've seen families with children there. The minstrel shows are great fun, and there are song-and-dance acts. We make sure to go when women get in free on Fridays. I don't know which night is better—on Saturdays they raffle off hams and turkeys. So even if you have to pay to get in, you could win something. My friend won a dress pattern, and her mother is going to sew it for her and she'll wear it this Friday. Come on and go. Even families from the nice neighborhoods are there."

Dovie and Shelagh went with girls from the block to Pastor's Opera House. Before they became regulars, Dovie and Shelagh went only on Friday nights, and at first, they looked around and clung to each other. At the intermission after the minstrel show, the spacious lobby was a place to promenade and buy refreshments.

Dovie was now fourteen, and when she looked at herself in the opera house mirror she saw cornflower blue eyes and long red hair that was coiled at the nape of her neck. Shelagh was sixteen and usually led the way in her new lavender dress. Dovie followed her, walking fast with a determined little tap, tap, tap. When Dovie first saw Shelagh with her hair up and wings of auburn hair framing her wide eyes and pink cheeks, she gasped. She hadn't known Shelagh was beautiful.

The women were busy assessing the other women's outfits and hairdos and flirting with young men. A young man tried to catch Dovie's eye as he handed her a cup. She looked away, confused, and tasted the sweet, fruity punch. Later, Dovie remembered only scattered details of the evening: loud remarks and shouts of laughter, a boy who smelled of soap and asked her name three times.

Ruby's brother tried to hold Dovie's hand as he walked them home. By the second Saturday, she had been coached by Shelagh on how to keep would-be suitors at bay. He hung around Dovie and talked a line about how he might be lying dead on a battlefield this time next year.

Dovie told him, "You know you work in a munitions factory and won't be taken. So, keep this to yourself," and she lifted his hand and daintily held it up in the air before dropping it as though it were a dead fish.

Soon, one frosty glance from her was enough to elicit a stammering apology from any of the boys. Like a flock of sheep, they gathered around her all the more, each hoping for a kind glance.

One Saturday night, Lolly, a girl with a booming laugh, saw that her boyfriend had joined the group around Dovie. All evening Dovie felt her glare. As they left the hall, Lolly called her a slut and shoved her on the stairs. Dovie started to walk away, but suddenly rage overcame her and she whirled and pushed with both hands on Lolly's chest. Before she fell, Lolly's fist clipped Dovie's eyebrow. Blood ran down Dovie's face as she bent over and grabbed the girl's hair. She heard the delicate sound of hair roots ripping from Lolly's scalp even as teeth sank into her other wrist. It took two boys plus Shelagh to pull Dovie off Lolly. Both girls were red-faced and panting. Lolly got to her feet and ran. They could hear her whimpering until she reached the corner and turned. Shelagh shook Dovie and berated her all the way home.

After that the two combatants kept their distance from each other in the lobby, and if one saw the other she turned her back ostentatiously. But sometimes in the middle of the night, Dovie remembered the small sound of the hair roots ripping out of a scalp and the storm of rage that had shaken her. She would twist uncomfortably in the bed she shared with Shelagh and another girl. Once, she fell off on the floor. She heard people grumble and curse at her before they turned over and slept again.

Mrs. Bebbins, who also lived in their room in the tenement, shook her head and said to Dovie, "No good will come of it, out at night this way. Mark my words, you'll be sorry—only bad girls run wild. You should come in at dark like a respectable person."

Dovie replied, "I don't have to do anything you say. Only I know what's best for me." She felt the big cut over her eye throbbing. "I can take care of myself," she said, even as the bite on her wrist hurt.

Then a morning came when a policeman stopped by her cart as Dovie stacked boxes ready to load. He watched silently as she worked, tapping his nightstick lightly in his hand. She looked up when he spoke.

"You'll want to be careful. This is a bad neighborhood."

"What do you mean?" Dovie stopped work and wiped the sweat off her forehead with the back of her hand.

For a reply he tapped the cartons with his nightstick. "These could get stolen or broken. I expect you paid good money for them. But it costs money to be safe around here."

Dovie gave him the same cold look she had practiced on her would-be beaux. He turned to leave and smirked back over his shoulder. Dovie felt uneasy but went on working and tried to forget him.

Life seemed simple: fill the wagon, drive the horse, sell the goods, and count the change. Dress up and go out at night, frown if someone got out of line, move on. Dovie hardly needed sleep, it seemed; she flew from one thing to another, lying on her bed and sleeping afternoons, tired enough that the noise and crowding didn't keep her from it. As evening came, she got up, threw water on her face, and started in again.

She wore her blue dress to the shows. It had flounces at the neck and hem, and she had squandered a week's earnings on it. "But it was worth it," Dovie told Shelagh, "If I can't have something pretty to wear, life isn't worth living."

This Saturday morning the two girls had been out late the night before at the opera house. She had no time to change clothes, and so Dovie still wore her patent leather, dress-up shoes with grosgrain ribbon bows on the toes. She had thrown on a smock over her blue dress. The flower in her hair was from a boy whose name she had already forgotten. Jimmy, was it?

There were so many who said the same things, "I saw you last week and hoped you would be here." The pink rose, bedraggled now in the dawn light, hung over her ear.

As she and Shelagh began to load the wagon, her mind was still full of the music from the stage. She lived for the nights of music and admiration. At those times, she was full of smiles and laughter, and her eyes shone and glittered over the rim of her punch cup. The intense glances and admiring eyes of these evenings fed something hungry in her.

She got back in the wagon after their regular stop at the bakery. Ginger had paid them, and Dovie's hidden purse was heavy with coins against her side. Shelagh worked in the back to arrange their wares. Dovie picked up the reins and flicked them. It was the first light of dawn. She noticed something dark leaning against the seat beside her. The wagon swayed, and it fell to the floor. At the next corner, she slowed enough to poke the bundle of black clothes with her foot. It fell against her leg. She stifled a scream as an arm rolled to the side and revealed the white, dead face of a man. Blood trickled out the nose; a gash, purple in the early morning light, went across one temple. Dovie gasped and remembered the cop's smirking face and his last words: "If someone doesn't cooperate—well, they get a nasty surprise."

She clamped her lips shut and whipped the horse. The wagon wheels bumped rapidly over cobblestones. She turned onto Houston Street, deserted at this hour. As the wagon careened around the corner, she shoved the dead man with one twinkling patent leather shoe. It took another kick before he fell out the side of the wagon. The horse galloped on.

Shelagh crawled forward to the little window and shouted, "What's wrong with Penny? Too fast, three pies have fallen down!"

Dovie stood up and braced her feet on the boards, pulling back with all her might. The horse, frightened by the rattling, swaying wagon, ran faster. Dovie couldn't turn the horse at their usual street. Conry's Hotel flashed past and the bank, but an uphill pull slowed Penny down. The horse was panting, her sides heaving.

Dovie sank to the wooden seat. She could hear Penny's shuddering breath as she struggled up the hill and turned.

Tree branches met over the street; the houses had marble fronts like Greek temples. It all looked familiar. There was the house front with four pillars and two doors, one of which she knew to be false, and the brass trim she had polished many times. The horse trotted past the house Dovie had left just months ago. She looked at it as though she were in another world—the cart had a smear of blood on the floorboards, silver hung heavy in her pocket, and dancing shoes were on her feet.

The less anyone knows, the better, Dovie thought as the wagon pulled up late at the shirt factory. The street was still empty except for Ginger with a basket of food over each arm and a scowling face.

"Well, you got here," she snapped at the small figure of Dovie now slumped on the seat. The horse's sides still heaved a bit. Dovie stared at Ginger unable to speak.

"Where's Shelagh? We got our work cut out for us to set up before the first trolley."

Shelagh was already opening the back panel of the wagon and placing their wares in stacks ready for sale.

"You make change and Ginger and I will make the sales," she ordered Dovie.

In minutes the horse-drawn trolley drew up across the street and disgorged a bunch of workers, hungry and already counting out their coins for pie and sandwiches.

✲ ✲ ✲

Months went by with work crowding the girls' good times. The sight of a uniform and brass buttons made her nervous, but Dovie had not seen the policeman who had threatened her. The cop on the beat was a new face. The whole incident receded in her mind.

It was July, hot and steamy. The first week of the month, people were talking about a great victory for the Union at Gettysburg and then the capture of Vicksburg that once again meant clear sailing on the Mississippi River.

She did overhear rumblings of anger among the factory workers who bought lunch from their wagon. On the docks stevedores on strike had to stand by and watch as the police led Negroes right past them to keep the cargoes moving. The strikers were mostly Irish, and their anger was building as they talked about the draft.

"They'll send us to fight the war for slaves to take our jobs!" they said.

Some wanted no draft at all, and some said it was unfair because the rich would be able to buy substitutes and not have to go.

The draft lottery began on a Saturday, and by the next Monday morning feelings had hardened among working people.

When Dovie and Shelagh started out that morning, the streets were empty as usual, but by seven thirty they realized something was wrong. The shops along their route were closed. They headed the wagon for the west side wharves.

They heard the noise before they saw anyone. At Eighth Avenue they came upon the mob. Angry faces, shouts, placards on sticks saying *No Draft* jerked along atop the jumble of people filling the avenue and swarming uptown.

Dovie drew back to watch. She heard raised voices. Mr. Jake, the owner of a machine shop they knew, was arguing with marchers. Then, with his hands up in front of him, he backed off. Soon his workers came out and joined the parade. The metal gates banged shut as he closed his shop up tight.

Shelagh climbed up on the seat. Dovie turned to her. "How can we sell anything with all the shops closed?"

"Turn this thing around and go over to Seventh," was all Shelagh said.

"We'll be out a lot of money," Dovie said. "They don't care about that."

At Grand and Broadway, they saw that Lord and Taylor's store had brigades of employees building a barricade of merchandise. Cartons, sofas, and tables were piled high between the store and the dangers of the street.

Curiosity drew them, and they turned the wagon up toward the park where the marchers were congregating.

They heard "Lincoln" and "Greeley" jeered and shouts of "Down Republicans, unfair to the working man."

"Where's Ginger? We need to talk to her. She'll know what to do."

When they finally found her, Ginger told them, "Get off the streets. They beat up Police Superintendent Kennedy and almost killed him. You can't tell what they'll do. Go home and make sure the liveryman locks the horse and wagon up good."

The sisters stopped at a shopkeeper's to try to sell some of their supplies.

He said, "They tell me it's the Confederates behind it. Someone saw two men tear an American flag up, and they even cheered Jeff Davis. They want to take over the city. You girls better get to a safe place and stay there. I'll buy your pies. But I can only pay half price, and I'm doing you a favor at that."

The next day the girls waited around their building until noon, and then all day because they heard rumors that what was a no-draft parade yesterday had become a full-fledged riot. The people they talked to in and around their building were afraid. They said that Negro people had been dragged out of their houses and attacked and mutilated, and at least one had been hanged. Anyone who employed Negroes was in danger. It looked like the war was going to end slavery but people feared what would happen as a result.

By evening they had to go and see that their horse was fed. In the livery stable, a group gathered around a man who told them in a shaking voice that a mob shouting, "Greeley! Gibbons!" had invaded the Gibbons house. Dovie flinched when she recognized the name and remembered the splendid white house lit up in the snow that she had seen blackened with pitch.

Everyone in the barn leaned forward to hear.

The man got his breath a little and in an excited rush of words said, "They threw the furniture out the windows. I saw a woman take a pickaxe to a piano. It made some notes like music playing, and then you saw it crack open and keys scatter on the pavement. I was there and saw it," he said. "Then they piled up the books and papers from Mr. Gibbons's library and set them on fire. A whole mob went in and smashed the china and mirrors. People acted like animals. They carried off even torn pieces of carpet. You wouldn't believe your eyes." The man took a breath and then, unexpectedly, covered his face and began to sob.

Dovie looked at Shelagh and saw her troubled face. At the horse's stall, they whispered together.

"Even the horses are nervous."

"Penny needs walking. She's been cooped up all day."

"We won't take out the wagon, though."

After dusk the sisters harnessed the horse and cautiously led her along the streets near the livery stable.

They were approaching a lighted street and heard yells and noise. Staying in the shadows, they looked out. They saw a man hold an American flag aloft surrounded by shouting men and women.

Suddenly, a man in a white hat with a feather rushed to the front of the mob. "Niggers with white girls—I've seen it. I say we burn the place."

Shelagh nudged Dovie. "Jimmy," she whispered, pointing out a boy near the front of the crowd. He was the fellow who had given Dovie a rose one evening at the opera house.

Dovie's eyes widened. She watched him pick up a brick from a pile against the wall and hurl it at the brothel door.

Others threw bricks that thudded against the wood. The crowd rushed forward. The door was thrown open, and there stood the owner. He aimed a gun and fired rapidly at the leader, who jerked backward and fell to the ground. Blood spurted on the people behind him, and they turned and ran. Screams filled the street as people fled, knocking each other down and trampling over the fallen.

Blood ran over the pavement. Shelagh had her hand over her mouth to keep from screaming. Jimmy ran past, so near Dovie could hear him panting. Blood from his shoes splashed on her skirt.

The horse whinnied, and a nerve twitched in her haunches.

"We've got to get out of here," Dovie said, and she put her head down and tugged Penny through the side streets, praying she wouldn't bolt.

When they finally got back to the livery stable, they had to rouse the man who slept there to let them in.

They dragged themselves back to their crowded room, where it was impossible to talk or move around with people snoring in the dark. They had to lie in their bed, tense and upset, hearing every creak of the bed frame all night. Dovie replayed in her mind the man in the white hat hit by bullets, the way he fell straight back. Then she saw the blood soak the white feather on his hat, heard the screams. Did he die? She would probably never know. Her heart thudded with fear and apprehension.

The sisters woke the next morning to hear more stories of the riot. "They tore up the railroad tracks, cut the telegraph lines, looted and burned."

"I heard they were going to send in the army to put this down. Don't go out there. People have turned into monsters," said Mrs. Bebbins, who was never short of dire warnings.

Gunfire was heard from further uptown. "They've sent in an artillery troop from Gettysburg," someone came in and reported.

This went on day after day. Dovie and Shelagh had given away all their store of sandwiches to people in the tenement before the third day was over.

The trouble had begun on Monday with the march; by Friday there were sixty thousand military troops in the city. This news came from a shopkeeper who came to check on the building. "I turned against all the violence. Now, they made me a deputy. We are going block by block in every neighborhood to see that it's safe."

The two sisters were hungry but heard the boom of a howitzer being fired far uptown.

"You could get killed out there," Shelagh said.

"I'm staying right here," Dovie replied.

Finally, the rioters' anger seemed to have run its course. People began to come out of their houses. They needed groceries, and then they needed to see if their jobs were still there in their shops or factories.

Dovie and Shelagh cautiously opened the door of their room and went to the stairs. It seemed quiet, and they started down. At the last flight of stairs, they could smell the ever-present odor of sewage that was seeping into the basement of the building.

Shelagh stopped and leaned on the wall. "What if the fighting isn't over yet?" she began.

"Oh, never mind, I'll go out and take a look at the street," Dovie said.

When she pushed the door open, a large, brown rat darted in as though it had been waiting for her to open the door. She turned to warn Shelagh. The rat brushed past Shelagh's foot, briskly going in as the sisters came out. Shelagh had seen nothing in the dark hall, and Dovie left it at that.

Shops near the Bowery had cautiously reopened. Dovie and Shelagh went in for supplies. They had been eating cold beans on crackers and bits of cheese for days. The girls bought bread and hot sausage for a dime and stood in a doorway to eat hungrily. Through a café window they saw a balding man hunched over reading the newspaper while one hand brought a fork to his mouth regularly. Some news arrested his attention, and he held the fork suspended in air as he read. Dovie and Shelagh bent over a scrap of paper and figured their money.

"It's a big step. We really don't know where to go if we leave here." Shelagh said.

"I got used to it here—bad as it is."

They remembered the violence and how it had shut the city down. Like mice they had nibbled cheese in their dark corner afraid to go out.

"I don't want to live this way," Shelagh said.

On the sidewalk they watched the growing stream of people walk past. The sisters had decided.

"Yes, it's time to get out of the city." Shelagh said. "We'll tell Ginger tomorrow."

Going West

In the train station people hurried in all directions as bells clanged and engines hissed steam. The sisters had each bought a cardboard suitcase that snapped open and shut. The handle on the luggage was cutting her hand, and Dovie stopped to set it down. The crowd parted and passed around her as though she were a stone in a rushing river.

Shelagh stood in front of a billboard with many times and places written on it in chalk. They studied it for some time. Chicago, Albany, the names meant nothing to them.

"Everything has to be west of here," Dovie commented, watching a group of four soldiers in new, blue uniforms walk past. One turned his head and she saw what a boy he was with fresh skin and curls of hair on his pale neck. "Any of these places means going west for us."

"What we have to do is get in one of these lines," Shelagh said.

They looked around the big, echoing space. It seemed to Dovie that the sun never came into this dim place. Shelagh was about to step forward when Dovie grabbed her arm and pulled her back.

"What's the matter?" Shelagh asked.

"See that metal cover?" Dovie pointed to the sewer cover at their feet. "If you step on those," she bent close and whispered in

Shelagh's ear, "there are bad people waiting down below and they grab your feet."

"What?" Shelagh said. "I never heard of such a thing."

"They grab your feet," Dovie went on with her eyes wide, "and pull you in and you have to stay there and dig their tunnels until you find them sleeping and then you can escape."

"I don't believe you," Shelagh said.

"It's true; at least I think it might be true. Mrs. Bebbins told me to watch out."

Shelagh said, "I don't believe Mrs. Bebbins knows anything, but—maybe we'll wait for another day. We could come back tomorrow." Her voice quavered.

"No, we can't. We've given up our place in the room. Look," Dovie said, "we can walk along the edges; there aren't any metal covers there."

They picked up their bags and walked, staying well away from the sewer covers. In front of the food stand there was another round cover. The sisters stood and watched to see what others did. People hurried past, but no one was seen to step on the sewer cover.

Instead most people bought food for the journey then got in one of the lines. Dovie and Shelagh saw that at the little windows people gave money to a man and he gave them tickets. Then the passengers went off to the tracks where they pushed their luggage up and boarded the train by some steps.

"Come on, we can do that." Dovie said. "Just be careful where you step."

They joined one of the lines. Each time the man ahead of them would pick up his bag and move forward a few steps, they imitated him.

At the window, the man leaned forward and said, "One-way ticket to Pittsburgh." He put down his money.

The girls counted their money again. Then Shelagh was at the window with Dovie's serious face right at her shoulder. The ticket seller looked bored under his green eyeshade.

"One-way ticket to Pittsburgh," Shelagh said and held up two fingers.

"Two?" he asked.

"Yes."

"Track four, half past eleven."

The two sisters looked at each other.

"Next!" the man said impatiently.

They went to buy food. They spent a dollar each and got pie, a paper carton of ham and cheese sandwiches, and apples. This had to last them to Pittsburgh, however far that was. Fourteen hours, the woman at the counter told them.

"And," she said eyeing their luggage, "you look like you've got no chamber pot. The trains have no lavatories. Better get one over there."

In the next line the girls bought a chamber pot concealed in a basket. While waiting in line, they studied an advertisement for gents that showed a long tube strapped along the leg under the trousers. They averted their eyes when they realized what this was for.

"Fourteen hours!" Shelagh groaned.

"That's all right," Dovie said. "I've lived fourteen years and it just seems like a minute."

Dovie and Shelagh found their seats after anxiously checking the signs and tickets many times. Looking out the train window, Dovie thought she saw the leader of the street thieves, Elsie, and leaned forward. But the thin girl with a scarf on her head moved so quickly through the crowd that she couldn't be sure.

A girl about Shelagh's age was seated across the aisle in the train. She wore a plaid dress, a hat with streamers, gloves, and shiny boots. Her dark brown hair was pulled behind her ears and fell in bouncy ringlets. Her mother and father, two portly figures, had moved along the corridor to speak to the conductor. The girl took advantage of their absence to lean over and strike up a conversation with Dovie.

"Mystery, that's my horse, has a chestnut coat and a saddle with silver trim. My riding instructor told me, 'Annabelle, I hope you know what a stylish getup that is!' Do you keep horses?"

Dovie thought of Penny, who plodded the stones of the city pulling the lunch wagon.

"Well, I've certainly been around horses a lot," she replied, though Penny, with her scarred flanks from years in the wagon shafts, was not what this girl meant.

"I brought my riding habit," the girl went on, "just in case there are any decent horses to ride out west. But I doubt they'll be to my satisfaction. I'm rather hard to please," she added.

Dovie leaned toward the window. She saw the girl in the scarf again, and it was Elsie, who lingered close behind two ladies and their pile of baggage.

"Everyone says, 'Annabelle, you are so hard to please!' The young men all say so." She smiled, bending her little bow of a mouth.

Dovie watched Elsie and the ladies' baggage.

"Do you have a beau?" Annabelle asked.

"No, not really," Dovie replied.

"Oh, you can tell me." The girl looked appraisingly at Dovie. "Blue eyes like that! Now don't tell me you don't have a serious beau! Though Mother says it's too early for me to be serious. I'm just to have a good time. Go to as many dances and picnics as I want."

Dovie watched Elsie walk behind the suitcases, scoop up a small case by its handle, and keep walking. Dovie leaned forward with her hand over her mouth, as nervous as if she were the thief. She watched to see if Elsie would be caught this time, but the two ladies had their heads together, talking, and noticed nothing.

"How many marriage proposals have you had? I have had two, almost three," Annabelle announced. "If only I could count Mr. Simms, who was overcome by his feelings, and then supper was announced. But I am as good as sure that he was on the verge of a declaration. I think I can count it, don't you? I will say three, and I am only sixteen and a half years old."

Elsie went through the crowd as smoothly as an eel in the ocean. The train lurched and started. The last thing Dovie could see was alarm on the face of one lady as she pointed to where her bag had been a moment before. The train left the station and began to pick up speed.

"However," Annabelle was saying, "I do think it selfish of the young men to want to marry before they go off to war. They say 'Oh, I will be on the battlefield this time next week, and I do love you so.' Why, what if he got an arm or a leg shot off?

Then, I would be married to a cripple, and I have the rest of my whole life before me. Selfish!"

As Dovie looked at Annabelle, the whistle screamed and the train clung to the curving track. At this moment, the girl's parents came back. One glance at the two sisters in plain brown dresses traveling alone caused the adults to frown and turn their backs. Seeing that they were being snubbed, Dovie and Shelagh looked at each other and sat back. The chugging of the engine was already becoming a familiar sound.

Many hours later the train pulled into the station at Pittsburgh, Pennsylvania. The sisters climbed down onto the platform. Shelagh brushed furiously at the cinder and ash from the train's smokestack that littered her clothing. Dovie felt dazed by the cessation of the long, rocking motion of the train. The two looked at each other with tired, smudged faces.

The conductor had told the sisters that most of his passengers took a boat in Pittsburgh and traveled the Ohio River to go west. The girls bought their tickets on the steamship *George Rollins* to go west. They were becoming more adept at travel and in the station bought passage as far as Louisville, Kentucky, where they had to change boats to continue.

Fort Pitt and Fort Duquesne were near the railroad station at the confluence of three rivers. The girls stood on the dock near Fort Pitt and could see the Allegheny, Monongahela, and Ohio rivers.

"Which one is the Ohio River? That's the one that will take us west," Dovie asked a woman sitting with her children on some boxes. She pointed to one of the rivers, and the sisters looked at its rushing waters as though they would see their future there. The conductor had told them they would pass Cincinnati, Ohio, and reach Louisville, Kentucky.

It was Saturday, and a parade came down the street with American flags waving grandly in the breeze. Dovie and Shelagh ran to join the crowd and see a band of piccolo and trumpet players in bright uniforms march smartly along. The two drummers in tall hats pranced, and between beats they twirled their sticks in the air. Soldiers in their Union blue marched to the music.

"They were at Gettysburg three months ago!" a woman near Dovie said, and shook her head. "The hospitals are still full from the battle."

Near the end, a wagon draped in black bunting and chains rumbled. It carried a tall effigy of Jeff Davis, the Confederate president, that swung from side to side or bent and bobbed and made the crowd laugh. A chorus of "We'll hang Jeff Davis on a sour apple tree" sprang up in the crowd. As he passed, the sisters could hear the yowling of live cats stuffed inside the cloth figure. When the man beside the figure shook and waved the attached pole, the cats howled and screeched and writhed even more. The crowd jeered and hooted. A donkey with a sign, *Follow me*, ended the show. People ran after the parade to see Jeff Davis and the cats inside burned at the edge of town.

"Look," Dovie said to Shelagh, "the parade and audience stepped all over the sewer covers and nothing happened."

"What is under those?" Dovie asked someone.

"Oh, you don't want to know," the person replied.

"But we do! We want to know."

The man shrugged. "It's wastewater that drains down to the river."

The sisters looked at each other. "No people down there?"

"Oh, no, no one down there."

Once the boat was on the waters of the broad Ohio, the two sisters stood at the railing with the other passengers.

"Where you headed?" the man next to them asked.

The girls looked at each other. They were weary of traveling, and their money was running low.

"West. We're going west," Shelagh said.

"Webster is the name," the man said and tipped his hat. "We're going back to Indiana."

"Are there Indians there?"

"Well, I don't know. I saw some once. Afraid, are you? Well, look, I was born in Rockport, Indiana. It is just a fine place to live. It's a bustling little town from all the traffic on the river. You can take a raft there and go all the way to New Orleans."

"How do you get there?"

"I'm going as far as Evansville. You can follow me. You take this boat to Louisville and then you change there to the *J.B. White*. It stops in Rockport, then Evansville. What do you girls do?"

"I can do tutoring or teach school."

"Well, now a schoolteacher is always in demand. 'Course, it'd be country schooling."

Dovie spoke when he looked at her. "I can do lots of work. I can do any kind of work. Not serving work though. I tried that."

At Louisville, they had to get out and walk to another dock carrying their belongings. The price was high to ride on a hired wagon the whole way. Dovie and Shelagh could only afford to ride to a halfway spot and then had to get off and walk with a few other people. The wagon set them down beside the road and then passed them. Dovie and Shelagh walked carrying their suitcases.

A few miles later, they saw the muddy edge of the river where a wooden dock led out into the water. The passengers waited, sitting, standing, or strolling along the path at water's edge.

There was a little shanty perched up on the bluff with a sign, *Eats*. Prices were high there at the one and only store. The girls were alarmed that their money was going so rapidly. They had begun to count their coins over and over before they parted with them.

The woman behind the counter hardly looked at the latest in the long line of travelers who came through and were never seen again. A man looked around at the mostly empty shelves, saw three eggs in a bowl, and ordered scrambled eggs. The proprietress cleaned her ear with the end of a wooden spoon and then stirred the eggs with the other end.

The girls choked down a dry piece of bread and a cup of something brown like coffee.

"What is this stuff?" Dovie asked indignantly.

"It's 'don't die till the next county' coffee." Mr. Webster said.

There were cobwebs and rough, unpainted splintery boards in the smelly outhouse. The girls were tired and discouraged. They walked outside arm in arm to take the air. Shelagh pointed

111

out to Dovie a flock of sparrows. "Look, they 're making a home in the hull of a wrecked boat near the shore."

"Some people would only see that the boat was ruined," Dovie said. "You see a shelter for birds."

Word came down that the boat wouldn't be in until the next morning and they would have to camp out on the riverside. They prepared to spend the night out on the banks.

Dovie went for a walk just before dusk. The sound of an axe splitting wood followed her for a while. She walked on deeper into the woods. The ground was soft underfoot, thick with pine needles and decayed leaves. Her feet made no sound. She saw the gleam of water off to her right through the trees and knew she could find her way back keeping near the river. Thick tree roots were slippery underfoot. She smelled pine needles as her feet trod on them. Vines touched her face and caught in her hair. She began to walk with one arm above her head to clear the way. In the top of the trees a bird called.

At the edge of a slight clearing, she stopped. All was green and gray in dim light. A large owl, its wings spread out, swooped silently down to perch on a branch. Dovie must have moved, for the owl lifted off and flew swiftly away between the trees. The forest seemed to darken. She turned and began to run back to Shelagh. She stumbled and caught herself on a tree trunk. Something near her hand moved and scuttled away, and she ran on.

They had to pull out warm clothes from their suitcases, whatever they had to cover themselves as the evening turned chilly. For warmth, Dovie and Shelagh curled up together against a tree trunk. When Dovie opened her eyes next, the river was silver and the woods black. The sky was gray tinged with pink. Twittering, rustling sounds began as the birds shook themselves awake. Thin clouds turned orange, and the line of woods took on a faint green. Dovie felt empty and weak from hunger and lay on the ground watching the sky lighten.

People pushed and shoved to get on the boat when it finally came. The towns and farms they saw from the river seemed to be small clearings of civilization cut into a dense forest. They looked with interest at a house built with rough logs fitted together. It had one door and one window, and smoke came out of the chimney. Around the house was a field of corn. Inside a zig-zag, snake rail fence they saw a pig, a cow, and a horse.

Later, the boat made a stop in a place where the river narrowed. Dovie walked along the bank, where she found stones and skipped them across the water. She picked up a stick and dragged it in the dirt. She came near to stepping on an insect several inches long, black with a yellow underbelly. She jumped back and threw the stick at it.

She walked on along the bank. Across the water she saw a man in strange clothing, a fringed shirt and trousers. He had dark hair to his shoulders. He put his hand to his mouth and called in an incomprehensible tongue. After a moment, he repeated cries that sounded like the clacking of sticks. Dovie shuddered.

A shaggy head rose out of the water and moved to the shore. Climbing up on the bank, a big dog shook itself and sent rings of bright drops whirling in the sunlight. Dripping and brown, it ran after the man. He strode away, and a long black braid with a bright feather in it bounced on his back. Dovie found that she was holding her breath and knew she had reached the boundary of all that was familiar.

When the boat arrived at Rockport, Indiana, they stood next to Mr. Webster and his son ready to say good-bye. Someone on the boat was sure they needed a teacher round about Rockport, and the sisters had decided to try their luck there. They looked up at a stone bluff one hundred feet high at its tallest.

"See that, looks like a stone pillar tilted out from the bluff? That's Lady Washington. There used to be another called George Washington, but it tumbled down in an earthquake way before I got here, even," Mr. Webster told them.

There on the banks with tree trunks piled all around them, two men worked with axes and saws cutting logs for the steamships. It was autumn, and though the nights were getting crisp, the days were warm and sunny.

Dovie first noticed the stocky, strong one when he spoke to Shelagh and said, "Pardon me, miss, is the captain of that boat a man name of Billings?" He just spoke to get a closer look at her and then blurted out, "What blue eyes you have."

Dovie looked at him. His hair was plastered to his forehead with sweat, and he had peeled off his shirt. He wore long underwear, red, with the sleeves rolled up. This person was smiling at Shelagh, and she was smiling back. Dovie grabbed her sister's arm and turned her toward the wagon that had come to meet the boat.

Dovie and Shelagh and several barrels of sloshing kerosene traveled in the wagon bed up a long incline to the crest of the bluff. As they went uphill, the driver pointed out the high water marks from past floods. There was a cave-like gouge in the stone where the first settlers, Lankford and family, had lived in 1808 above the waters of the river.

The driver pointed out a home, Miz Bradford's, and said, "She's in on everything that goes on. That lady knows everything without ever leaving the house." He shook his head admiringly and let them off at her door.

It was a fieldstone house with a lean-to. The two girls set down their suitcases and looked at each other.

"You knock, you're the oldest," Dovie said.

"No, it's your turn. You do it."

"What will I say?"

"Depends on who answers," Shelagh replied.

Dovie tapped on the door.

"Louder, no one could hear that."

"Then you do it," Dovie said and stepped back down to the road. Shelagh angrily rapped on the door. They waited.

"Ma'am, I heard you are looking for a schoolteacher," Shelagh said the minute the door opened.

The woman was drying her hands on a cloth. She stopped and looked the girls over. She turned to Shelagh. "Can you read and write?" she asked.

"Of course."

"Can you keep discipline?"

"Yes, but the parents have to back me up."

The woman finished drying her hands and tucked the cloth in her waistband. "I'd say you're hired, but let me go next door to Mrs. Babcock first." She started out the door.

"I have my diploma right here," Shelagh said reaching into her bag.

Mrs. Bradford paused. "Are you hungry? Come on in."

She motioned them to sit down at the table and from the stove took up a dish of boiled beans and a round, yellow cake for each girl. Silently moving her lips, she read the paper Shelagh held up in front of her. She nodded, and then she was out the door. The sisters ate at once, and the taste of the beans and the corn cake were delicious. Mrs. Bradford called the lady next door to the fence. Dovie and Shelagh could see the two women out in the bright sunshine.

The girls overheard the neighbor say, "I figure twelve children of school age from five families. We can have a real school at last."

Mrs. Bradford was back in a whirl of enthusiasm. "You're hired," she said to Shelagh. "Your salary will be room and board and fifty cents per pupil per month. That would be, let me see, at least six dollars free and clear a month. That's pretty good, I'd say."

"Besides reading and writing, I intend to teach the students arithmetic, penmanship, and public speaking."

"Will the minister's wife ever be glad. She's been trying to teach reading and writing, but now she's got another young one to care for. Five families, and between us we'll pay your salary each month."

"Where is the schoolhouse?"

"Well, we don't have a proper building, but there's Grandma Grant's kitchen or, better still, the blacksmith shop that's empty now—he's off soldiering. We'll get that, and the men will have to make desks and benches."

Dovie spoke up, "I have experience. I want to teach, too."

"We can only hire one, the older. I'll have to find something else for you." She frowned. "How old are you?"

"Almost fifteen, and I've taught French and singing."

"French lessons! Law, out here all you need is to read and write your name and figure a little bit. I need to find a family you can live with. We are going to go over to the Thompsons'. They have some room with their son off in the army."

Mrs. Bradford brought them to a stone house with woods behind it. Dovie and Shelagh waited outside. They saw strange-looking animals in back of the house.

"Hogs," Shelagh said positively.

"But they don't look like the ones at home," Dovie protested as she watched them. Razorback hogs, they were long-legged and wiry and trotted fast as they went in and out of the woods foraging for food.

The Thompsons' house was long and low with a steeply pitched roof of brown shingles. White-painted doors gave it an inviting look. They could see the Thompson Feed and Supply Store around the corner on Main Street.

At the Thompsons' door, Mrs. Bradford announced, "I've got us a teacher. Says she's almost seventeen." She turned and beckoned the girls to come in. "Two sisters and they need a place to stay."

"They can't stay here." Mr. Thompson spoke from his desk. "What if Joseph comes home?"

"Well, Poppa, we need a teacher," Mrs. Thompson said. "Our Ingrid won't have any school this year unless we get a teacher. Let's try it until spring. And if Joseph comes home—well, haven't I always managed these things?"

"All right, do as you please; you always do anyway."

"What we'll do is get most of the families in town to agree to contribute wood for heat." Mrs. Bradford was racing ahead with her plans.

Mrs. Thompson looked the girls over, their clothes neat but plain, their serious faces. The first words Mrs. Thompson said to them were, "I'll be glad to have a real teacher for my Ingrid, who is such a good student. You can lodge with us."

"The younger one—well, I'm going to ask for her, she's shy." *Shy*, Dovie thought *I can't get a word in edgeways.* "She could be a lot of help at the store," Mrs. Bradford was saying. "I know you are shorthanded with your boy in the war."

Mr. Thompson did not like being put on the spot, even though he could use some help. He frowned, drawing bushy, gray eyebrows together. Grudgingly, he said, "I could try her. No promises though. She might not work out."

"At first, I would like to help Shelagh fix up the blacksmith place for a school," Dovie managed to say before Mrs. Bradford totally fixed her fate.

Before nightfall, the two girls were settled. They helped Mrs. Thompson clear her son's bedroom for them. She put a quilt she had made on the long bed. Its patchwork was cheerful in the plain room, and she gathered a bunch of wildflowers in a jar on the homemade dresser. When Dovie saw the touches of color and window for fresh air, tears gathered in her eyes, and the room wavered until she blinked them away. *I can forget the tenement and the dirty bed and the smell of sewage. I live in a real home now.*

"Oh, I'm glad to be here," she told Mrs. Thompson who nodded and said nothing.

Enthusiasm ran high for the start of a school. Dovie and Shelagh began to fix the building for classes. Each family made a bench for their child and delivered it to the schoolhouse. Desks were lengths of board nailed to a support. Shelagh decided to put the unfinished floor to use and practiced using a long stick to write arithmetic problems or spelling words in the dirt. The windows were small, and the door was left open for light and air. To keep flies out she hung a curtain of light cloth over the door.

Dovie planned the games for recess. They would have relays, races and games of tag. She had a moment of wishing she could be in school; she had always been particularly good at the games that required speed. She had to go to work full days for Mr. Thompson once the schoolroom was ready.

Right away, Mr. Thompson told Dovie she needed to learn how to keep the account book for the store, stock the shelves and help the customers. When she worked well he gave a curt nod of approval and she felt rewarded.

She went with Mrs. Thompson to a seed swapping because the poor lady wanted so much to go and needed help driving the wagon back in the dark. As Mrs. Thompson drove, Dovie turned over the paper packets and read the names lettered on the outside: lettuce, cabbage, peas, mustard, even flowers like hollyhock.

"Each season I gather the seeds from my garden and fold them in papers. My mother brought seeds for most of these plants when she came west from Tennessee," Mrs. Thompson told her.

Dovie observed that Mrs. Thompson seemed to have no head for business but was a wonder around the house. The woman's cures were much in demand she began to realize when a farmers' wife knocked at the door one day. She had come about a rash on her neck. Mrs. Thompson looked intently at the affected area and then sent Dovie to the cupboard for her remedy book. When Dovie opened the worn leather book a faint smell of rosemary emanated from pages covered in spidery handwriting. Here was help for all kinds of ailments. Dovie found it hard to read but could make out the recipe for skin salve which Mrs. Thompson had told her to mix. From the cabinet of jars, Dovie took dried leaves and the mortar and pestle and went to work, adding just a few drops of oil, until she had made a paste.

As Mrs. Thompson applied this to the ailing woman's neck, she said, "This is an Indian medicine. They know the use of many roots and herbs, like sassafras tea for cures. I also know charms passed down to me from my mother's people and written here in this book."

When the farmer's wife left with her salve, Dovie sat beside Mrs. Thompson and listened as she read. "Here, here are some from my own mother. A spider web worn around the neck will cure ague, water in which nine eggs have been boiled will end infertility, a toad will draw out rattler-bite poison, and an onion in the pocket will prevent snakebite."

"It must be a good feeling to know that you can help people," Dovie said.

Mrs. Thompson clapped the book closed and said, "I have many ways to help people but I do draw the line at using the saw or knife. People have to rely on someone else if they need surgery."

At the start of school, Shelagh came home at night and told Dovie about the problems she faced. "We need money to buy books and slates and a better stove before winter comes. There's no end to the things we need."

"What you would get first if you could?" Dovie asked her.

"A stove. But then a dictionary and a teacher's desk. We have only one book, a school with only one book! The Bible."

"It's a book. It has words and stories."

118

Shelagh's first lessons from the stories in the Old Testament were of wise Solomon, cruel Pharaoh, and fearless David. She reported, "There was something for every age in it: spelling for the younger ones, vocabulary words for the older ones, and a moral for all."

Dovie nodded. "You are doing a lot with a little."

Tom Cornwall, the fellow from the dock, heard of the needs at the school and showed up one day with a desk he had made for Shelagh. The legs were crude sticks of wood nailed to the sides, but the top had been carefully sanded smooth. The feature he proudly showed was a shelf under the desktop for her papers.

"Some pupils," Shelagh told her sister, "ride horses in from farms. They bring their own corn, and I give breaks during the day when they feed and water their horses. One brother and sister row across a river to get to school. On rainy, fall days, if I see low, dark clouds gathering in the sky, I have to let school out early since students have as much as ten miles to go."

"I envy you the time off. I am kept busy all day because Mr. Thompson's hip and back pains are getting worse as winter comes on. In the evenings, he's teaching me to record and re-order inventory for the store," Dovie said.

Shelagh's students were to give a performance to show the town that it really had a school at last. Dovie was there early and saw almost everyone in the town arrive. Some ladies made their best cakes for refreshments; one father brought his fiddle for music. Soon the room was full to bursting and Shelagh nervously began the program. The audience was vocal with opinions, yelling, "Speak up," or cheering when a boy took a heroic stance and recited, "The boy stood on the burning deck."

When it was her turn, Ingrid Thompson hesitated on the side of the makeshift stage. Dovie was especially excited to see her perform because she had helped her practice and been impressed that she composed her own skit. The audience began to stomp their feet, Ingrid stepped out onto the platform and looked at the crowd with wide eyes. Her subject was a choice of trades. She held up a medicine bottle and began to recite, "When I am grown, a doctor I will be, if I can and I can. Broken bones..."

A man shouted, "A female doctor! No hen in petticoats is gonna to treat me!"

There was laughter. Ingrid stood holding her medicine bottle aloft with a stricken look on her face.

A woman called out, "Oh, hush you, Perkins!"

"Let her finish," Dovie shouted.

Ingrid spoke into the noise: "Broken bones and aching backs, old Mrs. Jones and poor John Flax..." She had great big tears on her cheeks as she finished in a tiny voice, "I'll help them all, great and small, when a doctor I will be."

Shelagh was upset. She tried to make herself heard over the din and called, "Quiet, please."

Tom jumped to her side, and when people didn't quiet down he stood up on a chair. His grating voice cut the noise. "I want a round of applause for this girl and for her mother, too. Will you please stand up, Miz Thompson? I want you to know this lady cured my foot; it was swole up big as a melon."

"So what?" someone yelled.

"So, she's a female, and you'll be lucky if you can go to her when you get the croup this winter." This was met with clapping and whistling.

The heckler said grudgingly, "That's different. Let her cure all she wants but just don't call herself a doctor."

After this, Shelagh and Tom were allies. He slicked himself up after work and attended the school performances regularly. Dressed up in a beaver hat, a tan boxy jacket and red and black-checkered vest over work pants and boots, he looked young and, Dovie thought, countrified.

Dovie noticed that he was uncomfortable dressed up and dug at the stiff collar where it chafed his neck. He helped Shelagh close the school up so he could walk her home. He took charge of hurrying people out. When Dovie lingered to talk, Tom shooed her out too. Dovie was very offended when he closed the door in her face and she sputtered angry comments all the way home.

At the Thompson house a letter arrived from their son, Joseph, a soldier in the Union Army. After dinner they all assembled to hear Ingrid read the letter aloud.

"'Dear Mama, Poppa and Ingrid,

"'September, 1863. I hope this war is over soon before I have to go through another winter. I still have good shoes, but my jacket from home is getting pretty ragged. However, I consider myself lucky. The uniforms have not come for all yet. Only our officer has a complete uniform with cap and...'"

Here Ingrid faltered over a word and came to a stop as she frowned at the paper in her hand. Mr. Thompson grabbed it, grinding his teeth in impatience. He tried to read it with his spectacles and then without. He thrust the paper at Dovie.

"Here, you read it."

Dovie took it and skimmed until she recognized the place. "'Only our officer has a complete uniform with cap and insignia.' That means the marks that tell his rank."

"Joe's a corporal. Go on," Mr. Thompson said.

"'I am hard to find a coat for. I am the tallest in my regiment, and on my seventeenth birthday one of the youngest. You would hardly recognize me though. I am cultivating a beard—now down to my breastbone. I think it makes me look older.

"'I have had two of your letters written the tenth and the twentieth of last month after none for a while. I was so happy when my name was called, I let out a whoop. The postman was new and watched amazed as the men shouted and laughed when their names were called, and then some cried when they had letters in their hands. Please write to me as often as possible; your letters mean everything to me. It is so good to hear of home.

"'I am glad to hear that Father has got some help; any at all is better than none.'" Dovie made a face over this.

"'Tell Ingrid to take advantage of having a school and to do her studies with diligence.

"'How are Miss Collins and Ella Thatcher? Give them my regards. I was never kissed by so many young ladies as when we enlisted men went off to the war. Then when we arrived at New Albany, the ladies gave us quite a banquet. There were chicken, ham, and pies galore, served up by the pretty cooks. It all made me think, why settle down to one girl when there are so many?

"'The army food is good enough. We have provisions of flour, beef, rice, coffee, sugar, and beans. When supplies run low, we *have to forage in the countryside, and the farmers don't like to see us coming. The other day I saw an old farmer and his wife working in their cabbage rows. She ran away. He stayed, looking grim. I saw myself as they saw me—the enemy.*

"'Eggs and squawking chickens—we carried them off to feed our unit. What's right and what's wrong? I don't know anymore.

"'I got my paycheck, ten dollars; the first cash I have ever earned is from the army.

"'The nights are getting cool here, and I am glad to have the blanket you gave me with my name embroidered on it by Ingrid. I can wrap up in it and think of home after a day on the march. We named our place here "Camp Indiana."'"

That night, Dovie fell asleep thinking of Joseph's letter. *He is grateful for small comforts—the blanket from home, a warm jacket, things he probably took for granted all his life. Just like me, I didn't know what a good life I had at home. Do people never appreciate anything until it's gone?*

When, shortly after that, Mrs. Thompson slipped and broke her leg, they were in need of so much in both the house and office that Dovie hardly knew where to start. Mr. Thompson was troubled with his bad hip. He tended to sit in his office chair and direct Dovie to do the work. His face was often haggard after a painful night.

Mrs. Thompson had tried to find a cure for his trouble. Hot baths helped only temporarily, and the next day he was in pain again. A poultice of flaxseed, ground mustard, and boiled onions made his skin blister and peel. "The cure hurts as bad as the hip," he said to Dovie.

With both parents of the family ailing and Shelagh busy with her school, Dovie tried to do everything. Her days were spent jumping on and off horses, unloading wagons, parceling out provisions, managing old people and children, cooking, and sewing.

When a letter arrived from Joseph, the family gathered around Mrs. Thompson, who opened the envelope and handed it to Dovie. The family had been in suspense after hearing of the battle of Chickamauga. The losses were heavy on both sides, and though they did not know for certain, they felt pretty sure that Joseph was in that battle.

We have had a big battle—our commander was General Thomas. We ran out of ammunition and fought with bayonets. It was hard to tell Rebel from Union in the smoke. The battle went on for three endless days. Sometime in a lull I fell asleep. I don't know for how long, but when I opened my eyes I saw my friend in front of me. Dickinson was sitting against a tree. At first, I thought he had only fallen asleep. When I leaned over to shake his arm, I saw that there was a hole in his forehead and blood all over his jacket. Why I wasn't hit I'll never know.

I have often wished I was not over six feet tall, for I make too good a target. Maybe hunger will shrink me. I am always hungry. We eat mostly hardtack, beans, and bacon. Rations are short lately. Our cook is as big a drinker as I ever saw. Lucky, he has an assistant who sees we get our meals.

How did the crops at home turn out? Any more problems with worms in the corn?

I am writing this letter on the back board of a wagon and that accounts for the poor look of it. I hope you can read it.

I hope for good health for all of you, Joe.

In January 1864, the family received another letter.

Now that we are in winter camp, we have a roster and take turns cooking. On my turn I made biscuit, which turned out quite tolerable. I don't know how many times I have watched Ma make her biscuit dough, and the memory came in very handy.

The captain sent Stokes and me to a farmer's house yesterday to requisition some farm animals. I knew they were rebels, but the farmer's pretty wife opened the door and spoke in such a soft, fine voice I was captivated. I have heard only men's curses and complaints every day for months. The Southern drawl is easy on the ears and we were exchanging some pleasant talk until she found out that they were going to lose their animals. Her voice turned coarse so fast my head was ringing. She called us "dirty Yankees" and slammed the door in our faces. The pigs squealed something terrible as we took them away.

I got three of your letters since I have been here. Dovie is a good correspondent, and even when her news is not good, her letters are. Just wait till I get home; I'll take over the work Father can't do and see about Ma. I hate to think you need me and I *am so far away. I am very grateful to Dovie for helping the family. I hope Ingrid takes her example and pitches in.*

How about Miss Ella throwing me over and getting engaged to the Kenner fellow? Well, I am probably lucky to know now what kind of a character she has. She got tired of waiting after a pretty short time.

When you see her, ask Evelyn Collins if she remembers me.

My love to all the family and regards to Miss Dovie, Joe.

One day Dovie was stewing the family a chicken while she added sums in the ledger at the kitchen table. A riverboat had docked, and the captain would be coming in to buy supplies, she knew. A fellow knocked at the door and entered. Dovie looked up to see an old man looking at her from under a big hat with two turkey feathers stuck in the crown.

"What is it you need today?" Dovie asked, busy over her ledger.

"I come to see Mr. Thompson."

"Mr. Thompson is ill and I am handling the business."

"I only talk to the man of the place."

"I'm in charge here while Mr. Thompson is recovering."

"Well, I don't deal with women."

"You'll have to deal with me or not deal. Now, we have the grain your ship usually buys already counted out. All you need to do is check it and load it."

He went off in a huff to inspect the shipment and came back mollified. "Anyone to help me load it?"

"No, sorry—"

"Well, it seems to be just you and you're just a girl. And here I am," he said, signing the invoice, "doing my business with a chit of a girl." He shook his head.

Dovie finished a column in the ledger and said, "It's the same grain if you bought it from me or a man."

On the next trip he brought her a buffalo horn with a rose carved on it. "This seemed just right for you. No disrespect, miss."

She hung it from a nail over the counter, and soon the customers began to call her Buffalo Rose.

When Shelagh heard this, she laughed and hugged Dovie. "I don't understand where my sister Dovie went—the little girl with the Welsh lilt to her voice."

Dovie frowned. Shelagh was so happy and bubbling over with smiles lately. Dovie knew it had to do with Tom Cornwall. *Oh, no*, Dovie thought, *he ruins everything*.

One Saturday, Shelagh was in the store when Tom came in. Tom greeted her by her first name. Dovie thought he should have said Miss Lloyd. He and Shelagh eagerly began to talk. Dovie stood behind the counter. *I might as well not even be here; they only see each other*, she thought.

"It's late," she said harshly to Shelagh, who didn't seem to be listening.

Tom was telling one of his stories, which Dovie found long-winded. "About forty years ago our president worked as a fer-ryman right near here on the Anderson River."

"I think it's time to close up the store," Dovie said and began to lock up the cash box.

"I've talked to men on the docks round about Troy who remember him, Abe Lincoln from Pigeon Creek."

"I thought you were going to help me," Dovie said to Shelagh.

"Shelagh is coming with me," Tom replied.

"Oh, do you mind?" Shelagh said. "Mr. Cornwall is going to walk me along the hill to see the boat that just docked." Without waiting for a reply, Shelagh put on her bonnet and left with Tom. Dovie slammed the doors unnecessarily hard to lock up.

☆ ☆ ☆

To raise funds, Shelagh and some of the school parents held a basket social. Women prepared a basket dinner that men bid on and the proceeds went to supplies for the school. Once a man had bought a dinner, he matched the tie inside the basket to the dress of the woman or girl who prepared it and then shared supper with her.

Dovie wanted to prepare a dinner she would be proud of, but she got busy with a shipment at the store and had to hurry. Her cake fell, but the Indian corn pudding seemed just fine.

Tom kept bidding on her basket because he had seen Shelagh carry it in and thought it was hers. When he took out the cloth tie and found it matched Dovie's dress, his face was so disappointed that Dovie got her only smile of the evening.

Tom looked into the basket. "I don't like corn and I hate all Indians."

"Well, they were here first," Dovie said.

"The only good Indian is a dead Indian," Tom said.

"They should be left to live their own way. If we didn't bother them they wouldn't bother us," Dovie shot back.

"Ha! You are one of these people who think everything is going to be all right till you are scalped in your own bed. They steal and kill wherever they please."

"I think there's enough country for all."

Tom took one bite of the heavy cake and dropped it back in the basket. They quit conversing.

Shelagh looked over and saw them staring away from each other. When she got Dovie alone, she said furiously, "I can't even trust you to be civil to my friend," and marched off.

"He's the one that picked the fight," Dovie called after her, but Shelagh didn't answer. "He wouldn't eat the cake I baked." Shelagh was gone, but Dovie said to the empty air, "And I don't like the way he bosses you around."

After that evening, weeks passed in which Dovie and Shelagh spoke only a few words to each other when absolutely necessary. One day, Shelagh opened the door to the store where Dovie was working.

She set down her suitcase and announced, "I am marrying Tom Cornwall. Tom wants to go west and I'll go with him. There's a wagon train gathering in late February."

"You're going without me?"

"You and Tom don't get along. In fact, you two make me miserable. I'm the one in the middle. You have to see my position." She paused. "You can take my share of the money."

Dovie looked at the coins Shelagh put in her hand. Her mouth twisted. "I would never have left you." She turned her hand and let the coins spill to the floor. Bowing her head in a long silence, she heard the door open and felt a breeze flutter her hair as it thudded shut.

Dovie heard that Shelagh and Tom were married in a ceremony held in the minister's front parlor with only his landlady and the minister's wife in attendance. The day the wagon train left town, Dovie broke the silver-framed mirror Shelagh had given her long ago. She went out to the woods and smashed it on the rocks and then kicked it into the underbrush. When she came back to the house, she saw the boy next door going hunting and called to him to wait, she was going, too.

She had hunted only once before and gotten nothing. This time, her eyes narrowed with concentration, she shot two rabbits for the Thompson family dinner.

✷ ✷ ✷

The world Dovie had come from seemed far away since Shelagh had left. Misty Wales seemed unreal; so did bustling New York City, where in Mrs. Llewellyn's quiet parlor, among tables waxed and shining like mirrors, she had taught French to Meredith and her brother. Here in Indiana, the sun did not penetrate dense woods pressing in around the little town, and the bright sky hung above like a far away dome. Dovie woke some mornings and had to lie still and think where she was.

She poured all her energy into working. She could lift boxes she never thought of lifting before. If the shelves in the store needed organizing, she would work at it without a break, going up the ladder and down all day until it was finished. She was determined to do it all herself. Mr. and Mrs. Thompson were still unable to do their usual duties, so she tried to run both the house and store. There were practically no able-bodied men left in town.

Dovie thought once, *This could be home for me right here. I don't mind working hard if I have to, in fact, I like it.* Dovie was preparing a bowl of hot soup for Mrs. Thompson when she thought, *My life could have been satisfying like this if Dad had not remarried. Shelagh and I would still be at home in Wales, busy and needed in our own home.* But then Mrs. Thompson called for her soup and Dovie had no time to waste on regret.

Thoughts of Wales and a sense of loss remained with her all afternoon, a leaden feeling in her legs and arms as she measured out rose hips and brewed a pot of tea. Dovie brightened a little as she thought how store-bought tea was so very expensive, but she had gathered and dried this tea herself. She had a whole tin of it, enough to last the rest of winter if she was careful.

Dovie and Mrs. Thompson often sat together looking out the window at the bare, black branches. Sometimes they were silent as they sipped cups of tea near the fire, sometimes Mrs. Thompson told about her life in bits and pieces.

Dovie began to keep a diary as she had in Wales. It filled up the evenings in her room after dinner was cleared away. Formerly, she and Shelagh had used that time to tell about what happened in the store or at school.

Since Mr. Thompson was not up to it, Dovie made the next trip with a neighbor to shop in Evansville. She bought for the family and put in Mr. Thompson's order of supplies for the store. In her diary that February night she wrote: *The creek was full of ice when we crossed it in the wagon. Heard wolves howling. Awful cold. I am fifteen years old and have no real home or family.*

Weeks passed filled with constant work. In her diary she wrote, *Killed my first deer. He took three pistol shots before he fell. Took one more to the head before he died. We will have venison for many a meal.*

Dovie sometimes brought out her box of mementos from home. Her old journal was a book with a green cover. She sat back against the pillow on her bed and began to read. A steamboat passing by the town sounded its whistle, a tune of four notes repeated. *We had cake and custard today. It was my twelfth birthday and Grandma Howells gave me two gold coins.* Dovie could hardly recognize her life of only three years ago.

Folded in the pages was a note from her father when he was away on a trip on her eighth birthday. She looked at his handwriting; the ink was growing faint. She could not read because her eyes were blurred with tears. She could see her life all stretched out as one long journey, the cart bumping up and around the mountain in heavy mist, ocean waves restlessly lapping the sides of the ship, the city a stream of noise, carriages, and people channeled along narrow streets, on a ship again; this time she and Shelagh with their hands tightly gripped together as the broad river opened out before them going west.

She opened the new book she had bought to write in, a notebook with unlined pages inside a brown cover. Last week, she had written, *Saturday at dusk I saw a thin, gray wolf come to the edge of the woods behind the house. He must have been hungry to venture in so close. He seemed to be curious about the place. Later, I went hunting with the Garwood boy. I shot two rabbits; they made a good stew. Mr. Thompson not well again.*

Where would she go now without Shelagh? She got up and moved restlessly around, closing the window tighter, pulling the curtain to cover the drafts. She didn't know. She had no answers.

In the next week, there came a letter from Joe Thompson on a piece of paper curled at the edges and hard to read. The lines were written first across the paper and then the paper turned and the rest was written longways on the page.

April, 1864

Dear Family,

As paper is scarce I think before using each word and often as not leave it out. I will only say on the matter of Ella: I did give her a brooch and she did accept it and so maybe we were engaged, but she has decided differently and that is fine with me. I was never that keen on the romance; it was just nice to have someone at home thinking of me.

I saw an odd sight on our last march. It was a row of "Quaker Guns." These cannon are not going to shoot any more than a Quaker would. They looked real from a field or two away, but as we drew near, we could see that they were only logs painted black and even had wheels attached. The Rebs are low on artillery to try a thing like that.

We are deep into Johnny Reb's territory now, and when we march through a town people turn their backs on us or children make fun of our shabby appearance. We have to be ready to kill men who may be their fathers and husbands, or they would kill us. It's a miserable business.

I would consider myself lucky to plow uphill in scorching sun on the rockiest field in Spencer County—if at night I could sleep with no thought of killing or being killed. So many of my friends have been shot down around me that I can't help but wonder when my time will come.

Must close off this letter and get it in the next mailbag. I am looking at my fingers stained purple and a nearly empty pail. I and a couple of other warriors happened upon some vines clustered near a creek. We attacked with full force and no retreat. I have eaten as many wild blackberries as I could cram into my mouth. They were ripe and delicious.

Ingrid says she has picked out just the girl for me—well, thank you very much, but I don't know if I'll need a wife. I can even mend my own uniform now.

Love to all, Joe.

Dovie read this ending with a feeling of jealousy. Then the next minute she thought, *I feel sorry for Joe; he might never live to have a wife.*

Later, Ingrid whispered to Dovie, "It was you I picked out for Joe."

Love And Marriage

"I'd like to send a man but they are all away at war. It's a big sale and I'm not well enough to travel. I've thought about it, and you're the only one to do it. I'm asking you to make the trip for me," Mr. Thompson said to Dovie.

Dovie said yes. It was a chance to go farther west, all the way to a frontier fort in Nebraska Territory.

Mrs. Thompson gave advice. "Once you board the ship, stay in your cabin. Your meals can be brought to you there. Never allow yourself to talk to strangers. I have sent for my sister, Lavinia, to come and help here and she has started her journey."

"We don't need Aunt Lavinia," Ingrid protested.

"No, no, your mother needs the help and company even though her leg is healing," Dovie told her. "You are in charge at home. Go to Mrs. Bradford if anything serious happens before Aunt Lavinia arrives."

Dovie boarded a steamship to complete the sale and delivery of tools, shovels, and pickaxes needed by western troops in their territorial skirmishes with Indians. She felt quite efficient and important. She ordered the cabin boy around, and the steward when she could. The captain addressed her respectfully as Miss Lloyd. Near St. Louis she oversaw the unloading of the goods and reloading onto the ship that would take her on the Missouri River to her destination, a supply point and trading post. *Omaha, Council Bluffs, strange and exciting names,* she thought.

The ship arrived at Kansas City. Off the gangplank and onto the ship stepped a man that made her stop and stare. Later, she congratulated herself that she had worn her good, dark blue dress.

The man, so handsome in a linen suit and Panama hat, had ruddy skin, clay colored like earth. When he removed his hat, he had thick black hair, combed back off his forehead, and his smile dazzled her.

By instinct she glided right across his path. No bird in a mating ritual ever moved so deliberately as she. At the ship's rail, she turned and heard the shock of his voice, a deep, soft voice, and faced his brown eyes looking into hers.

"It looks to be a pleasant trip, Miss—?"

"Lloyd," she whispered. "Gwendolyn Lloyd."

"Gwendolyn Lloyd. Is this your first trip up river, Miss Lloyd?"

"First," she repeated.

"Well. Then you must allow me to show you some points of interest since I have taken this trip several times." He eyed her red hair, orange and gold in the sun, and seemed startled by her bright blue eyes. After a moment he recollected himself and said with a slight bow, "I am Grover Ames."

The ship was leaving the dock as Grover Ames offered her his arm. She took it and never thought twice about who he was or where he came from. The whole familiar world seemed to have broken into bits and scattered over the churning water in the ship's wake. It was a strong arm. He helped her up the stairs, bending over her tiny form.

That evening, Mr. Ames leaned over his guitar as he played. The ladies in the salon sat forward to hear.

"Grover, Mr. Ames, looks a bit dangerous," a lady, Mrs. LeBeau, said.

At her side, Mrs. Waltham crisply put him down. "He's an Indian. Oh, he's got some white in him. That's what makes him so good looking outside—but he's just a red Indian inside."

"So full of feeling," her daughter murmured as she got a glimpse of the golden brown eyes.

132

Wonderful eyes, Dovie could hardly look at them and yet couldn't look away. He didn't look at the ladies as he played. He seemed absorbed in his thoughts.

The rest of the night went by in a daze for Dovie. The group moved to the deck after the music. Dovie stood at the rail, and Grover leaned next to her. There were quiet moments when no one spoke and there was just the sound of the water rushing past. For Dovie, never had the night held so much mystery, shadow and light moving as the lanterns swung with the motion of the ship.

Mr. Ames spoke in a low voice as he stood next to her. "This promises to be a very special voyage."

Then there was a burst of noise as a group left the salon. When the door swooped closed, Mr. Ames moved away. She did not speak directly to him again, and he said nothing else to her. The night ended. Tired and weak, she drifted away from the group and into bed. As soon as her head touched the pillow, she slid from her waking trance into sleep.

The next morning was Sunday. When she went to breakfast, the other ladies were dressed for church. Dovie went along with them to the ship's chapel. Church service would be a good place to be alone with her fantasies of the handsome man in tan linen.

Her thoughts lingered over him as she had never lingered over anything in her life—except once when she was ten back in Wales. She had wanted a paisley shawl displayed in the window of Mr. Tuttle's shop on Broad Street. The shawl glowed with deep reds and jewel greens. Draped over a stand, the gold fringe seemed to flow. Dovie thought if only she could wrap herself in that cloth she would be beautiful and serene. Each day she bent her path through town from the shop where she sold the day's eggs to Tuttle's. There her steps slowed. One day she might notice the sheen of the cloth, another time the intricate pattern.

She never got the shawl. Her mother, who might have given it to her, was ill and died. While Dovie was still grieving her death, her father brought Ada into their home. *That was the end of any special treatment. I never got another gift and even had to fight to get food that was my right*, Dovie thought.

The minister spoke of love for one's fellow man, but she thought of one man only. The vision of his eyes with the golden lights made her feel a little faint. She sighed deeply. The lady next to her looked over reprovingly. It was Mrs. LeBeau, who had her hymnbook out and opened. Dovie had not even heard the number announced. When the congregation began the hymn, she recognized the song and closed her eyes to sing. She knew the words without looking at the book.

At the phrase, "How can I keep from singing?" she opened her eyes. It was a shock to find that the very eyes she was thinking of were quite near and looking into her own. They stared at each other a moment, and then Grover reached for her hymnal. She surrendered it and leaned weakly back in the pew.

Grover's hand brushed hers. She actually felt her heart jump in her chest and was hot and shivery at the same time.

Reverend Maxwell spoke in a high voice of a "choir of angels."

Grover smiled at her. She looked at him, and then avoided looking at him. He dropped the hymnal on his foot. Looking down she saw that he wore brown shoes. This was a source of wonder to her, brown shoes, she thought, just like any mortal.

The minister, ending his sermon, thundered his hope that, "by the practice of virtue all here present will be saved." Quite lost, Dovie fluttered her downcast eyelashes.

Mrs. LeBeau wanted a stroll on the deck, and Mr. Ames was only too glad to accompany them. The *Ben Bartlett* was a luxurious ship. On the promenade deck there was no shortage of spittoons for the men; one of polished brass was furnished every six feet. Mrs. LeBeau found the deck too windy and the ladies' salon too pokey. They entered the main salon and walked on parquet floors under stained glass that threw colored reflections over the floor and people. Huge mirrors allowed the guests to admire themselves and the others promenading there.

Dovie sat in a group of upholstered chairs with her companions. She picked up a pretty silver bell on the table beside her and toyed with it as she talked. In a few moments, a white-coated waiter appeared at her elbow. She tried to ignore him and continue her conversation with Mrs. LeBeau and Mr. Ames, but she could see out of the corner of her eye that he remained there.

With an amused smile, Mr. Ames said, "Would you care to order something?" and gestured to the waiter.

Dovie hastily put the bell down. Her face flushed red.

"If you pick this up and it rings, a waiter will appear. Nothing just now, waiter." Mr. Ames said.

He seemed sophisticated, and Dovie did not want to appear ignorant. She, who had been praised for her singing of French songs, got up and strode to the piano. She wanted to make an impression on Mr. Ames. She sang and imagined him seated behind her with a look of bliss as he listened. She was very confident and put on her most charming airs as she played and sang. Afterward, a lady with a *pince nez* leaned forward and corrected one word. Dovie swung around on the piano bench ready to collect Grover's compliments. His chair was empty.

The lady was still peering at Dovie through her eyeglass. Dovie blushed; the woman was correct. She had made a very public mistake and felt embarrassed. Was her French that she took such pride in faltering?

"*Merci*," Dovie said curtly to the woman, closed the piano, and swept away.

Mrs. LeBeau took this opportunity to follow Dovie and speak to her. Putting her hand on Dovie's arm, she said, "Mr. Ames, I believe, bears watching."

Dovie refused to take her meaning. "Where is Mister Ames?" she said.

Mrs. LeBeau spoke with the most honeyed concern in her voice, "There's a rumor that..."

Dovie didn't stay to hear.

It was a shock to see Grover deep in conversation with an attractive lady at the edge of the salon. Dovie left the room. A day passed in which she stayed mostly in her room. Her feelings were confused, and she tried to get hold of herself. The boat was coming into Omaha, Nebraska Territory, where she was to sign over Mr. Thompson's shipment to the military representative. She knew that Mr. Thompson was waiting eagerly for her telegram that the deal was done.

Once she had seen the materials unloaded, she received the signed receipt and with relief sent Mr. Thompson word that the business was completed. Soon he could collect the money for his spring restocking of the store. That done, Dovie walked along the deck enjoying the sound of the whistle as the boat left port.

Ames found her on the deck before she had walked half the length of the ship. Without a word, he offered his arm. As they walked, he began to talk.

"My father was English, from the Midlands, a trapper. My mother is a Cheyenne Indian. My father never took me back to England, though he said he would. He's dead now, or disappeared, it's all the same to me. So I had to go back with my mother to the tribe when I was twelve. Dakota Territory, that's the place I was happiest in my life. The Black Hills, the Dakota sky, blue, gray, different in all weathers and times." He scowled. "The white man will soon ruin it.

"The Cheyenne believe a new world will be built to the west and will move and overlap this one as the left hand covers the right." He moved his hands one over the other. "There will be a great fire that will burn the white man and drive him into the sea. The elders smoke their pipes on it and dance and think it will be so. When I am with them, when I put my eagle paint on—my Cheyenne name means Young Eagle without a Nest—I believe this also.

"But I am part white man; will I be burned or saved? When I am not with them but here," he stared in deep gloom at a lady opening a fancy parasol, "I know that they, the Cheyenne, will be snuffed out. They cannot understand the way things are done. They would not be Cheyenne if they could do that. They are doomed. If I want to survive, I must become like the white man. I am a white man, but never totally." He looked down at Dovie.

"You have the whitest skin I have seen. What would my Cheyenne mother think if she could see you? Red hair is of fire but blue eyes of water; this must carry magic. She would have to think a long time about what it means."

The thought amused him, and he began to walk faster. Dovie caught up and looked up at him. Ames gave her his most charming smile. Like her partner in a ballet, he led her along the promenade. "I am tempted," he said aloud. He seemed lost in thought. At the stairway, he grasped her gloved hand, lifted it, and looked at the inside of her exposed wrist. He saw the tracery of blue veins visible through the pale skin.

He proposed marriage, she accepted—she had in a sense accepted whatever he proposed from the minute she saw him.

He had a scar on his jaw that Dovie had wondered about but not dared to speak of. That evening, she got up her nerve and pointed to it. "How did this happen?"

"Melvin Thomas did that. Melvin was my best friend—until he shot me. Shot me with my own gun. Made me mad as hell, er, sorry."

"Why would your best friend shoot you?" Dovie asked, astonished.

"We had a fight in St. Louis."

Dovie didn't know what to make of that. Grover fingered the scar.

"When he died, I dug his grave through frost on the ground. It was a day in December. We, the Cheyenne, say it is the time of the cold, hard faces. I had to use a pick and a shovel." Grover shrugged.

They left the boat at the next port, Fort Pierre, Dakota Territory. She composed a telegraph message to the Thompsons. She was allowed ten words but had so much she wanted to tell the Thompsons that she rearranged them many times. Finally, her message was: "Met wonderful man getting married Dakota. Letter follows. Affectionately, Dovie." She looked around to see if anyone was watching and kissed the form. *To my family—or the closest I have to one.*

Grover hastily purchased a horse and wagon near the wharf, and they drove to the trading post. He began what seemed to Dovie a frenzy of purchasing. He bought black kettles, ten of them, and ten Hudson Bay blankets of heavy wool, then steel knives, twenty of these. He paid, throwing down the money on the counter with a flourish. He didn't explain. Dovie was mystified but out of pride didn't ask, just got into the wagon. Grover pitched their things in the back and drove to the edge of the Bad River.

They were the only passengers on a flatboat carrying many barrels. The boatman tied the horse and cart on with ropes. Before they had left the town, Grover was leaning forward over the railing and lost in thought. On the river, the boat passed through vast open spaces, a rolling sea of tall grass. Everything seemed to slow down.

The boat stopped at a pier, really only a mud rise on the shore with a few wooden stakes in the ground. Grover and the boatman maneuvered the horse and wagon onto land, their feet slipping and sliding in the mud. Dovie climbed into the wagon. Once on solid ground, Grover began to drive swiftly and in silence. The sun overhead and their shadow running along under the wagon were Dovie's only company. He drove on and on toward dark hills in the distance.

Towards midafternoon, Grover slept as Dovie drove the horse. Out of the empty prairie came a stag running toward the moving wagon. It grew larger as it neared them. Dovie began to fear that it would crash into the wagon. She yelled and waved the whip in the air. The stag veered as it came close and ran beside the galloping horse. Dovie looked over at the animal. Every detail stood out in the strong light: its liquid brown eye, the points on its horns, the gradation of colors in its fur, steel gray mixed with brown. It was magnificent, galloping beside her, and she yelled with pure excitement. The stag turned, veered off, and was gone from view as suddenly as it had appeared.

Grover only stirred in his sleep and didn't wake. Dovie felt alone in the vast bowl of earth and sky. It was the loneliest road in the loneliest territory she had ever been in. She wished they would see people and exchange a few words, get water and food.

They were high in fir-covered hills when an eagle flapped up from a meadow right beside them. In its beak dangled a thick, black snake. At sunset, she saw the moon in an orange sky.

It was almost dark when they finally arrived. There were strange, rustling sounds in the grass.

"Rattlesnakes," Grover said and turned the wagon away from the area.

Dogs barked an alarm as they approached an encampment below the hills. Dovie's first sight of the Indian camp was smoke from fires drifting across a wide valley where two rivers met. Many white tepees gleamed in the last light, horses moved slowly over the field, grazing. Nearby, were flatbed wagons and a river that meandered between grassy banks.

Grover led her inside a tepee, pulling her by the arm after him. Inside, he spoke in Cheyenne to the old man and women gathered there as he gestured roughly to Dovie. They stared at her. The old woman signaled Dovie to come near where she sat. The woman reached out and touched Dovie's red hair. The Indian loosened it from the bun, pulled the hairpins out, and held them in one hand. Dovie felt the rough fingers tugging at her hair. The woman spoke in wondering tones. A younger woman approached and, poking her neck forward, looked Dovie over. Dovie felt her breath, which smelled like wild grasses, on her face. The young woman turned to the others, speaking rapidly and tapping her knuckles beside her eyes. Another female was behind Dovie and pulled some red hairs out of Dovie's scalp. Dovie cried out and swatted with her hand. They all stood back.

Only then did Grover speak again, roughly issuing orders Dovie could not understand. One of the women, Half Sister, Grover called her, took Dovie's wrist and tried to lead her away; but tired as she was Dovie resisted.

"Go on," Grover told her. "Half Sister will show you a place to sleep."

They went out in the dark and into another tepee where the woman led Dovie to a pile of buffalo robes on the floor. Dovie went to it and, exhausted, fell asleep the minute her head lay on the fur.

The next thing she knew, she heard low, rasping voices and opened her eyes to slits. People were coming and going, raising the door flap, admitting flashes of daylight. When someone touched her hair, she snapped open her eyes. There was a collective gasp at the sight of her light blue eyes. A little boy, who had been kneeling on the floor beside her, scrambled to his feet and ran out of the tent, whimpering in terror. Blanketed figures stood all around her pallet with their faces intent on her. A woman with long braids poked the one next to her and they whispered excitedly. The flap lifted, and someone else entered and jabbered, pointing to Dovie. Dovie sat up suddenly and they all surged back.

Dovie clutched her blanket and yelled, "Grover, Grover!"

Some backed away but stayed in the tepee. A girl with the most liquid, dark eyes Dovie had ever seen seemed to take in what was wanted and ran out the open flap. Dovie tried to straighten her clothing. She pulled the blanket around her and stood up. The girl returned with Grover.

"Get these people out of here," Dovie said. If Grover wanted to show her off to his tribe, he would have to give her time to wash and comb.

Grover flapped his arms and shooed the women and children like a flock of chickens.

"Times are bad here," he told Dovie. "Soldiers prowling the trails have attacked peaceful Cheyenne camps. This has happened on the South Platte River recently. The attack was done with no warning. There was a parley at Camp Weld near Denver." His face was an angry mask. "These people, my people, will be betrayed again." He turned his back.

Dovie struggled to take it all in. "What will happen? To us?"

Grover rubbed his forehead. His mind seemed to be far away. "I've fixed it up with the elders. It's not the time for the usual celebrations, but the wedding will be tonight." He went out the door opening and yelled, "Half Sister, come and help."

When she appeared Grover spoke to her and told Dovie, "I've told Half Sister to take you to the creek to bathe. She and Yellow Star will have to see to your wedding dress. I want a splendid dress."

When his sister began to protest, he cut her off and persuaded her.

Grover turned to Dovie. "I have told her, 'Remember when I gave you and Yellow Star Sister fine, new blankets before last winter's snows came? This time, I knew I would ask your help, and I have brought each of you a strong, new knife and iron pots to help you prepare the food for my wedding.' You have a lot to do, our ceremony is this afternoon."

As she started to speak, he made a curt motion. "My sisters will help you in all that you must do." And he was gone.

Dovie called after him, "Grover, Grover!"

The two women stood watching her. Dovie turned to them. She made motions, scooping with her hand and chewing.

The two laughed together, and then each took one of her hands and pulled her. They took her to a place where women worked using a smooth rock with a knob for a handle to grind corn on a hollowed out slab of rock. They reached into a storage chamber of mud plastered over a frame of twigs and gave her a gourd filled with squash, corn, and beans. As she sat on the ground and ate, she saw a hawk on the dead branch at the top of a tree. It was there for a long while, calmly surveying the countryside.

Grover came walking up, in his arms a wiggling, tan puppy. He dropped the little dog in her lap. He sat down by her but spoke with his sisters.

"What are they saying?" Dovie asked.

He turned to her and translated, "Yesterday, Half Sister had her knife in her hand. She was carving meat and hanging it up to cure. The children splashing in the creek called her, and she went to them. When she returned the winter meat was gone, pulled down and eaten by the dog, the mother of this puppy. With her knife, she slit the dog's throat."

Dovie recoiled as Grover rubbed behind the ears of the brown puppy.

Half Sister was eager to tell her brother what had happened since his last visit, and Grover repeated it for Dovie.

"Red Dog gambled too much and has even gambled away his wife."

Half Sister handed Dovie more food to eat and continued speaking.

"Half Sister says 'This squash was planted in early spring while rain fell. It is good to have a storm to water the new plantings. Now we need rain and a ceremony is planned. These berries were gathered by children on the other side of the creek.'"

Dovie asked, "Do your sisters know the history of every bite they eat, who planted or gathered it, and when?"

"Cheyenne share everything among themselves, food and game."

Hours later when Dovie saw herself in the still reflection of a pool of water, she was amazed. Fitted over the top of her

141

head was a decoration beaded and woven of dyed porcupine quills. From this hung, almost to her eyes, strands of red and blue beads with shiny discs at the end that clattered and swung when she moved. Red braids of her hair framed her cheeks and hung down over her chest. A high collar woven of quills encircled her neck, and three thick ropes of white shell necklaces mingled with necklaces of blue beads. Her dress was of soft deerskin heavily beaded at the neck and shoulders and fringed at the bottom. The short, stumpy tail of the deer decorated the center front below the beading.

Half Sister nodded with satisfaction and tapped the beading on Dovie's dress. She made sewing motions and tapped herself. Dovie understood that Half Sister had decorated the dress. Dovie pointed down at her moccasins, beaded in yellow and blue designs, and the Indian girl nodded; she had done those also.

Dovie stared at her reflection in the stream. She was filled with a sense of wonder that she could be so transformed in the space of a few hours and a change of clothes.

The two sisters motioned Dovie to come. As she started to walk, the weight of the beaded dress on her shoulders nearly made her fall. Escorted by the sisters, she walked up from the creek over a sunbaked field of low brush. It was July; Dovie was sure of the month but had lost count of the days. She heard the sound of hidden rattlesnakes like dried seeds shaken slowly in a gourd. The hair stood up on the back of her neck as she walked forward trusting her guides. The sun was in her eyes, and she felt the heat of the clay under her shoes. They neared the tepees and a loud noise began. Dovie saw all the men and boys pounding their feet in rhythm on boards over a hole dug in the ground. It made a deafening noise. They began to chant.

Dovie was shocked to see dancers with bare chests and only loincloths around their bodies. They ran and jumped on the boards, and each jump made a noise like thunder. Shells tied around their ankles jangled as they stomped in rhythm. Dovie covered her ears and stared at their wild, tossing hair decorated with feathers and beads.

Suddenly, in front of her, a man's face appeared with red paint up to his eyes and white stripes across the forehead.

With a shock, she recognized Grover. Around his neck was a leather strip with three bear claws.

"The drumming is to bring rain from the mountains," he said in her ear.

They walked to two heavily laden horses. Grover took the bridle and led them. Dovie walked behind him as he led the horses to the chief's tepee where he ceremoniously unloaded the blankets, kettles, and knives he had bought from the trading post. He spoke to the chief who received the goods and replied with many words.

There was muttering among the older people. Dovie had no family there to give or receive gifts. They shook their heads; it broke with their customs. She was not a full-blooded Cheyenne or even from another Indian tribe. Grover told her he had pointed out to them that her eyes were the blue of the sacred lake in the Black Hills; it was something in her favor.

Now, from the circle of men came the noise of howling wolves, barking coyotes, and chirping birds. Next to her, Grover lifted his garishly painted face and uttered the scream of an eagle as though the spirit of the wild bird were inside him.

Women carried in the food and drink. Dovie turned to see them, though the beads dangling in her eyes obstructed her view. Again she almost fell under the weight of her heavy dress. Half Sister caught her but spilled some food from a gourd she was carrying.

The elders looked at each other over the meat spilled on the ground. Half Sister backed out of sight with her head lowered. Grover stood tensely next to Dovie.

"Any mistakes in the ritual can cause sickness or death to the tribe. Every person must do his part perfectly," he told her as the men muttered uneasily.

The priest strode to Dovie. As he loomed over her, he shook as though a great power possessed him. He did not point his fingers at her, but carried a short stick, lifted it high, and pointed it down at Dovie. She thought she was being witched and drew back.

Grover, at her side, whispered, "You, all of us, are protected now. This is strong medicine."

Grover led her to a place in the circle. There was a roll of thunder in the distance. Mumbles of satisfaction came as the people scanned the dark clouds in the sky. Dovie and Grover sat down on the ground with the others.

"Now we are married," Grover said in her ear.

Dovie was astonished. Her wedding march had been the rattle of snakes and roll of thunder; she had been blinded by sun and witched by the priest. Now, she was breathing in a cloud of tobacco smoke as the priest smoked a long pipe.

She thought briefly, *This is what you get for marrying an Indian*.

"He will bring blessings on the family," Grover said, breathing in the smoke. "And no one will tease me anymore and call me 'Rain-in-the-face' from all the tears I cried when my mother first tried to teach me Cheyenne ways. Now, I am Golden Eagle."

Dovie took hold of Grover's sleeve. "Golden Eagle," she said uncertainly.

After the wedding feast, men danced around a fire. Dovie watched the jumping black silhouettes against the flames until, at a signal from Grover, she went into a tepee and got out of the heavy dress. She folded it in her bag before she put her shift, corset, and dress back on. She and Grover left, slipping away on two horses he had ready.

They rode up into the mountains; he knew the way in the dark. They went to a cabin he lived in at times, a trapper's cabin his father had built. Their excitement led them as though in minutes up the hills and to the cabin. When Grover undid the lock and threw open the door, Dovie heard something swoosh and depart. It was an owl perched on the roof. But she had no time or wish to think about that with Grover so near, and all her love for him making her dizzy.

The air in the room was damp and cold. Grover lifted a quilt off a hook on the wall, and the two of them held its sides and tossed it in the air. It sank slowly to cover the rope bed.

Later she remembered a lace ruffle tickling her bosom as Grover worked to undo the buttons, six of them, that held together the pale pink scaffolding of her corset. Grover untied the laces that let her round, tender flesh expand from its nipped waist. Petticoats, high buttoned boots, silk ribbons, jet-beaded shawl, all fell in a heap on the dusty floor. The couple soon made the room warm.

The next morning when Dovie stepped out of bed, the air was chilly. A big coat of animal skins sewn together hung from a nail on the wall. She pulled it around her. It had no buttons, only rawhide ties which she fastened. On the cabin doorstep she stood as though poised to step off into the thick, lavender mist that covered the valley between her and a jagged mountain. Ranges of pointed firs so dark green they appeared black stood out against the sky. She took a few steps on steep but solid ground. A cottontail rabbit in the scrub grass nibbled busily, its ears a translucent pink in a slanting ray of sun.

I am fifteen and a half and a married woman, Dovie thought, hugging the coat around her for warmth. *I may have given Grover the impression that I'm a little older.*

She had told him she was a storekeeper and left out that she was once a servant. She had made the decision to put that behind her, the humiliation of taking orders, bowing to Miss Eleanor, being told to tidy herself up and cover her red hair with a cap.

Her mother had often warned her about her tendency to tell stories, embellish reality, and not be scrupulous with the truth. *I know I need to be more truthful, but what's the good of going all this way for a new life if I have to drag the old one after me?* Dovie thought. *After all, I've crossed an ocean and half a continent on my own, and I deserve something. I won't tell him yet. I know the way he dresses he would not like to be married to somebody's maid. I wish things could be the way I want them to be.*

Her new husband seemed citified and smooth, but he had told her that his father was a trapper who had built this cabin with his own hands. The place looked neglected to her, vines grown over the roof and weeds in the doorway. Funny to think that beaver hats caused this cabin to be built on a mountainside. And then when the style changed to silk hats there was no market for his beaver pelts anymore. That must have been when Grover's father moved on and left his Indian wife and child, Dovie thought, and felt sorry for the young boy, abandoned.

Grover had said he lived here at times with only his dogs for company. *It's a harsh life*, she thought, looking at the mud-daubed logs. *In this wilderness people survive how they can. How will we manage to live here?* A little fib seemed like nothing in the face of that question.

A Gambler's Life

After a few days a young Cheyenne came up the mountainside with a message. A passing band of Arapaho had brought the Cheyenne camp a warning. A party of white men was approaching; they did not seem to be soldiers but had guns. Because Grover spoke English, he was needed to find out what they intended.

When he returned, Grover told Dovie all that had happened. Four warriors accompanied him; they remained concealed below the ridge of a hill while Grover rode out alone to meet the group of ten men. The group tensed at the sight of Grover riding toward them. They stopped and drew together. As he came near, they looked at him with grim faces.

He had high cheekbones, dark eyes and hair and was dressed in fringed buckskins. Dovie laughed, delighted, when he told her of the sensation he caused when he spoke to them in proper English.

"What did you say?" She wanted to know everything that had happened.

He repeated for her, "Good afternoon. I am from the Cheyenne; Grover Ames is my name. I have come to parley. You are too near our camp."

A slight man in a broad-brimmed hat and a little pointed beard came forward. The man just behind him had a rifle balanced behind the saddle horn.

"We are a hunting party," the first man said. "We mean no harm to any Indian tribe."

"What sad, pale eyes he had," Grover told Dovie. "I told him, 'These are dangerous lands and times. The Cheyenne and Sioux are in a warlike mood. They may think you come to attack.'"

Then, the man said, "I am Lord Bermondsey. You speak like an Englishman but appear to be an Indian."

"My father was an Englishman and a trapper, Harold Ames. He was from the Midlands."

The man appeared to be very relieved. "I know the area."

"You know the Midlands! It is a place I would have seen if my father had lived longer."

"I will describe it to you if you like. Here, we have heard of a strange, blighted landscape and are looking for it. It is said to be in this area," he said.

"The Badlands," Grover replied. "There is no hunting there. Here, there is grass. Bison in some seasons, mud in others."

"I want trophies to bring back to England, buffalo, mountain lion, and eagle. I have heard that there have been discoveries of gold and silver." He pointed his riding crop at the mountains. "I might want to buy a mine."

Grover told Dovie, "I told him, 'That place is sacred to the tribes. It would be dangerous for you to even be found there.' The English Lord seemed to think. Then he told me, 'We need someone like you who speaks both languages. I would hire you as a guide and hunter for our group.'

"I named my price and Lord Bermondsey accepted. I was hired on the spot. If only I had asked for more, I could have gotten it. Next, he asked me, 'Can I meet your chief?'

"I told him, 'I could bring you into the Cheyenne camp, but only if you pledge peace. You would smoke pipes of peace with the chief, and this would give you protection even with other tribes. It will have to be arranged,' I told him.

"'You'll dine with the group,' he told me. He considered me presentable enough. The others were watching all of this. They were all curious about me, and when I told him I was newly married he said, 'But of course, your bride will be welcome at the table tonight.' He'll be surprised when he sees you and your fine table manners."

Grover was jubilant as he began to pack his guns and ammunition. "What luck! He's a lord, he knows the place my father was from, and he's going to tell me about it. And we dine with them tonight. Lord Bermondsey has come out to see the huge buffalo herds he's heard about. They all want to hunt and bring back trophies. It's a great opportunity."

Dovie tried to be enthusiastic since Grover was so excited about this. She wanted to find a place to call home and settle there, not follow some English Lord around on his travels.

"We'll make a lot of money—for the future you're always talking about," Grover said.

Dovie began to rummage through her things in the cabin. She would wear her wedding dress, which was the most special dress she had, and she needed to assemble the headdress.

That night, everyone who entered the room waited respectfully for Lord Bermondsey to make his appearance. Dovie stared up with the others at the top of the stairs. The balustrade was made of a giant tree trunk skinned of its bark. The steps were logs cut in half with the flat side to step upon.

The English lord traveled with a retinue of cronies and servants, among them a Boston newspaperman to record the trip. They traveled with four mules pulling wagons and five horse-drawn carts. They were all housed in a rancher's cabin and in tents on his place.

Lord Bermondsey appeared and paused for a moment. *A real English lord!* Dovie thought and observed that he was slim and held in one hand a black *cigarro* from which smoke plumed. He had a moustache and beard, and his hair was neatly parted and combed. He wore a short, dove-gray coat; a waistcoat over a cream shirt; a black, flowing tie; and gray trousers. He displayed his long-nosed profile with the elegant nonchalance befitting a fashion plate straight from London or Paris.

She approached him on the arm of Golden Eagle. Everyone turned to watch, and conversation stopped as Dovie padded softly across the room in deerskin moccasins. She was busy observing every detail. She noticed that Lord Bermondsey was startled to see that the Indian's bride had red hair and blazing blue eyes.

She had braided her hair and stuck two bright feathers in the braids. Lord Bermondsey stared and stared, and then broke into applause. Dovie blushed from the attention. He inclined his head slightly to her. Now she felt really self-conscious.

"I thought—but you are no squaw. Do you have an Indian name?" he asked.

"My husband sometimes calls me Red Blossom," she replied. "You are far from home," Dovie ventured to say. "Is your family with you?"

A pained look came over his face. He took a slim, gold case from his pocket. "No, but I carry this. Painted of my daughter in Paris," Lord Bermondsey said and held it out.

Dovie opened it. She stared at a miniature of a world that seemed solid and rich. The child's pale brown hair was drawn up and tied on top of her head. She wore a blue taffeta dress with a sash and a gray fur collar and cuffs. She stood with her hand on a table near a vase of roses. Dovie sighed and returned the gold oval.

"When I have a daughter I want her to look just like this," she told Lord Bermondsey.

"You don't want her to be a Cheyenne Indian, then?" he said.

He moved on to greet others but left Dovie troubled. *Of course not*, she thought. *My children won't be wild Indians!*

There were only two women in the party. The other lady sought Dovie's company. She was Countess Charlotte, the wife of Count Leonard Durnil, who stood next to Lord Bermondsey. The countess's fair hair framed a pretty face.

She took Dovie's hand and spoke in a lovely, low voice. "I would like to call you by your Indian name," she said, smiling.

Her manners were very graceful, befitting a countess, thought Dovie, dazzled.

"You should know that Ned, Lord Bermondsey, is a man who thinks that he will never be happy again," she said. "He has come so far to try to forget the death of his wife."

Dovie watched Lord Bermondsey and saw the unsmiling demeanor with which he greeted others in the group.

Dinner was announced. Women were such a rarity in the West that Dovie had been given a place not too far down the table. The count sat opposite her. His hair was gray and worn collar length, parted in the middle. He sat back very relaxed. He paid little attention to Dovie, who was busy casting about in her mind for a topic of conversation she could broach with a count.

Lord Bermondsey traveled with a staff and his own cook. The centerpiece of the meal was a whole boar roasted and displayed on a silver platter. The tusks were strong and yellow, and the jaws held an apple. This delicacy was surrounded with roasted potatoes decorated with sprigs of wild rosemary. A serving man carved the roast at the sideboard.

Dovie sat before a plate with gold designs and on it a two-handled cup on a saucer. The array of silverware was dazzling. There were three forks to her left and a meat knife, a fish knife, and two spoons to her right, as well as four wine glasses. None of this intimidated Dovie; she remembered it well enough from the Llewellyn's sumptuous table. This time, she was thrilled to sit down as one of the guests. She looked up and down the table at the sparkling glasses, the candles and silver, and at the head of the table saw Lord Bermondsey's unhappy face. *How strange life is*, she thought, *that none of this splendor could bring a smile to his face.*

She read the handwritten menu beside her place: cream of turtle soup, melon, filet of speckled trout, cutlet of wild boar au jus, quail with watercress, potatoes and fried celery. For dessert, there were meringues a la crème.

Serving dishes were brought to the table and offered for guests to help themselves. White gloved hands holding a silver dish offered potatoes to Dovie. She remembered the times when Cook had told her, "Keep an eye on those potatoes." She had wound the corner of her apron around the handle to lift the pan when they were done. Tonight, she lifted the silver spoon and served herself a small portion. She felt too excited to eat.

The count was saying to the rancher on Dovie's left, "You would be surprised to know the number of women who smoke cigars, not little *cigarros*, but full-bodied weeds in many cases."

"Not in America, surely."

"No, no, I'm talking of Paris, and not only in Montmartre. I mean in the salons."

The rancher, a Russian, had rented his lodge to the party at a handsome sum. He and his Indian consort were living in a tent in the meanwhile.

Countess Charlotte said, "I have seen a photograph of your Madame 'Arriet Beecher Stowe. *Quelle surprise!* Only a modest and small lady."

Dovie remembered what she had heard at another banquet. She told the countess, "You and Mr. Lincoln are in agreement on that point. He called her *'la petite femme,'*" Dovie spoke a few words of French to impress the countess, "'the little lady who caused the big war.'"

"How charming of your Mr. Lincoln. I would like to meet him."

The man on her right wore rough clothes and said he was one of the hired hunters. He had on a calico shirt and his pants legs had leather coverings. When Dovie asked about them, he told her they were to ward off snakebites or cactus thorns. Though his fingernails were ragged with a rim of dirt under them, he held his knife like a dagger and carefully cut the bread.

Dovie and Grover had spent several weeks with the hunting party when Lord Bermondsey said he was very pleased with the trophies he had shot since Grover led the hunt. That day Lord Bermondsey had bagged a mountain sheep with big curled horns. "It will look wonderful in the great hall at home, mounted on the wall."

Dovie and the countess had been allowed to go out several times with the group when there was some special sight to be seen. Both women wore big-brimmed, western hats and bandannas to keep from breathing the dust. They would need to ride for hours. It had been a long time since Dovie had ridden the horse at home in Wales, but she managed to keep up with the group. The servants filled large canvas canteens with water from the spring before the riders departed. Two horses were loaded with these, and there were regular water breaks for the riders.

Dovie marveled at how surely Grover led them through the vast spaces to what he knew was hidden in the canyons and cliffs. The first trip was to a garden of petrified trees that lay fallen on the ground, so ancient that they had turned to maroon and yellow stone. Dovie looked down from her horse and recognized the grain of wood in the rock; sometimes she saw knotholes or bark, showing that there had once been a forest in this arid place.

Another day, the party passed by great walls of cliffs striped in ribbons of red, brown, white, and tan. Not a green or living thing was to be seen. Grover had brought the party to the wind cave where cliffs trapped the wind and made it howl. The sound of a long scream and then a constant moaning unnerved the riders as they drew near.

"I am going no farther," the count announced. Most agreed and moved their horses into the shade of an outcropping of rock.

Lord Bermondsey stopped his horse and listened with his head lifted. "This is the sound of my despair," he said in a tone of discovery. "Weary, weary of civilization. I seek a total break with my old life."

He signaled to Grover to bring him closer. They rode out of sight between huge boulders.

While waiting, two of the men ventured to climb some rocks. They were looking around at the view when rattlesnakes began to appear around them in droves. They ran and jumped down screaming. Dovie was relieved when the men returned and the group could ride away.

The two ladies joined the group again to travel to Jewel Cave. Grover left a man in charge of the horses, and the party entered a dim cave in the rock. Dovie left the hot glare of the desert and crouched in the low passageway. She felt her way with her hands on the walls. A cold, clammy wind brushed her skin as it rushed out of the place. The line of explorers walked almost in the dark following Grover, who held a smoking torch. At one point, Dovie, along with the others, had to pull herself over a boulder and through a hole.

She gasped to find herself in an underground room filled with strange formations of rock. The flickering light of the torch made shadows leap along the walls. No one spoke; the place cast a spell over the group, and the regular drip of water sounded loud in the silence. Dovie, hardly breathing, looked at shapes like castles and mountains in pale green and lavender.

When they finally emerged, Lord Bermondsey sighed and shook his head. "The dead might inhabit such a place."

Usually Dovie waited at the lodge for Grover to return from the day's hunt. Late in the afternoon the sun was low behind cottonwood trees as they walked down by the stream. Hundreds of the seeds in clumps of white down floated in and out of beams of light.

"I am thinking of our life together when we leave here," Dovie began.

Grover was dressed like an Indian in fringed buckskins and with a knife in his belt. She looked at him as though at a stranger. He wore a bandanna rolled and tied around his forehead to keep the long hair out of his eyes. He had dropped most of his American ways with his change of clothes, it seemed.

"When this job is over and our real life begins, I would like to have a small farm. It would be near a river like this but with neighbors and a town nearby." Dovie said.

"What would I do? I'm not a farmer; that is woman's work."

"Well, maybe we should live in a town. I do know how to run a store." Dovie answered.

"I am not a storekeeper, either. I am a hunter. Or I can do alright on the ships." Grover looked at her appraisingly. "You can help me, you would bring me luck. But you would need the right clothes. On the ships people only notice you if you are well dressed. You could attract a lot of attention being a redhead."

They sat down on an outcropping of rock. Dovie reached down for a stone she saw in the streambed. She held it up. "It looks like a bear, see? There's the head and..."

To her surprise Grover grabbed it and studied it closely. Very excited, he said, "Yes, the curved back, and there, the eye." He rubbed it on his shirt. "Good medicine for the hunt tomorrow."

Dovie laughed, but saw that he was serious.

"This means we will get our bear tomorrow," he said earnestly.

It was at moments like this that Dovie felt a great distance open between them. *I believe in luck, yes, but a rock I found has nothing to do with it*, she thought.

"Today, Lord Bermondsey had the perfect shot," Grover told her. "There was a buffalo in his gun sights. He had his favorite gun, 'Old Reliable,' fifty caliber and about twenty pounds in weight. He has learned to stand and brace the gun on his saddle. I taught him that. The buffalo had a massive head; it would have made the trophy he wanted. Everything was going fine. I'm the hired hunter; I have to make sure of everything. At the last second, wind blew his hair in his eyes and he shot but missed. No more buffalo. Then, he copied this." Grover touched the rolled bandanna. "The English Lord likes to look like an Indian brave," he said and laughed.

Dovie liked to see him laughing, but already she realized it was rare.

One day the next week, an Indian party came to the ranch with things to sell or trade. They were stopped well away from the lodge because they had a reputation for stealing. The European group was rounded up and went out to a low place out of the wind to see their wares.

The Indian women, wearing blankets and braids, stayed at a distance in the two wagons. The Indian men were on horseback. Some wore felt hats banded in grosgrain ribbon, and ragged, coarse, black hair hung halfway down their chests. The Europeans stared at them, remarking on their soft deerskin boots almost to the knee.

This group wanted to trade buffalo robes with thick fur and designs painted on the skin side. Dovie and the Countess Charlotte held them up one after another and exclaimed over them.

"See the arrows and deer," Dovie pointed out.

"Oh, a primitive hunting scene! Leon, we must have these," Charlotte said.

He examined them with interest but then patted his pockets. "Unfortunately, I brought no money."

"But he will take five dollars for the two. I've bargained a good price. Only five dollars," the countess said.

Dovie had exactly five dollars in her purse.

"They would look splendid n the chateau," the countess said.

My new friend wants the blankets so much.

"In Europe there is nothing like them!" Charlotte lamented.

Dovie opened her purse and found the bill. Her fingers touched it but she hesitated.

"This may be my last opportunity," Charlotte said.

The bill felt crisp in Dovie's fingers. It was for railway tickets when she and Grover left.

"If only there were a way," the countess said, turning her pretty, distressed face to Dovie.

Dovie held out the five.

"Oh, what a friend you are!" the countess said, and the five was aloft in her fingers. "I never borrow, you understand." She mimed embarrassment. "I am making an exception only this one time."

She turned slightly, and the count took the bill and told the seller, "Wrap them well."

"Oh yes, you must roll them in a cloth." Charlotte busied herself with her back turned to Dovie.

Just then, one of the cowboys, Jim, cursed at an Indian and shoved him to the ground. The Indian rolled to his knees and crouched on the ground. The other Indians swiftly gathered by him. One pulled a knife from his belt.

"He was stealing from my saddlebag," Jim cried.

Other ranch hands pulled their guns and muttered threats. The Indian showed his empty hands.

Lord Bermondsey pulled his gun and fired. His shot tore a line of dust from the ground and sent it whirling between the two groups. All faces turned to him.

Lord Bermondsey motioned with his gun at the Indians. "Get on your horses and go."

Jim started for Lord Bermondsey, raging and cussing. He swung at Lord Bermondsey, who stood his ground and landed a blow on Jim's head. Lord Bermondsey wound up and delivered another blow. Jim fell to the ground with a thud.

The Indians rode off whooping, and Lord Bermondsey's face was lit up by a big smile. He made an exhilarated leap onto his horse and rode away, rubbing his fist. The incident seemed to signal the end of the trip; Lord Bermondsey soon announced his intention of returning to the East Coast.

The same day she heard that news, Dovie found rainwater caught in a tree stump and hurried back to the lodge to get a towel and wash her hair in it. She would be glad to go anywhere water was not scarce and she could wash without thinking, *I'll have nothing to drink later.*

On one of the last days, Dovie was seated at a table next to the count.

The Russian gentleman who had rented them the lodge was saying, "Our trapper is leaving. He says he'll work as a buffalo hunter..." when Dovie felt a foot and a leg press against her leg.

She moved quickly away and glanced at the count's face, but it had a bland, humorous look as he said, "This, I hear, is the government policy, to kill off the buffalo."

Dovie moved slightly and resettled her skirts. She raised her teacup. A hand grasped her knee under the table and squeezed. Her raised teacup began to shake. She slammed it down into its saucer and stood abruptly. As she turned to go, she carefully brought the heel of her shoe down hard on Count Durnil's toe.

She turned, grinding the shoe, and murmured, "I've just remembered...You must excuse me." She saw a slight spasm cross the count's smooth face.

In the next room, Dovie came face to face with the countess.

"Oh," Dovie said, still flustered, "I am so glad to see you alone. I need the, uh, are you ready, that is, to repay me?"

"What?"

"The five dollars."

"Now? Now is not a good time. No, it is a very bad time."

"But the five dollars are for tickets. We are leaving soon."

"Don't even speak of it to me!" the countess commanded and stared coldly at Dovie.

Then, Countess Charlotte swept away. Dovie, standing empty-handed, had the uncomfortable realization that she had just been taken for a fool. *Nobility*, she thought bitterly. *The lowliest villager in Wales would have acted better than the count and countess.*

She overheard the Russian in the next room comment, "Grover was lucky at cards today."

The count replied, "His cards are too good. I'm not accusing anyone of anything, but I think there may have been a 'one-eyed man' in the game."

"If I catch any SOB cheating—I will shoot his other eye out!" the Russian replied, and both men laughed.

Dovie heard this and frowned. *What do they mean?* She thought, but her mind was really on what a temper Grover showed lately when things didn't go as he wished. She dreaded the time when she would have to tell him the five-dollar bill was gone.

Later that same day, as the group gathered for dinner, she heard with trepidation Grover asking her for the five dollars.

She pretended to search in her purse and then said, "I can't find it. It must be lost."

The countess watched this with one charming hand curled at her chin but said nothing. Grover's face reddened with anger, but he didn't speak. Dovie was glad he had asked while others were present. She didn't like to think about it, but she felt a shiver of fear when he seemed to swell up with rage over something.

☆ ☆ ☆

Within days after Grover received his final pay, he mysteriously acquired a shipment of guns and went off for a few days to sell it on the frontier.

Dovie protested as he left, "But these guns will almost certainly be used against Indians." For a reply, she heard only the door of their rented room slamming behind him.

When he returned they traveled the riverways until they could board a steamship. Grover carried a gun and a knife, Dovie observed. On the steamship, he didn't need those, she thought, but had already learned not to question what he did.

Grover had specially requested a room with a nice mirror. Dovie came into their room and found him seated before his own reflection shuffling his deck of cards. He shuffled and cut the deck dexterously as he watched himself. By now Dovie had grown used to the importance he placed on the evening of card playing. She realized that he made money from these card games, but she found it boring. When she heard Grover lie and say he was from St. Louis or Kansas, she excused him to herself, thinking he only meant to be sociable. She retired to her room as soon as he became absorbed in the game and she was able to slip away.

In December, reading an old newspaper, Dovie first became aware of what was being called the Sand Creek Massacre. It had happened back in November in Colorado. Now the passengers could talk of nothing else, it seemed. A Cheyenne and Arapaho camp had been attacked without provocation by U.S. troops. It was far south of the Dakota Territory camp where she and Grover were married.

"Listen to this, Grover, 'The scene of murder and barbarity,' the paper says. It was 'conduct to disgrace the veriest savage. Women, children and warriors were slaughtered.'"

Dovie read with growing revulsion. She threw the newspaper she had been reading to the floor of their room and stood up.

"It was murder!" she cried. "Guns! The guns you sold were probably used against your own people."

The blow came as though out of nowhere and sent her reeling against the door.

A week passed, and the bruise on the side of her face was fading but still needed to be hidden. She looked in the mirror and pulled the curls forward on her cheeks. *He chose profit over loyalty to the people who raised him. And he seems to hate me for pointing this out.*

He had been apologetic the next day and sworn that he would never again raise his hand to her. She stared into the mirror. She wouldn't make excuses for him anymore. Her eyes were opened now. She had found a second knife, small but deadly looking, fitted in his boot when she had moved his shoes. There seemed to be clues everywhere, but she had been oblivious to them.

All those months ago when she and Grover were leaving the Cheyenne camp, there was a squaw with two clinging children. She had spoken urgently to Dovie and pointed to the two children. Dovie looked at them; they were like two dolls. She picked them up and held one on each hip to admire their shiny black hair, bowl cut and falling like licks of paint on their round heads.

"What did she say?" Dovie had asked Grover as she climbed aboard the wagon to ride away.

Grover was busy adjusting the harness. "She wants you to remember them," he said laconically.

Dovie waved good-bye to the woman who stood staring after them.

Now as she watched the steamboat come in to dock, "Yes, yes, I remember you," she whispered.

The ship's whistle sounded two long and three short blasts. At a church near the waterfront, the doors were thrown open and people came running out. They took off their hats and waved them.

Dovie waved back, but she was thinking, *Of all the Cheyenne in the camp, only that woman came forward to say, "Remember me and my children."*

Dovie turned abruptly and went to her cabin. Grover was sitting in front of the mirror dealing, shuffling and cutting the deck.

"The ship has docked, did you hear the whistle? That means new passengers and that means," he watched himself in the mirror as he cut the cards, "opportunity. You must wear your new dress tonight. I would like to sit in the salon after dinner with my beautiful wife."

"Before the card game," she said.

He looked up, gauging her mood. "I think, yes, I will play cards this evening. There is usually quite a swell crowd boarding at St. Louis. Is anything bothering you?"

Dovie didn't answer but went to the wardrobe and took out her new dress.

"I was looking forward to wearing this."

She turned holding the dress in front of her. She held out the skirt with lace scallops caught up by pink rosettes that she had been so thrilled with in the shop.

"I'll sit with you—and attract men to play cards."

"No one will look anything as beautiful as you will in that blue gown. They will talk of no one else, believe me."

"Why, thank you. Even though I am only wife number two?"

"What?"

"I know about wife number one; she brought your children to show me when we left the Cheyenne camp."

Grover was silent. Then he shrugged and began to deal four hands out on the table.

"That is our custom. You are wife number two. If we were to go back, you would have to be a helper for her. Wife number one rules; that is our way. Now, there may not be a camp to go back to."

Dovie was silent, listening. Her hands smoothed and smoothed the lace on her blue dress.

"It is hard to belong to two worlds," Grover went on. "Sometimes they get mixed up. Yes, that's wife number one. Yes, the children are mine. I spend too much time away, I know that. But I bring them good provisions when I return." There was a long silence. "Now you know everything. Dovie?"

This is as bad as the days with Ada, Dovie was thinking. How long ago that seemed. She carefully straightened the stem of a pink rose on her new dress.

"We can be partners," he said. "These cards, they are my luck. What do you notice about these cards?"

Grover held two playing cards facedown in front of her.

"Do I know everything about you, Grover?" Dovie said and looked up from the picture on the cards of a boy on a unicycle riding along a lake's edge. She felt very sad.

"Notice one difference. Look, I know that this one is a king." He turned the card. It was the king of diamonds. "The shoreline is v-shaped, not straight as on the other card." He picked another card. "This one is a black king. See? The extra spoke on the wheel. Here, an extra mark in this petal of the flower means an ace." He sat forward, excited. "I know what marks to look for."

"How do you make sure your deck is used?" Dovie asked. She felt as though she were watching him from a great distance.

"I may even call for a brand new deck if a player seems suspicious." He produced an unopened package. "A special deck." He winked.

Dovie sat, silent, and then asked, "Are you the 'one-eyed man' in the game?"

He didn't answer but said, "You don't ever have to go back to the Cheyenne, I promise. We can have our life here on the boats."

That evening Dovie went through the motions of dressing, meeting young Mr. Tolliver and seeing his youth. She flirted with him knowing this was to get him to the table where Grover would cheat him at cards. She didn't yet know how, but she knew she must change her way of life.

A few nights after the incident with Mr. Tolliver, things got too hot for Grover. He awoke Dovie and told her to pack. They sneaked away from the boat before dawn.

"Meet me aboard the train; I have some business to take care of." He dropped their bags and walked rapidly away.

Dovie bought their tickets and waited to board. There was a commotion at the door and a man, a passenger from the ship, entered. He was angry and had two sheriff's men with him. They looked carefully at all the men in the waiting room. Dovie stood very still, watching. The porter called all aboard.

A woman, very fussily dressed in a bonnet and curls, entered the waiting room. Dovie eyed the woman's lumpy hips and bust. Dovie turned away and then turned sharply back to her. There was something about her; her hands in gloves held a shawl, something familiar. As the woman passed by, Dovie saw a flash of golden brown eyes, just a flash. She stared after the lady, whose head was modestly bent with her bonnet frill fallen over her face. The whistle blew again and Dovie hurried onto the train.

I know exactly who he is— now, I see him for who he is, Dovie thought. She felt a wave of shame burn her face.

When Grover joined Dovie hours later, he wore his usual outfit of cutaway coat, checkered trousers, and shirt with cravat. She was almost asleep. When her eyes fluttered open, he said brusquely, "Don't bother to talk. I want quiet."

✣ ✣ ✣

Dovie and Grover got off the train in northeastern Kansas. Dovie still didn't know what they were fleeing; Grover wouldn't talk about it. They walked into the town and encountered union troops. The captain was suspicious of Grover.

"I wonder why you are not in the military, sir."

"I am a supplier for the troops," Grover said in his smoothest manner. He showed his receipt for the shipment of guns. "I believe in the cause; the Union will be preserved."

The captain handed back the receipt.

Grover asked him, "We are very hungry, sir. Can you tell us of a place to eat?"

"I heard that there's an inn down that road, not too far."

Dovie and Grover had not eaten since yesterday's midday meal. They walked down a country lane until they could see the frame building behind a packed dirt courtyard. There was no activity along the road or outside the door. Grover frowned and motioned Dovie to wait in the yard. He moved cautiously up the porch stairs and looked in the open door. He signaled to Dovie to join him, and they stood in the doorway looking into the inn.

Breakfast was on the table. Their eyes saw the plates of food first of all. Then they saw that one chair was turned over on the floor and the others pushed back. The room was empty of people and the back door open. Dovie walked over to the coffee pot and touched its side. It was warm. Half-eaten eggs congealed on the plates. Dovie looked around hungrily. One bite was taken out of a biscuit. She daintily picked it up and bit out of the other side.

She perched in a chair, took off her hat, and threw it down on the table. She reached for the plate of biscuits just as she heard the sound of horses' hooves in the yard. Grover picked up a loaf of bread off the counter and ran out the back door. Dovie got up to follow, but her skirt caught on a hook. She struggled to loosen it, but her fingers were clumsy and slow while her mind raced to the back door and down the steps.

There was the thud of boots on the porch. With the clink of swords, soldiers burst in the front door. Dovie ripped her skirt loose from the hook and turned. A serving girl screamed as a soldier tore away a curtain that covered the women hiding in the pantry. Dovie mingled in with the women as they went into the kitchen. One girl cried into her apron as the proprietress, called Miss Amy, was questioned by a sergeant named Tilley.

"Who were they?"

"I don't know anything. I'm just a poor, widow woman."

"How many of them?" The one they called Harry grabbed Miss Amy's arm. He had a bandage wound around his head with his cap over it. She cowered and he let go.

"How many? Too many." She walked painfully across the kitchen floor, dragging one leg after her. "See, I have only a few eggs left, and this bone was a whole ham."

"Was there an officer? What did they call him?"

"What did they call him? I'm so upset I can hardly think. I'm out so much for supplies." She put her handkerchief to her face and blubbered.

"The name, ma'am. I need the name."

The sergeant turned exasperated and questioned Dovie. She shook her head dumbly.

"You," he said to the next girl. "Speak up! There's nothing to be afraid of, miss." He adopted a soothing tone. She opened her mouth but no sound came out. "Ten men? Twenty? How many were here?" The girl nodded. "Twenty?" She nodded again.

The sergeant dispatched three men to search the building and one to ride back to report to their commander. Three of the soldiers in blue uniforms sat down at the table.

Harry mockingly said, "We'll finish Quantrill's breakfast for him." He crooked his little finger as he slurped from a china cup. "You girls, better cook up more eggs and fry some ham."

Dovie moved to the stove with the other women, who looked at her with questioning eyes but said nothing.

The soldiers clattered down from the second story, holding up two whiskey bottles in each hand. "They's a whole closet full of the stuff!" they announced to the others.

"Lead me to it," Harry said, bounding to the stairs.

The girls exchanged glances, and Dovie followed two of them out the back door to the pump. One began to pump the handle while they scanned the yard. At a sudden noise they whirled around. It was Miss Amy running full tilt, the limp forgotten now that she no longer needed it.

"Run," she hissed, and they all ran as lightly and soundlessly as deer until the trees hid them.

A man's figure appeared from the shadows, and Dovie saw that it was Grover. The others ran farther into the forest. Grover took Dovie's arm and led her quickly after them.

"Quantrill!" he muttered when she told him what the soldiers had said. "That bloodthirsty devil!"

They lost the others but could occasionally hear crashing sounds in the forest and went in that direction. Later they saw the edge of a town through the trees. Dovie and Grover watched for several hours for signs of Quantrill and his dreaded raiders. They had heard how the raiders swooped down on a town, killing and burning. Fear drew them together, and when Grover held out the loaf he had pinched, Dovie tore off chunks and ate. Finally, they dared to approach the houses and find a way back to the riverboats.

In a scenario that was becoming dreadfully familiar to Dovie, she and Grover soon were back on a boat and ensconced in one of the best rooms. But this time there was an alarming change. Grover had been drinking until he passed out the night before.

That morning, Dovie got up and tiptoed past him sprawled in a chair. She stepped over the bottle rolling on the floor and went to the dining room. There, on sparkling linen, she ate breakfast alone.

"And just where have you been?" Grover said ominously when she returned.

"To breakfast," Dovie replied, noticing that he was freshly dressed and shaved though his eyes looked sunken and tired.

They had hardly spoken since their eyes had met under his bonnet ruffle during his escape dressed as a woman. Dovie's feelings for him had undergone a drastic change, and he seemed to hate the sight of her.

Grover scowled at her and went out. Dovie heard the sound of the key turning in the lock. She ran to the door, suspecting but not believing until she tried the handle—he had locked her in. Her first reaction was shock. She tried the handle more carefully. It did not turn. A scream came up in her throat, but she closed her lips on it. She ran to the window. It was high up, and she needed the metal rod hanging on the wall to open it. To still the panic rising in her, she breathed fresh air in gulps. She tried to think. She was furious. Locked in—how dare he?

When he comes back, she thought, her mind racing. "Money," she said and dropped the rod on a chair. She went to the wardrobe where she had hidden her cash in the toe of a shoe. She picked up the shoe and shook it. Nothing came out.

"Mean, conniving sneak, he found it," she muttered to herself with tears of frustration springing from her eyes.

Frantically, she reached in with her finger and clawed. Something came loose and her money scattered on the floor. She got to her knees and swept it up.

Several hours later, the sound of the key turning in the lock woke Dovie. She had dozed off seated in a chair. Grover came in. His face had the slack-jawed, drunken look she was becoming too familiar with. Dovie watched him try to replace the key in the inside lock. It took several tries before he could connect his wavering hand and the lock. She remained where she was and said nothing.

"Get me a glass." Grover put a rum bottle down on the table and sat heavily in a chair.

Dovie moved carefully to the opposite side of the table. She got a glass from the cabinet and placed it in front of him.

"Remember Mr. Templin?" she asked. "The man who called me 'little lady trickster' last night? He said he has something for you."

She noticed the metal rod within reach of her hand. She relaxed her hunched shoulders and let her breath slowly out.

Grover questioned her. "Well, what has he got?"

She answered coolly, "He wants to settle with you."

She was alert and awaiting Grover's next move. Her mind furnished, unbidden, the picture of the squaw woman cowering when Grover spoke harshly to her in the Indian camp.

He stood up and, rocking from side to side, started toward her.

"But what about Mr. Templin? He's waiting for you." Dovie's back was to the wall.

"Too much freedom, you..." Grover said slurring his words slightly.

His hand lashed out and hit her face. She couldn't see for a moment and her head was ringing. *He means to leave me in some Indian camp in poverty with children to raise and no support.*

"He said he had the money for you," she said.

Grover's face flushed. "Damned weasel, almost got away."

He downed the rest of the rum and tilted the bottle over his glass. When nothing came out he cursed and leaned over to get another out of the trunk.

Dovie grabbed the metal rod in both hands and struck him a quick, sideways blow to the head. He remained hunched over, still, for a long moment in which her heart seemed to stop beating.

Then his jaw dropped. "Aargh," he said and fell sideways to the floor.

Dovie felt rooted to the spot, unable to move. Her heart was jumping in her chest as she leaned over him to see if he was still alive. She forced herself to put a hand on his chest. He stirred slightly, and she recoiled and scrambled to get away. She grabbed up her bonnet and reticule.

He moaned. She ran for the door, where her fingers scrabbled nervously at the key. The voice of Mrs. Thompson seemed to speak in her mind, *Get out and keep going.* Dovie took a breath, stopped her shaking hand, and made it turn the key slowly. She opened the door and walked rapidly away, putting on her bonnet as she went. The cabin boy passed her in the hall, and she thought he stared at her face. She reached up and felt her temple. She saw blood on her fingers. She pulled her bonnet lower and kept going.

Up the stairs she hurried and down the gangplank, across the street, and around the corner to the train station. There was a train on the tracks with the engine going. She boarded it.

Dovie went into a crowded car and sat to the side. She found a seat with no one facing her, where she bent her head as though dozing until she heard the train whistle and felt it lurch into motion. She wiped her hands on her handkerchief and dabbed at her forehead.

The door to the car opened, and she whirled defensively, sure she would see Grover coming at her with blood streaming from his head. A lady in a green bonnet nodded to her and took a seat.

The train gathered speed. They quickly left the town behind. Out the window, Dovie saw bushes, a stream, and cows grazing in a field. She leaned back. She thought of her wedding, which had been a sham because he was already married.

There was the distant sound of an explosion. The train traveled around a bend in the river, and the passengers ran to the windows to look back at the ship in a mass of flames.

The conductor ran to the riverside and looked out. "That's quite a fire; the whole ship looks like it's going. The boiler must have exploded."

"Cotton cargo," a man next to Dovie said, shaking his head. "A ship like that will burn to the waterline."

"Oooh, ma'am, you look bad. Watch out, she's going to faint."

"There you go," said a man, assisting Dovie as she tottered. "See if you can get her a sip of water, conductor."

Dovie saw the flames and smoke envelop the boat and dropped into her seat with her eyes closed. It flashed across her mind, the sympathy she felt when Grover told her the painful truth that he was trying to forget: he was a despised and cheated Indian that people would rather see dead than alive. She doubled over, her stomach tightening in knots.

Later, when the train had traveled a while, she asked the conductor, "Where is this train going?"

"Hmmph. Probably on the run from something," a woman said, taking out her lorgnette and observing Dovie's fancy boots and lace hat.

"Don't you know, ma'am? Why, it's going to St. Louis," the conductor said.

"I'm going to a sick relative," Dovie said, thinking quickly. "And I've had no time to prepare. I'll buy my ticket on the train."

"Where are you going?"

"Near Louisville."

"Well, you'll have to change at St. Louis to get there."

Dovie noticed others who looked as though they, too, were on the run. Three shifty-looking men were traveling with an Indian who had his hair braided into a big knot on top of his head. Some of the passengers objected to him being in the car. He was their guide and a very important shaman, a medicine man, the men protested. He was allowed to stay, but only in a seat at the end of the car.

That night Dovie finally got to sleep very late. The sound of chanting woke her, and she opened her eyes to see the Indian bending over her with antlers on his head. She shrieked, waking the people who dozed near her.

"She moaning in sleep," the Indian shaman said. "I take demons, demons in her, go away."

He chanted and waved a bunch of herbs to keep the bad spirits from entering him or others in the railroad car. Dovie screamed and screamed until the shaman was hustled out of her sight.

Later, in St. Louis, she heard how the ship went down, burned up in fifteen minutes, its cotton cargo aflame. Only the captain, some of the crew, and a few passengers who were on the deck at the time of the explosion survived.

One man escaped on a bale of cotton and was floating in the river. But when a rope was thrown to him, he reached for it, rolled off, and was drowned.

She read the list of those lost—Grover Ames was on it—but so was she. Mr. and Mrs. Grover Ames. She went in to report to the port authorities that she was alive, had left the ship that afternoon.

"But my husband is dead," she said and began to cry.

"Oh, my," the stationmaster said and called his wife. He couldn't stand to see a woman cry.

"How old are you, dear?" the wife asked her.

Dovie managed to quaver, "Fifteen," through her sobs.

"Why, she's just a child and already a widow," the wife said. "Now, now, I'm sure he didn't suffer."

Dovie cried even harder. He could never threaten her again. She could go her own way with no fear. She was so relieved she smiled through her tears.

"Oh, the poor darling! Don't even try to be brave, ma'am. But, young as you are, you must have a proper dress for mourning."

Dovie went to a dressmaker's shop that specialized in mourning attire and bought a dress of black silk taffeta with a tiny ruffle of white at the high neck and two rows of braid in a V across the bodice. She stood before the mirror in the shop and fitted the hat on her head. It was black straw with a high crown and a veil that flowed down her back. She looked at herself. With tendrils of red hair curling on her forehead and pink cheeks, she looked like a child dressed up in her mother's clothing.

"You will need to wear this for a year and a day," the saleslady said, but her voice sounded uncertain. "You know," she said confidentially, "what with the war and things moving so much more rapidly, I doubt but that you'll be engaged to some nice, soldier boy before then."

"Oh, no," Dovie said, "I don't ever want another husband."

Armistice

"I can't decide how to wear my hair for the party," Ingrid said, lifting her hair in front of the mirror.

"Stand still!" Dovie took a pin out of her mouth to speak. Wearing her widow's weeds, she sat on a stool in front of Ingrid to alter her hem. "You are becoming such a young lady, I think you could put your hair up. But not now! Now, you need to stand still if I'm going to have this dress ready for the party in two days."

"I don't know that it is right to have a party at all," Aunt Lavinia said.

"Well, Lavinia, why not?" Mrs. Thompson asked, irritated.

Lavinia took two infinitesimal stitches on her needlepoint. "Circumstances."

"What about circumstances?"

"I do think that the sanctity of mourning must be observed, for one thing. It has been only—how long has it been, Dovie, since Mr. Ames crossed over?"

Dovie and Ingrid had their heads together giggling at Lavinia, always so gloomy. "Ohhh," Dovie said, and the laugh died.

"I, for one, cannot—" Aunt Lavinia punctuated each word with a push, then a pull of the needle.

"Really, Lavinia, I wish you would relax for once. I, myself, feel that with the armistice being signed and the war over, we have

171

many things to celebrate at Ingrid's birthday," Mrs. Thompson declared.

"Perhaps I should not attend," Lavinia said. "My thoughts are always with poor Joe, lying in a hospital somewhere, alone, and no family at his bedside."

Mrs. Thompson turned her back to the room. The others could see her shoulders heaving as she fumbled for her handkerchief.

"Miss Lavinia! Look what you have done!" Dovie exclaimed.

"Oh, Aunt Lavinia," Ingrid said, exasperated. "How could we go to Joe when we don't even know where he is?"

There was a silence in which Mrs. Thompson could be heard sniffling.

"Sister, do you want me to attend the party?"

Mrs. Thompson only raised one hand but kept her face averted.

"My dear, if you wish me to be in attendance, I will put my own feelings aside."

"Of course, I want you to be there; you are my only sister," Mrs. Thompson wailed and hurried from the room.

"It's all settled then," Lavinia said. The devastated faces of the two girls turned to her. "I think my lavender taffeta will do nicely. It has triple rows of ruching at the bodice and again at the cuffs. I don't believe any of you have seen it."

It was a few days later as Dovie went down the stairs to the party that she caught a glimpse of herself in the mirror, a drab figure, all in black with her hair pulled back severely in a net. *I am sixteen and my life is over*, she thought. *I'll never be happy again.* She sighed and pushed open the door. *Celebrate*, she asked herself, *what is there to celebrate?*

When she entered the parlor, there were other ladies, young and old, wearing black because of war losses. Ingrid and her mother were setting out the platters of cake and a bowl of preserved, spiced peaches on the table.

"I may not be here next year for any parties," Lavinia announced with one hand in a net glove placed over her heart. This was the site of the palpitations of which she complained.

Her sister looked into Lavinia's face and forced a smile. "Of course you'll be here. Dear Lavinia, we couldn't get along without you. Could we, Ingrid?"

"No, ma'am, we could not." Ingrid exchanged glances with Dovie.

Mr. Thompson leaned his head back and said loudly, "Lavinia, you're going to outlive us all. I don't know what this darned rigmarole is all about. You look strong as a horse to me."

Ingrid put her hand over her mouth to hide her laughter, and Dovie thought, *You can count on Mr. Thompson to get at the truth or at least try to.*

"I am so glad you are back. This is what it's been like the whole time with Aunt Lavinia," Ingrid said in an undertone to Dovie.

✫ ✫ ✫

"Your son Joe, where was he wounded?" one of the guests asked Mrs. Thompson.

"His left leg."

"No, no, the battle, what battle?"

"Ooooh..." At the mention of wounds and battle, the widow, Mrs. James, made a sound like a punctured balloon and swooned.

"Oh, Miz James, you'd better have some of Mother's hysteric water," Ingrid said.

Mrs. Thompson hurried to her cabinet and produced a bottle. Her recipe had an excellent reputation and was often requested. It contained several ingredients including wild parsnip seeds, oak mistletoe, and one-quarter pound dried millipedes.

As she shook the bottle, Mrs. Thompson named off the ingredients and then instructed, "Beat all this together and pour over it three quarts mugwort water and two quarts brandy. Let stand in a closed vessel for eight days; then distill it. Draw off nine pints water. Sweeten to taste and mix. Mind you, let it steep the full eight days. And my advice is don't stint on the brandy; you won't be sorry."

Mrs. Thompson administered a small glass of the brew to the fainting lady. Mrs. James first moistened her lips and then drank it down. She sat up in her chair and fanned herself with a hand-kerchief with a queer expression on her face.

"Joe had to have his birthday in a hospital in Philadelphia or Washington, we don't even know which," Lavinia said. Mrs. Thompson, who had been such a rock a few moments before, began to cry into her handkerchief.

"Will he be an invalid?" someone asked. She cried harder.

"A farmer needs to be able-bodied," Mr. Thompson said and shook his head.

Mrs. James's daughter brought out her banjo and offered to play. After only one tune, Mrs. James thought she had better go home and rest. Her eyes had become quite sleepy looking, and she departed leaning heavily on her daughter's arm.

When Dovie first returned to the Thompson home in February, the atmosphere had been thick with worry. Mrs. Thompson held out a letter, which Dovie took and read. It was written by a vol-unteer nurse telling that their son, Joe, was wounded in his leg at a battle in Nashville, Tennessee, about December 16, 1864. When the letter was written, he was in a train on the way north to a hospital. Dovie read the brief note quickly and then looked up to see all their eyes on her.

"Is this all you've heard? No more letters?"

"No, none. We searched the papers for news. The battle was a Union victory, but there were thousands of casualties on each side," Mrs. Thompson said.

"We don't know where Joe is. We've written letters but had no reply. His former captain said he is looking into it." Mr. Thompson rubbed his forehead as he spoke.

The whole family was troubled, but Mr. Thompson brooded over his son's injury and said, "If he is crippled, he won't be able to work."

"He survived, we have to be grateful for that," Mrs. Thompson insisted.

"Where is he? If he's alive why can't we find him?" Ingrid voiced what they all were thinking.

"We are glad you've come back, Dovie, and we sympa-thize with your loss. You are young to bear this. As you can see, we still need your help," Mrs. Thompson told her, patting her shoulder.

Dovie did not tell them much about her short marriage. They were preoccupied and she was reluctant even to speak Grover's name.

The house was crowded, and Dovie had to share a room with Miss Lavinia. She began to take solitary walks in the woods wrapped in her big cloak. She cried a lot and held the heavy wool hood to shield her face from icy wind. Her mind churned with chaotic thoughts. If she had not run away from Grover, he might be alive now, but she would still be tied to him. She never wanted to have a husband again. But didn't she want to have a family, a home, and be a respectable person? Then she would start over again: if she had not run from Grover she might be dead, too, burned up with the ship and people on it. *I am lucky to be alive but I don't feel lucky or even very much alive.*

"I still need you in the store," Mr. Thompson said. Dovie could see that he was better, though he walked with a cane and favored his bad hip. "I'll need to look for a man to replace you, though, when they begin to return from the war and need work."

I need the work, too, Dovie thought. *Without wages how can I remain in the house?* Her mood sank even lower. It had seemed like home when she was welcomed back to the Thompson house. She had cried with relief to be there. No one would threaten her; the worst that could happen would be Mr. Thompson's irritated remarks when something didn't go well.

Mrs. Thompson embraced her and whispered in her ear, "You poor, grieving girl."

By the end of April, the first of the soldiers heading home began to appear on the roads. Dovie knew that soon she would not be needed. The men were ragged and dirty as they made the long trek home. Dovie baked big pans of cornbread and poured the soldiers glasses of buttermilk to wash it down. They could afford to feed many with this cheap and plentiful food. The Thompsons did not charge for it; they thought of their own son and that he could be in need as these men were.

The first day, Dovie poured milk for a man who, she couldn't help but notice, had on two shirts, each one torn in different places. She had to laugh to herself and admire his delicacy; he was fully clothed and no skin showed through the holes.

Mrs. Thompson, Ingrid, and Dovie took turns in the kitchen and yard and together fed the men and sheltered them at night in the barn. Though they touched her heart with their forlorn eyes and weariness, Dovie also knew that it would be only weeks or months before one like them would pick up the pieces of his life and take her job away.

A letter came for Dovie that May. She recognized the handwriting, a schoolteacher's handwriting, the round and perfectly formed letters that she had always teased Shelagh about. "You write better than the teacher," she used to say. Her hands tore open the letter while her mind filled with questions.

Dear Dovie, she read, *I am writing to tell you that you now have a namesake in the world, my baby daughter born December 15, 1864, and named Gwendolyn Muriel for you and our mother. She is precious to me with her red hair and a face that reminds me of our family. She is really a Lloyd. She was born early one cold morning here at the foot of snow-covered Pike's Peak.*

We came this far with Tom seeking the right work. As it is, he is gone a lot on hunting trips, but I manage just fine. There are several nice ladies living nearby who have been a world of help to me. I get along fine when he is gone because he is one who wants to manage everything, but I have always had my own ideas, as you know.

You can write me at this address, and I would be very glad to hear from you.

There was no invitation for Dovie to come. It sounded like Shelagh was managing and didn't need her. Dovie would have liked to be asked to come and live there. She read the letter over again, but there was no invitation. She would like to see this new person in the world who had her family's looks and names. She began to compose her reply in her mind as she moved cartons and shelved goods. *I should have tried to get along with Tom. It's too late now, anyway, but I could have tried even though I didn't like him.*

Finally, the family received a letter from Joe.

Dear Family, I am in a hospital in Washington now. I had pneumonia and was moved around some. My captain said you would be glad to hear that now I am on the mend. This is

176

the first time I have felt well enough to write a letter. I lost some time to sickness, but people have taken good care of me. I hope I will soon be able to get my discharge papers and come to you.

With this war over my life can begin again. I think about home a lot and hope nothing has changed in the years I have been away. Last night I fell asleep remembering how I would come in from working in the rows of corn feeling so thirsty. I would pump some water into the pail and fill the dipper that Mother always made out of a long handled gourd. Those gulps of cold water were better than anything I have tasted in several years.

In winter, I left my dirty boots at the back door and came in to sit down in front of the fire. My weariness from the long day would fall away as I toasted my stocking feet a few inches from the flames.

I hope the two big pines outside my bedroom window are still there. I want to go to sleep hearing them sigh in the wind. I remember so many things, how when it rained I slept so well hearing the rain on the roof. Up and down the narrow stairs I went and always had to duck to get under the low beam at the bottom.

Dovie, living the same house now, felt it inhabited by this shadowy soldier and imagined she saw a tall figure walking with long strides across the floors.

When Dovie got hold of the May 30, 1865, St. Louis newspaper, it was several days old. The headline read, "Congress condemns Sand Creek massacre. Country revolted by savagery." This was the massacre that she and Grover had quarreled over six months before.

Dovie read the story avidly. Finally, the country was showing that it knew it was a terrible thing that had been done to the Cheyenne and Arapaho. Mothers, babies, and elders of the tribe hacked down as they ran. It was wrong. *I am glad the newspapers now say it was wrong, but I still feel sad. I knew Cheyenne people. When I first saw their camp from the hill above, it was tranquil with smoke drifting from fires and horses grazing. I remember Half Sister's serious face as she bent over me arranging my headdress for the wedding ceremony. Half Sister might be dead now, with a bullet in her back as she ran.*

So many things are wrong in the world, there does not seem to be any end to them. Dovie sat back in her chair, the newspaper drooping in her hand.

At the beginning of June, Joe sent a card with one sentence triumphant on it: *On the way!*

The family watched for him. Every boat that came in on the river was eagerly met. They were in a state of suspended happiness; he was on the way. Days went by, and worry crept in. They reassured each other that nothing could have happened to him; the war was over.

Dovie and Ingrid were upstairs hanging curtains one clear and sunny June day. Someone was passing in the road. Ingrid stopped with the dotted Swiss curtain in her hand and listened to footsteps on the front porch. She let out a yell, dropped the cloth in a heap, and ran down the stairs as fast as she could go. Dovie looked over the banister and saw a hand opening the front door. Ingrid began to call out, "It's Joe! He's home."

Their parents found her clinging to her brother, both of them crying and laughing. She said, "I was the first to hear him! I was the first!"

They hugged Joe as Dovie stood back and looked at the returned soldier. They had all expected him to be thin and sickly; they had braced themselves for it. He looked healthy and strong.

"I was the first to hear him, before anybody else," Ingrid said and took Joe's arm. "This is Dovie."

Dovie looked up at an immensely tall, thin fellow with startling blue eyes and a black beard almost to his waist.

"How did you get here? How long did it take?" The family threw questions at him.

"Rode the train, walked, got lifts on wagons."

"Your leg, does it hurt?"

"I limp when it's tired; otherwise I'm okay."

"How did it happen?"

Joe held his head and shook it. "I am not going to talk about the war anymore. I am sick to death of it," he said.

A few weeks later, Mrs. Thompson pulled Dovie aside and showed her a letter she had received. "This young lady has written me a very polite letter asking if Mr. Joseph has received her letters. While in the hospital Joe apparently had a romance with a teacher who volunteered as a nurse. She says she has written letters to him since he got home, but he has not replied."

Dovie read the letter feeling more and more uncomfortable with each sentence. By the end of the letter, *"I used to see him every day, and now I hear nothing. I hope he is all right. From a small Pennsylvania girl, Catherine,"* she was frowning. It roused her sympathy, but she was glad he wasn't in love with Catherine because his presence in the house had made her life much more interesting. *I don't like the way Joe acted toward the poor girl, ignoring her. However, it's not my place to tell him how to act.*

Mrs. Thompson took the letter in her hand. "I don't know how to reply," she said. "I think Joe will have to answer and at least thank her for her care in the hospital."

Dovie thought about this development as she walked back of the house to the store. Joe was seated on a log at the edge of the clearing with his face lifted up to the warmth of the sun. He had refused his family's entreaties to shave off the beard he grew in the army. He took out a comb from his pocket and worked it through the beard. Dovie watched from the shadow of the house as Joe combed in short, choppy strokes and then longer, easy strokes. He went over and over it, top to bottom. Dovie watched as the beard became silky in his hands. He finished off the ends combed over two fingers and then slipped out his hand to leave a large curl. Dovie left him in his private moment and took another path to the store.

One evening, the family was invited to a gathering at a neighbor's house. Dovie dressed with care because she knew that Phyllis, the neighbor's daughter, would be wearing her best. In fact, Dovie saw Phyllis almost every day now that Joe was home.

The latest visit was yesterday when Phyllis, all smiles, brought over a cake she had made. Blushing, she said, "It's a spice cake with caramel icing. Welcome home." Dovie saw Joe's face light up.

Dovie knew she was expected to wear mourning for a year, but as she looked into the wardrobe, her hand veered from the black to a pale gray with just a bit of white at the throat and wrists. She put it on and tied her hair up with a few artful curls drooping down.

At the party there was some music and storytelling. Joe began to tell a story about a dog his troop had adopted in camp. People gathered around to hear him tell how Trixie, a tan hunting dog, was very good at bringing back the ducks they shot for meat. Joe gave the high-pitched whine of Trixie on the trail of something. Well, one evening—the whirr of cicadas in the woods—Trixie got a wolf on her back. Joe gave short, sharp yelps like the dog, smacked his hands together for the rifle blast, and then howled like the shot wolf. Walking his fingers in an uneven gait he clicked his tongue to show what the dog sounded like from then on walking with its spine clicking where the wolf's teeth had sunk in.

Dovie laughed so hard her face became quite pink and she got the hiccups. Joe appeared at her side with a glass of water. Each time Miss Phyllis beckoned to him, Dovie put her hand on his arm and detained him with a smile.

By the time the evening ended, he had spent most of it at her side, making her laugh and smile. As they started out the door, Miss Phyllis averted her head as she said good-bye. Joe seemed unaware of Phyllis's pique as he took particular care to wrap Dovie's cape securely around her shoulders. Dovie felt a wave of good humor and was even nice to Miss Lavinia on the way home.

Why didn't I marry someone like Joe, Dovie asked herself, *a man who went through the whole, terrible war and came out with his sense of humor intact?* He liked the earth and growing things. He started a small vineyard on a hillside where he grew Muscat grapes. He raised chickens and she had seen how gently he handled the new chicks.

She watched him as they each went about their tasks. With his great height he moved with a certain tension, as though holding himself together to keep from toppling over. At nineteen, he was still gawky and boyish. His shoes looked too tight on big feet, and his wrist bones always showed below his jacket.

One day as they worked side by side in the store, Dovie told Joe about her first marriage.

"The feelings are there at the beginning and there is a lot of love, but then the person seems to change and all the bad qualities come out. You see, he was so different; he came from..."

Here, Joe hushed her seeing she was about to cry. "I know," he said, "I know."

"No, you need to know. His father was English, but his mother was a Cheyenne Indian. I haven't told anyone else in the family because I know your parents would hold it against me. But I wanted you to know. People don't always behave honestly, but I want everything out in the open between us."

Joe combed his beard with one large hand. "I'm glad you told me," he finally said. "No, I'm not going to hold it against you, though you have to know I don't believe in marrying between whites and Indians." He picked up his pen, ready to resume writing in the ledger in front of him.

"I don't think we would ever lie to each other, do you?" Dovie said. "Besides, he was only one-half Indian. I'm sorry he died, and in flames—it's too horrible. But I didn't love him anymore; I was afraid of him by then."

"You, afraid? Dovie, you seem so brave to me. And my parents relied on you and you helped them. We all owe you gratitude."

"Oh, they've more than shown it. I feel like they are my own family."

Joe said, "I first began to know and love you in your letters while I was so far from home."

In January 1866, a little more than a year after she had been widowed, Dovie and Joe had their wedding. They had known each other for seven months.

My wedding is to be just as I want it this time, Dovie decided. Her dress was the redone pale gray since fabric was still scarce. Dovie felt happy with the skirt, which she and Mrs. Thompson had split at the front center seam to show a lavender under-skirt. The long sleeves had lavender frills added to the cuffs, and this, with touches of white lace, made the dress quite new. The two women sat back and congratulated themselves when it lay finished before them.

The refreshments were homemade also. A large cake, sliced roast beef, nuts, and sweets made an impressive spread on the dining room table. Only the family would be present for the ceremony in the parlor, and the guests were invited in for just after.

Some families forbade dancing, but the Thompsons allowed it. Two musicians were hired, a fiddler and an accordion player and they arrived with their sheet music under their arms.

One young lady looked around and commented, "With the war over, we have no shortage of partners!" She was asked to dance and said, "Let's have a good time, we'll dance till midnight if we want."

The next year, in 1867, Dovie was seventeen and her first son was born. The midwife wrapped baby Clarence Eugene tightly in a blanket and placed him in Dovie's arms. Dovie was on her side, half dozing and tired. The midwife sat behind her and with a comb gently worked to get the tangles out of her long hair. Both women were quiet, the midwife absorbed in her task and Dovie filled with happiness. Now she had the family she had longed for in all the lonely times. *We'll never be parted*, she thought drowsily, never. *Now, all I want is to have land and a place of our own.*

Even though Mr. Thompson had hired a man to work in the store, Dovie continued to help out. Often, she tied the baby to her by a cloth sling on her back. It was her version of the Indian papoose she had seen in the Cheyenne camp. When she found that she was pregnant again, she felt happy and energetic. She was building the family she wanted.

Before the next baby came, she and Joe decided that if it was a boy they would name him for Ulysses S. Grant, after the man who seemed a sure thing to win the coming election for president of the United States. Joe felt bursting with pride and loyalty for Grant. "My general," he called him. "We were his men and he cared about us."

Ingrid was now sixteen and married to a local young man. He was given half his father's farm, and she took up the role of woman with healing remedies alongside her mother.

Once they were a family of four, Dovie and Joe wanted their own place. Joe traveled farther west, scouting the area.

When he returned and said that prospects looked good, they decided to move on. So it was with two sons, Clarence Eugene, they called C.E., and Ulysses, that Dovie and Joe said a tearful good-bye to his parents and moved to Missouri in the spring of 1869. They were able to rent good farmland east of a village called Mount Vernon.

As they approached the place in their wagon, they forded a small creek running so clear that they could see every bright color of pebble, red, brown, and gray, in the streambed. Dovie saw a large stone by the road with some letters crudely hacked into it.

"Stop the wagon. I want to read that." She got down; it was quiet there except for the low, gurgling sound of the water. "Solitude," she said after studying the markings.

She climbed back up on the wagon. "This place is called Solitude."

Joe said nothing, just flicked the reins and the wagon rattled on over the rough road.

They arrived in early spring. It was a season of wild storms when the trees around the house were lashed by rain. Dovie often saw the oaks tossing in the wind and lit by flashes of lightning. When Joe first went into town after several days of rain, there were ducks swimming in puddles on the main street.

He had to find a midwife to help Dovie with the now-imminent birth of their third child. When the woman heard where they lived, she said, "Solitude! It'll depend on the river if you can get out or I can get in. If this baby comes when the water is up, you'll be living on an island and I hope you have a good boat."

Their farm was in Turnback County, so named because part of an early group of pioneers had given up here and turned their wagons to head back to the homes they had left only weeks before. Turnback Creek, which crossed their farm, had been a campground for various Indians, especially the Delaware tribe. After each plowing, Dovie liked to walk the rows and pick up arrowheads that had been turned up by the plow. Touching the pointed stones, she felt wonder at the life that had gone before her in this beautiful place. She saved the arrowheads in an Indian basket. The design woven into it by the Indian woman caught Dovie's eye and she traded some grain for it.

A party of four Indians came from farther west to revisit their fishing streams and hunting grounds. When Joe first encountered them, he returned home that evening and announced with a scowl, "Indians, camped just up the creek from our fields."

Some came to the door the next day. They had baskets to sell or trade for food or ammunition. That first group was on horseback, but others, one or two at a time, came on foot. They were dirty and thin. By the end of winter when their supplies were low they begged for food. Dovie always had cornmeal and dried apples to give them.

Dovie and Joe's third son was born at a time when the water that surrounded them was racing between its banks. When Dovie began to feel the birth pains, she looked anxiously out at the water and the sky as she went to ring the bell that would call Joe in from the fields. The creek was low enough for Joe to ford and bring in the midwife. Dovie chose her third son's name, Sylvester, for the forest that surrounded them.

In four years she had borne three sons. She realized as she looked at Ulysses, called Gus, and Sylvester that both had the large, round blue eyes and stocky build of her father. The thought caused her to stop where she stood at the stove, stirring the oatmeal. It bubbled and thickened as she stared unseeing out the kitchen window. The past was still with her, she thought, no matter how far she traveled or how much she changed her life. She sent a letter to Shelagh to tell her about the family she was raising. It was important to her to share with Shelagh how two of her sons looked like the sisters' dad, Evan. She was the only one who would understand the many ways this reminded Dovie of their life in Wales.

Dovie had settled down to a routine of work and having babies. She and Joe struggled against the weather and insects with their crops of wheat and corn. Joe worked hard in the fields all day, but sometimes at night he woke wild-eyed with terrors from the war.

Dovie saw to the farmhouse, the health of the children, and the raising of chickens and milking of cows; she knitted, sewed, and cooked. When she sat down her lap was full of socks and shirts to mend. She was twenty-four in 1873 when William was

ARMISTICE

born. From the beginning, they called him Rusty because of his red hair. Dovie looked upon her four sons as her riches.

A letter came from Shelagh announcing another move, this time to Wichita, Kansas. There were more jobs there for Tom as the town became a rail hub. They had two children now, Gwen and Tommy. Dovie saw that the two sisters might get to see each other with the distance not too great to travel by train. The daily chores and the children made it difficult but it was a possibility.

Many days, as Dovie went to the shed to milk the cows, she had to kill cottonmouth snakes with a shovel. Trailing after her, the little boys would climb up the fence and scream. Only Sylvester, now four, seemed as determined as Dovie and stood at her side slashing with a stick at the snake. She worked from dawn to dark, fell into bed, and slept in spite of her worries about weather, crops, disease, and money.

News that Joe's parents had died in a boat accident came to them by messenger. Joe returned to help his sister settle matters in Rockport. Dovie remembered how Mrs. Thompson had dug up bulbs for lilies that Dovie carried with her to Missouri. She planted them in a patch of sun near the water where the pink flowers announced summer every year. *They were good to me. I can't believe I won't ever see Mrs. Thompson mixing up her remedies again or hear Mr. Thompson give a bit of precious praise.* Joe would not show how he felt but became more silent. Now that he had a small inheritance, he began to look for good land they could buy or farm. He even went as far as Indian Territory.

The first night Joe was gone from Solitude, Dovie felt afraid as dark came on. Deep woods that were pleasant in the day with sunlight filtering through leaves, at night seemed full of menace with each shifting shadow. *If I were to call out*, she thought, *no one would hear except the children.* They sat wide-eyed, watching her.

"Come on," she said and called them all out on the porch. "See the sun setting behind those trees? Where will it come back up tomorrow?"

"The same place," C. E., now six years old, said wisely.

"You watch and tell me what you see in the morning."

The children played on the steps. Dovie sat on the porch and rocked baby Rusty but had a rifle ready at her side. At night, the four children all slept in her room for security. The children watched from the bed as she struggled and strained to push a heavy bureau to block the bedroom door.

When daylight came, C.E. went outside and reported that the sun had moved in the night and come up over the shed instead of the woods. With sunlight, Dovie got her courage back. She carried baby Rusty in a sling, and with her three boys trailing her, they went exploring. They took a rambling walk along the creek, jumping over ravines and cutting through the woods. The low places were dense with undergrowth, tangled vines, and tree roots. Nearby were two rounded shapes as tall as hills. Known locally as Indian mounds they had been there as long as anyone could remember. When Dovie and her sons walked along the high and dry ridges they found a trace of a trail, beaten by animals first and then Indians.

They discovered several springs deep in the forest. One had turned the rocks it ran over a rust red color from minerals in the water. Another came out of the ground so cold the children could not swim or wade in the pool of water even though the day was hot. Back at the farmhouse, the impression stayed with Dovie of deep, shadowed woods, crystal water—of a world very old, but living, breathing and harmonious.

At Solitude Farm the silted land deposited by the rising and falling of the river was fertile for growing crops. The oaks growing there could be sold for logs to build homes and the walnut and cherry made into furniture. The Thompson family began to prosper for the first time, and Dovie had found the home she longed for. That spring she transplanted some of Mrs. Thompson's pink lilies into clusters around the door so she could see them each time she went in and out.

In June of 1875, even though Dovie was expecting her fifth child, Joe found land he wanted her to see before he made a deal on it. So, their first daughter, Lily, was born in Indian Territory.

Dovie looked around at the wild and empty country. She held her newborn wrapped in an Indian blanket and told her husband, "I do not want to leave Missouri. I want a town and a school for my children."

Joe tried to persuade her. "We are on rented land in Missouri same as we would be here, but here we can have more land for the money."

After quarreling about it, in the end they rented farm-land there and hired an Indian man to work it but returned to Turnback County. Dovie was determined that they would use their savings and make an attempt to buy the farm at Solitude.

This time Dovie took out the box that held her most precious possessions. The two gold bracelets that had belonged to her mother were inside. They were still wrapped in the speckled paper, now brown with age, from her dad's store. She sold the bracelets to a jeweler in Springfield and saw them go into his safe. The sale helped her get the one thing she still wanted, a place of their own to raise her family.

Dovie had now been married nine years, was twenty-six, and had five children. Joe was twenty-eight and no longer a gawky boy. He had become a handsome man of imposing height with piercing blue eyes above his dark beard. He rarely showed his feelings, and Dovie sometimes wondered if she really knew him.

That year, 1877, was Grant's last as president of the United States. Though the newspapers wrote that his regime was cor-rupt, Joe always took up for his former general and said, "He is honest, I'd swear to it. It's just those so-called friends of his, crooks and politicians and moneymen, who are dishonest."

Dovie's second daughter and sixth child, Oleva, was born. As Dovie lay on her bed nursing her new baby, there was a commotion out in the yard as the dogs barked. Dovie combed her baby's hair with her fingers and wondered what was going on. After a while, her son C.E. knocked on her door and came in. His face was full of barely suppressed excitement.

"Mother," he said, "we've got two cousins. And the boy, he's just a year older than me, and he and his sister rode in on one horse."

Dovie sat up. "What are their names? Cousins!"

"Gwendolyn Muriel and Tommy, and their mother was..."

"Shelagh! Is she here?" Dovie got up and moved swiftly to the door with the baby in her arms. She saw the two children in her next glance. The girl had red hair in two long braids.

"We came to you to be raised.," the girl said. "Our mother died and the baby she was trying to birth did, too." The blue eyes, the tilt of her head, were so like Shelagh that Dovie's hand came up to cover her open mouth. "We didn't like our step-mother and she didn't like us and so we got on a horse and took off and came here."

The boy spoke up. "We're almost grown," he said hopefully. "You won't have much work with us."

Dovie handed the baby to C.E. and encircled them both in her arms. "My sister's children!"

Dovie broke into tears, Lily joined in, and baby Oleva began to scream. The boys were astonished to see their mother cry, and the younger ones began to blubber, too. Dovie stood still thinking, *Shelagh is gone. No one wrote to tell me. I can't believe I'll never see her again.* She turned to the two children.

"How did you get here?"

"We rode all night the first night. We were afraid they might come after us—but only to get their horse back."

"One of us slept across the saddle and the other held the reins."

"Why are we standing here? You must be so tired," Dovie said. "C.E., take Gwendolyn Muriel up to the girls' room and find her a place for her things. Boys, carry their bag up and help Tommy settle in. Let's see, C.E., you make some room for your cousin. I'm going to bake a cake and make dumplings—these will be the lightest dumplings you ever tasted."

As Dovie put on her apron and set to work, their story of a father's remarriage and a stepmother made her close her eyes a second. History had repeated itself. She measured out extra walnuts and raisins for the cake with abandon as though by doing so she could protect these two children from hardships like she and Shelagh had suffered. Dovie was thirty and vigorous. She was unfazed by having six children of her own plus two of Shelagh's to raise.

Dovie and Joe were now property owners with an ever-growing family. Their seventh child, Jack, was born in March

1880, followed by Noble, another redhead, two years later. In 1884, their ninth child, Pete, was born.

That same year, Joe and Dovie heard that former president Grant was dying of cancer and in financial trouble. As farmers they did a lot of trading and bartering, but for this they scraped together cash. Once Dovie had the money in her hand, however, she could think of at least three pressing needs they had: their horses both needed new harnesses, her children were wearing hand-me-downs, and the rear wagon wheel was so much mended she worried about driving on it.

"He was a great general, he cared about us—we were his men," Joe said.

Some things are more important than everyday needs, Dovie thought. *I guess we'll get along as we always have.*

They sent Grant twenty-five hard-earned dollars. They read in the newspaper that many of his former soldiers contributed money when they heard he was ill and in need.

The next year, Grant died. Then within a year, his personal memoir, which he had written to try to provide for his family, was published. Joe bought a copy, brought it home, and gave it a place of honor on the mantelshelf.

Inspired by Grant's example of public service, Joe ran for county sheriff and was elected. With his election, he and Dovie became personages in Turnback County. In their seventeen years of living there, the town of Mount Vernon had grown from a place where grass grew in the middle of the main street to a prosperous county seat surrounded by apple orchards and mineral springs. The courthouse was a three-story brick building set in the middle of the square.

After the election, Dovie and Joe made ready for their first walk to his office on the town square. With a new sense of importance, Dovie wore a store-bought hat and her best dress with braid trim. Joe had gone all the way to Springfield to get a suit and shoes because of his size.

He looked tall and strikingly handsome with his blue eyes and dark hair, but Dovie's eyes focused on the long beard that reached halfway down his chest. She had come to detest it. His true self seemed always hidden from her, and she hoped that if she could see his whole face she would know him better.

"There," Dovie said to him as she brushed lint off his coat, "you do look handsome, but you would look even better if you shaved off that beard and moustache."

He put a protective hand over his chin. "My beard! I went through the war with my beard." He shook his head and started out the door. "Now I'm sheriff, I need my beard."

Once they arrived in town, shop owners hurried out to greet Sheriff and Mrs. Thompson as they walked around the square. It was Mr. Wyatt, at the door of his blacksmithing shop, who first called him Sheriff Joe. Joe tipped his hat and smiled.

"Once you pin that star on your chest, your first name becomes Sheriff the rest of your life," Mr. Wyatt said and saluted with the tongs in his hand.

They walked past the livery stable with a fenced yard for the horses. Then the millinery shop in a log cabin, and next to it the Union Hotel. It had a bell out in front, which Dovie had heard sounded for fires or funerals, but people told her that the owner's wife rang it during the Civil War to warn of the approach of rebel troops. A furniture store was open in its new building with a clock tower on top.

The jail was on the north corner of the square. As they walked up to it, Dovie saw the familiar two-story building of brown field-stone. Her husband now had an office and would spend his days there instead of in their fields.

He opened the door with a flourish, and Dovie walked in. Joe began to show her around. "Now, Dovie, this is a very solid jail. Each stone in the wall has a pocket cut into it and the one next to it. An iron ball in the pocket makes it impossible to chisel loose a stone and escape." Joe was lit up with pride about his new place, and Dovie nodded and smiled as he showed it off to her.

✷ ✷ ✷

Dovie and her sons farmed the properties at Solitude and in Indian Territory while Joe was busy with his duties as sheriff of Turnback County. Dovie bossed them all, from C.E., the oldest boy, at nineteen and Gwendolyn Muriel, twenty, down to the youngest, Pete, two years old.

"We must set an example now that your father is sheriff. People are watching the whole family," she told them. For convenience, they bought a small house in town just a block from the Baptist church. Dovie brought her brood to town Saturdays, and on Sunday mornings, Dovie got everyone all slicked up, washed, combed, and dressed in their best. The older ones had to help with the younger ones and make them keep clean till church began. Dovie gave them all the final inspection.

The eight boys had to show her their hands, both sides, so she could see if they had washed and had no dirt under their fingernails. Oleva tried to get away with slapping a bow on top of uncombed hair. Her mother sat the girl down and combed every snarl out while Oleva got red in the face from crying. Once each girl and boy had her nod of approval, Dovie would take a freshly ironed handkerchief and tuck it into her sleeve so the lacy points showed at her wrist. This was the signal that everyone had passed inspection, and she would march them off to church.

Dovie now saw the church as a civilizing influence. She tried to forget her mother's questioning attitude and had little time for her own doubts. She welcomed any help she could get with the household of eleven children.

Sylvester sneaked out his window at night to run around with his friends. He got away with it once, twice, and then Dovie became suspicious because the teacher said that he was falling asleep at his desk. She got up in the middle of the night and went to his room, where she found the window open and a breeze blowing the curtain over an empty bed. She pulled up a chair, wrapped herself in a blanket, and sat in the dark. She awoke to see him climbing in the window in the early dawn.

"Where have you been, young man?"

He jumped but turned wide eyes on her and lied, "I didn't feel so good, only to the privy."

In that instant she felt that she had failed as a mother. "Do not lie to me, young man. You will have extra chores for two weeks for this." From then on, she goaded herself even harder to instill the right ideals in the boys. She read her Bible daily and searched for guidance.

The new place in town needed furnishing, and Dovie could indulge herself for the first time since they were becoming comfortably well off. She purchased a print of *Blue Boy* by Gainsborough and then thought it needed a companion, so she bought a picture of Pinkie, a girl of the era. She hung the pair in the front hall where she could see Blue Boy and Pinkie every day as she came and went.

An itinerant artist showed her a painting of a wolf on a frozen riverbank, howling in a wilderness of ice and snow. Something in her went out to the wolf; she could almost feel its howl in her own throat. Dovie bought the painting and hung it above the mantel in the new house on Cherry Street.

When Joe came home and saw it, he snorted and said, "I don't know why anyone would want such a dismal picture in their house."

Murder And Scandal

Dovie leaned over to brush her hair and then grabbed it in one hand. With quick, practiced turns of her wrist, she twisted it into a bun on top of her head and stood up as she secured it with two tortoiseshell hairpins.

She walked through the silent house where the family slept in their beds. Pausing by Oleva's door, she heard even breathing and moved on down the hall. The bedtime mug of warm milk and honey had helped Oleva stop coughing. Deep quiet was like a blessing over the house.

She stepped out the back door onto dew-covered grass. In the eastern sky clouds were turning pink as the sun rose. Mildred Eloise, the baby, had cried and wakened her while it was still dark. Then, thinking about the peach preserves she had to put up, Dovie never got back to sleep. She struck a match and lit the fire under a large pot of water in the yard that she would use to clean the jars. It would have to come to a boil, and that would take some time.

At Dovie's breakfast table, little Milton was hungry and pounding on the table with his fist. She had taken in the boy because his parents died and left him an orphan. Milton demanded, "Cereal, I want cereal."

When Dovie got the oats cooked and put a bowl in front of him, he ate only a few bites before he picked up the bowl and dumped it on top of his straight, brown hair.

Sheriff Joe looked at the mess of pale cereal clinging to the boy's face and shirt and shook his head. "Dovie's going to whip you good."

Dovie said, "I'll do no such thing. Why, the poor, motherless boy." She got out a piece of peach pie and put it in front of him.

"Now, Milton, try this. You're going to like it."

Joe shook his head as he left. "You are so strict with your own children! There is no figuring you out."

C.E. was grown-up now and his dad made him a deputy sheriff. He came out fastening his new badge to his shirt. He was a robust and handsome fellow, and Dovie smiled down on him as he sat and ate.

"Now, don't you be late your first day on the job," she said.

He was the most serious of her seven sons, and when he said, "I won't be late," she knew he meant it.

The next day, Dovie was cooking breakfast again. Her son, Rusty, read aloud from the newspaper to her. "'Colby Carr, a boy only sixteen years old, took a gun and robbed and murdered another young man, Alexander Somer, seventeen.'"

"Where is this, Rusty? I don't recognize any of the names of folks around here."

"Over in Joplin. Seems that this Alexander, he took his mother's gold watch to work to know the time out at the engine house. Well, this fellow, Colby, had a gun concealed under his jacket. He stepped up behind Alexander Somer and 'moments later a gunshot sounded over the fields of scrub trees and brush at the edge of town.' Colby stole the watch and no telling how much money from the boy. 'He was reputed to carry large sums,' but his pockets were empty when his body was found."

"Just think, at the same time we were sleeping, just a warm, June night to us, this stranger was lurking with a gun. To take a young life! Even the thief, the murderer, is a tender age," Dovie said.

In July, they heard that the trial of the boy, Colby Carr, had been given a change of venue and moved to Mt. Vernon. Sheriff Joe escorted him over in handcuffs and booked him into the jail on the square. When C.E. took the handcuffs off, Colby raised his head for the first time. C.E. saw watery, pale eyes and a freckled face looking up at him. "This one won't give any trouble," he told his mother that night at supper.

The trial was held three months later in the Turnback County courthouse in Mount Vernon. Dovie read the local paper's front-page accounts every day. Everyone in town seemed to talk about nothing but the unfolding story. The body of Alexander Somer lying on the ground in a pool of his own blood and brains was discovered by the fellow who took the next shift at midnight. Colby had been seen in the vicinity of the engine house near the time of the murder.

When the police went to Colby Carr's house in the early hours of that morning, the entire family was there with the exception of Colby. They were packed up and ready to move but gave conflicting stories about where they were going. The mother said Pittsburgh, Kansas, but the father, questioned separately, said Sarcoxie. When asked where her son was, the mother said he had gone on ahead to look for work. The father said that he was looking after some livestock. The house was searched, and part of the striped cord that Alexander Somer used to fasten the watch to his suspenders was found swept up in a pile of rubbish. When Colby was arrested nine days later in Barry County, the gold watch was on him.

At the trial, the lawyer for the defense pled Colby's extreme youth; he was sixteen. The lawyer said that Colby had "grown up like a rank weed with little more guidance than a wild thing."

After a ten-day trial, Colby Carr was found guilty and sentenced to hang.

C.E. had escorted the boy to and from the courthouse each day, and Dovie waited to hear C.E.'s account of events each evening. On the day of the guilty verdict, there was a lot to tell.

After the verdict was read, C.E. brought the youngster into an anteroom of the court and offered his handkerchief to Colby. He had to watch while the youngster cried.

"Now, get hold of yourself," he warned the boy before opening the door to the hall where reporters and gawkers waited.

C.E. took hold of Colby's freckled arm and pushed through the clamoring crowd.

A red face leaned in on them and yelled. "Gotcha! We gotcha, killer!"

Blocking their path, a big man rocked back on his heels. His thumbs were hitched in the buckles of his bib overalls. He rocked forward and spat on Colby. The spittle, foamy at one edge, slid down Colby's cheek and onto his collar. C.E. put one arm around Colby, slightly lifting him off the ground. Then he charged forward using his other arm and shoulder as a battering ram until they were safe in the jail with the door bolted shut.

The next morning the newspaper headline blared, "Mere Boy a Murderer" and "Colby to Dance on the Hangman's Rope." Dovie folded the paper hoping C.E. wouldn't see the headlines but the first thing he did was look at them. C.E. crumpled the newspaper in his hands and threw it away. After barely a bite of breakfast, he left for the jail.

When C.E. returned home that night, he told with a grim face how he found Colby in his cell, reading the accounts of his trial.

"Listen to this," Colby said and found his place. "'This is an aw-ful doom.'" He read slowly, sounding out the harder words. "'A mere boy to be hurled into, um, e-eternity is enough to make the stoutest heart tremble.'" He looked up at C.E. "They wrote that about me," he said and carefully smoothed the creases out of the paper.

C.E. went on, "Colby has been in the jail half a year—that's as long as I've been keeping company with Minta. I realized that the boy's seventeenth birthday is approaching so I asked Minta to bake a birthday cake for him."

On the day, C.E. primed the other prisoners to sing "Happy Birthday." Minta had baked a white cake with pink icing. Her special touch was to spell out *Colby* in peppermint candies on the top. Dovie and Minta both came to the jail office to watch as C.E. carried the cake into the cellblock to the singing of the other prisoners. Colby watched open-mouthed. C.E. cut the cake and handed pieces around through the bars.

Colby chewed his piece of cake solemnly and said, "I never had a birthday party before."

"Well," Guinea Pig Porter, who was in for burglary, blurted out from his cell, "looks like your first was your last."

C.E. gave Porter a look that quieted him down.

Colby remained in the jail while his attorney made appeals. On a rainy, cold morning with the window streaked with water and the monotonous sound of wind coming in under the front door of the jail, C.E. was on duty. He needed to open the door to the cellblock so the prisoners could be fed.

There was a special metal compartment into which the cook's helper stepped with a tray of food. Then the door to the outside office was closed behind him before C.E. moved the gear to open the second door of the compartment into the cellblock. The outer door was solid metal, and the inner door was a metal grid to allow the jailer to see if anyone was hiding there. This contraption was called the latest thing in detention. C.E. took pleasure in operating the gears and showing it off to his girlfriend, his mother and visiting lawmen.

This morning the cook's helper didn't show up, so C.E. took breakfast in. He turned the gears and opened both doors in order to get through carrying the tray of food. There were two cells on the ground floor and a metal stair leading up to two cells above. As C.E. bent to set down the tray, a figure dashed past from under the stairway and made for the open doors.

C.E. straightened up and dove after the man.

He just managed to catch hold of the fellow's shirt and whirl him around. It was Colby, small but biting and kicking. C.E. managed to grip one arm and twist it behind the boy's back. Colby hung his head and fell to weeping. Guinea Pig Porter watched holding on to the bars of his cell.

Charlie Perkins, in again for vagrancy, commented, "Nice try, kid, but not good enough."

"He's got nothing to lose, if you know what I mean," Bob Adams, jailed for drunkenness and assault, commented.

C.E. got the boy back into his cell and examined the door. He removed folded cardboard which had kept the lock from closing. C.E. shook his head sadly at this point as he told Dovie the story. "I recognized it. It was from the box I carried his birthday cake in."

That year in November, 1890, Sheriff Joe was reelected to another four-year term.

When the New Year began, Dovie read accounts of a massacre of Indians by the Seventh Cavalry at Wounded Knee.

This had happened December twenty-ninth. She read on with the growing feeling that she knew that area near Pine Ridge, in the new state of South Dakota.

It was said that the Indians were followers of Wowoka, a Nevada Paiute. He prophesied an end to westward expansion of the whites. The Indian lands would be returned to them, and the buffalo would be seen in great herds again. To bring this about, Sioux and other tribes joined in the ritual of Ghost Dancing. Here, Dovie closed her eyes and remembered the chanting and dances she had heard long ago at the Cheyenne camp.

She gasped as she read that Wowoka's followers believed that the ghost shirts they wore would protect them from bullets. More than two hundred Sioux had been killed by bullets at Wounded Knee. *They are not going to be allowed to survive*, she thought. *We want them to become farmers like us, and they won't give up their way of life*. She put her hands on her pregnant belly and cried.

When Joe got home from his office, she tried to tell him how she felt about the massacre of the Indians. He patted her shoulder and said, "You're upset; it's only because you're due to deliver soon."

That winter C.E. married Minta and Dovie gave birth to Floy, her eleventh child, a girl sickly from birth. Dovie was forty-two and had already given birth to ten children, raised two of her sister's children, and taken in other needy children as troubles arose in families around her. She struggled to bring Floy to health, to give her a good color, and cure her constant wheezing.

The various appeals his attorney made for Colby Carr were finally exhausted. The execution day loomed up before Sheriff Joe and C.E. as a reality, barely a month away. Sheriff Joe wrote an appeal for a stay of execution based on the boy's youth and sent it off to the governor of Missouri. He and C.E. felt that they had gained a little breathing space.

Governor Francis's reply arrived while Sheriff Joe was out of the office for two days transporting a prisoner to Springfield. C.E. saw the governor's name on the envelope but in spite of his curiosity could do nothing but place it on his father's desk to await his return. When Sheriff Joe did return, he had many matters to attend to and left the envelope unopened. With C.E. standing over him, he reluctantly sat at his desk and cut open the letter. He read it to himself and then covered his eyes with his hand.

"How can I put this young boy to death?" he said.

He passed the letter over to C.E., who rapidly read to the phrase "I cannot see my way clear to further interference in the case. You understand what your duty is. Respectfully, David R. Francis, Governor."

The next morning they began to construct the gallows on the town square in front of the jail. The structure was built of wood, as was the fence in front of it to keep back spectators.

Dovie stopped by to see the construction with her two little daughters. She pushed Floy in the carriage. The infant wore a frilly bonnet, but her face was pale and her eyelids droopy. Mildred was three years old with white blond hair and a happy smile. Dovie had dressed her in a blue dress with pink trim and a hair bow to match. Mildred wore a delicate gold bracelet engraved with ME for Mildred Eloise, the same initials as Muriel Eloise, Dovie's mother. Now that they were prosperous, Dovie lavished on Mildred the best their little town could supply, even sending to Springfield for special shoes and dresses. Dovie had had fine things when she was a child before her mother died, and it seemed right to her to give the best to Mildred, the very sight of whom made her happy.

On the corner of the square stood the blacksmith's wife, Beryl, and Mrs. Livery Stable, as the lady whose husband owned that establishment was called. They greeted Dovie and Beryl observed, "Little Mildred has a new bracelet."

Mrs. Livery Stable sniffed, "A child never wore gold jewelry in my youth. We were not indulged in that way."

Overlooking her remark, Dovie said to her, "About that pony your husband has to sell. It's a nice little chestnut but Mildred has her heart set on having a white pony with brown spots. I hope he can find us one."

Dovie said goodbye and in a few steps paused to greet another lady. She was near enough to hear Mrs. Livery Stable say in low tones, "Nothing, it seems, is too good for little Mildred." Beryl, getting in the last word as she liked to do, said, "Well, every crow thinks its own is the blackest."

Dovie arrived at the jail. "How is Colby today?" she asked.

Sheriff Joe frowned and didn't answer. Dovie looked at her husband waiting for a reply. He turned to C.E. and said sternly, "From now on everyone will refer to the prisoner as Mr. Carr. Those are my instructions. No more cakes, no more parties."

"Yes, sir," C.E. said.

Dovie looked from one man to the other. They had seen Colby every day for over a year and taken care of him. *This will not be easy*, she realized.

The day before the execution, C.E. could barely force himself to make the motions of doing his work. The sentenced boy seemed animated by it all. He was attended by not one but two ministers determined to prepare his soul for the hereafter. Colby wrote farewell letters, a long one to his "Dearest Mother," another to his brothers and sisters. Dovie read his statement to the newspapers forgiving everyone. *It seems almost forgotten that he committed a crime. He took a life,* she thought.

Late that last afternoon, Sheriff Joe abruptly pushed back from his desk and left the office. He returned about half an hour later and tossed a large box on C.E.'s desk.

"What is it?" C.E. asked.

Sheriff Joe motioned for him to open the box. In it was a new black suit.

"The boy never had a new suit," Sheriff Joe said.

"Yes, sir," C.E. said. He felt like blurting out, "I don't want to be a deputy any more," but he was afraid his father would take it wrong. When he told Dovie later about his father's gift, he said, "It's an awful responsibility. I hope we can both get through this."

The Carr family drove into Mt. Vernon that afternoon with the intention of camping on the outskirts, but stormy weather brought them into town. Dovie was doing a quick errand on the square when she heard the shopkeeper, Mr. Beale, discussing with some businessmen that the Carrs had no money.

"We ought to take up a collection to pay for their lodging at the hotel," Mr. Beale said.

"It's the right thing to do," the mayor said, took off his hat and tossed a bill in to start the collection.

The hotel proprietor threw in an offer of free grub. His wife, standing beside him, looked surprised.

"Here's how I look at it," he told her, "they brought a lot of business into town for the hanging."

Dovie completed her purchase and hurried home to Floy, who was ill again.

The deathwatch began that night. C.E. and his brother, Sylvester, sworn in as a deputy for the hanging, stayed the night at the jail. The spiritual advisors, now numbering three, gathered round the boy "whose life hung on a thread, now ready to snap," as the newspaper said. Sheriff Joe remained at the jail until midnight and then went home to the house on Cherry Street where the family stayed most of the time now.

Even though she was caring for a very sick baby, Dovie noticed that he was quiet and full of dread. She had the teakettle set up with the spout issuing steam in Floy's direction. The child was propped up to breathe it in.

"Don't come out tomorrow," Sheriff Joe ordered Dovie. "It'll be crowds and confusion. There's a cold rain falling now." He felt in his pockets and brought out a paper which he threw down on the table in front of his wife.

She smoothed it out and read:

My Statement to the Public: If I should confess myself guilty, it would but heighten the desire of the public for revenge, while on the other hand if I should declare myself innocent I would not be believed and would brand myself a liar. I will leave my case to Heaven to decide. Colby Carr

The next day, December fourth, dawned sunny and cold. Colby rose at five and at once dressed in the new, black suit. He smoked several of the cigars provided for the condemned man, but ate little breakfast. He appeared watchful as events moved forward.

Curiosity and dread led Dovie to go to the hanging. She left Oleva in charge of her sick baby and by eight o'clock joined the crowd gathered around the jail. The gallows was built thirty feet off the ground at the front of the jail building. A few guards with loaded guns paced along the high fence surrounding the jail and gallows. Several people had climbed up to perch in the trees on the courthouse square for a better view of the hanging.

Colby was in his cell attended by a minister. At five minutes to ten Sylvester, as deputy, brought him up onto the scaffold where the officials stood. C.E. read the death warrant aloud. Colby stood by his side and moved his lips as he read the document around C.E.'s shoulder. He requested permission to say good-bye to the other prisoners. When this was granted by Judge Landrum, Colby sprang down the stairs to the cells and urged the men there to avoid bad company and strong drink. He returned to the gallows platform. Sheriff Joe stepped forward with the handcuffs. C.E. closed the cuffs around the boy's wrists and locked them.

Sheriff Joe put the rope around Colby Carr's neck. The judge asked the boy if he had anything to say.

"Could the rope be loosened a little so I can talk?"

Sheriff Joe looked to C.E., who stepped forward. When his fingers touched the boy's perspiring flesh, he recoiled but steeled himself and adjusted the rope around the skinny neck. Colby spoke, but to the dozen people standing around him his voice was inaudible.

Judge Landrum, in a kind tone, said, "Speak a little louder, Colby."

Colby cleared his throat. He looked out over the crowd of people in the square. "Whiskey and bad company..." he said, and then his voice stopped. He moved his lips, but only a hoarse sound came out.

They waited a few moments. The watching people were noisy and restless. C.E. looked to his father, who stood rigid and stared straight ahead. Finally Sheriff Joe signaled with his hand; C.E. tightened the noose and placed the black cap over Colby's head and face.

Colby stopped C.E.'s hand, clasped it, and spoke through the black cap, "I hope we'll meet in heaven."

Sheriff Joe placed Colby over the trap. One lingering shout hung over the crowd and then, absolute silence. With a sharp hatchet, Sheriff Joe cut the rope that held the trap door. There was a gasp from the crowd as Colby's body fell through and jerked on the rope. When his neck broke, the boy's head lolled to the side.

It was C.E.'s job to hold the watch and time the fifteen-minute wait before the boy was taken down and pronounced dead. He stood in place as the minute hand moved round and round the watch until it had circled fifteen times.

His duties were not over. He admitted the funeral director to the area to do his job. Then C.E. had to accompany the body in its coffin to the courthouse and set it up in the corridor. The family and then the public were admitted to view the corpse until the burial that afternoon.

Each step C.E. took dragged as though his legs had lead in them. He took up his stance beside the body and his mother, watching him, felt anxious. The broken body and the curious, even gleeful faces peering at it provoked horror in him. He returned home that night to his bride of eight months in a state of exhaustion.

The next day's newspaper carried the headline: "Jerked to Jerusalem!"

✳ ✳ ✳

Later that December, Dovie's second son, Ulysses, called Gus, married his sweetheart, Minnie. With the family growing, Dovie wanted a portrait of them all together. They hired a photographer and went to his studio. He posed the group. With Joe next to her, Dovie sat proudly at the center of her creation, her family. On the back row were the two oldest boys and their wives along with Sylvester, Lily, and Oleva. In the middle row were Dovie and Joe with three sons, Rusty, Jack, and Pete, seated around them. On the front row were Shelagh's two children with Mildred and Noble.

The photographer instructed that they would have to remain still several minutes while the plate was exposed. Mildred, the youngest in the photo, moved her head slightly and her image was blurred. Noble, a few years older, managed to remain perfectly still. Poor Floy was too sick to sit up that long and so was not in the portrait.

Later, to make up for this, Dovie waited for one of Floy's good days and brought her to be photographed. She needed propping up, and Mildred was put in the photo to hold her. So the two girls, one healthy and the other looking very ill, were pictured together.

Later in that year, 1892, a son, Raymond, was born to C.E. and Minta. Dovie cried and couldn't explain how deeply satisfied she felt to see the beginning of the next generation of her family. C.E. told Dovie, "The birth of my son has changed me. I must act on my resolve to change my occupation. I was sickened at having to put to death a young boy and I don't want to be in law enforcement for the next grim task, whatever it might be. I have avoided telling Father but I can't put it off any longer."

He took an acquaintance up on the offer of a job. Then C.E. crossed the square to the jail. He walked to Sheriff Joe's desk and blurted out. "I'm going to be a buggy salesman."

It was done. The look of surprise and hurt on his father's face was the worst moment of all. At the end of their talk, Sheriff Joe stood up and shook his hand. C.E. all but floated along the quiet, tree-lined streets to his home, his wife, his son—they had never seemed dearer.

In the new job he made good money and dressed well in a new gray suit with black piping edging the coat and vest. With his good looks and amiable manner he was successful, but Dovie, watching her eldest son, could see he was not satisfied. He looked around to find what kind of job he could care about and use to support a family. He decided that he would like to be a pharmacist and have his own drugstore someday.

He needed training, and there was a school that taught pharmacy courses in Kansas City. He began to save up the money to go. C.E. felt sensitive that, at twenty-five, he would be older than the other students, boys eighteen or so. He went in on the train and studied for several sessions, fall and spring, and got his certificate. He began to work in the drugstore in Mt. Vernon, mixing prescriptions and selling other products from patent medicines to sodas.

When Floy was two years and a few months old, she died from another bout of the croup that had plagued her short life.

Dovie felt that she had failed the child whose struggle even to breathe had been a constant worry, shadowing her days and nights. She relived the long illness in her mind, questioning herself, looking for what she might have done differently to save her child.

Dovie had trouble sleeping. One very bad night, she dreamed she was a child again terrified by the sound of her mother's racking cough. Dovie was too agitated to lie in her bed. She got up, walked through the dark rooms, and wept. Finally toward dawn she laid down on her bed and fell into a light sleep. When she awoke, Joe had already gone to work and the children to school or work. On the breakfast table Dovie saw the first fig from the little tree she had planted. It had turned a rich purple and was displayed on a green fig leaf. Next to it was a piece of paper that said, "With love, to Dovie from Joe."

That evening Dovie made a special effort to fix a dinner that Joe liked and to be cheerful when he returned home. As usual dinner began when she pushed open the swinging door with her hip and entered the dining room carrying a large platter. That night she had fixed Joe's favorite meal of roast beef, potatoes, carrots, onions, and rich, brown gravy. Everyone at the table straightened up in expectation. But Dovie heard a child crying out on the street and was so distressed that her hands began to shake and she dropped the platter. Joe and the children stared at her over the mess of broken china and oozing gravy on the floor. Joe led her to her room and told her she must rest.

After this, Joe seemed to avoid the house, which was so full of tears. Mildred was Dovie's greatest comfort. All the others looked up to Dovie as the boss, even feared her temper. But when Dovie sat down and fell into one of her fits of weeping, the little child did what the others wouldn't have dared. Mildred would go to Dovie and put her soft, small hand on Dovie's arm and bring her back to a sense of life and strength.

After many months, Dovie finally went alone to choose a monument for Floy's grave. Joe pleaded that he was too busy and had to be at the courthouse to assist the Widow Clayton with some property matters. Dovie chose a small marble pillar no taller than Floy had grown to be when she died.

On the way home from the stone yard, a boy was selling puppies out of a basket. Dovie stopped to look at them. At first she only saw a wriggling mass of white fur, and then a round face looked up at her and yelped in distress. Dovie immediately scooped up the dog and cuddled it. She brought it home to Mildred, and the two of them gently washed it and patted it dry.

Around this time, Dovie read an account of the Indian, Tecumseh, chief of the Shawnees. A speech he had given in 1810, before Governor William Henry Harrison, seemed so true that she found herself thinking about the meaning of it for people like herself, seeking land to settle and call it home.

When Joe came home that night, she eagerly read him Tecumseh's words: "What, sell land! As well sell air and water. The Great Spirit gave them in common to all, the air to breathe, the water to drink, and the land to live upon."

"His words have truth in them," she said.

"Yes. I know, I know," Joe said impatiently, "but that's just not the way things are."

"Is it the way things ought to be? I don't know," Dovie said.

Rusty, who was listening, said, "It sounds like it's fair, but I know I want my own land to do what I want with it."

Dovie was troubled, remembering the Indians who had come to her door begging and homeless because she and people like her wanted more than anything to have a home of their own.

At present, her family rented land and a house in Indian Territory from Cherokee Indians named Johnson, who ran a ferry across the Arkansas River. A hired hand saw to the crops when Dovie was in Mt. Vernon. The land was near the Cherokee Outlet on the most traveled road from Missouri.

The next time they went there to farm, Dovie looked at the countryside with new eyes because of Tecumseh's words. The smaller streams abounded in fish. The fields had game in abundance: deer, antelope, turkey, and prairie chickens. Wildflowers grew everywhere over the hills and valleys: purple ironweed, yellow mustard, red poppies, and wild strawberries. It seemed a paradise with room for all. It was small wonder that everyone wanted a home here. It had been given to the Indians, she knew, but there were so many others that needed land for homes and farms. The government soon would open this land up for settlement in the last of the land runs. *It will all change*, she thought. *I won't see this wild place anymore.*

They needed to harvest the wheat, and the five boys would do that. Sylvester was now twenty-three and Rusty, twenty, and could oversee the younger three. Her daughters, Lily, eighteen, and Oleva, fifteen, would keep the house and watch Mildred, who was five. As was their custom, Joe stayed in Mt. Vernon to do his job as sheriff.

The afternoon before the Land Run, Dovie went to the hay-stack to get food for the horses. She plunged her pitchfork in. Instead of coming up with a forkful of hay, she heard a muf-fled scream and jumped back. Then the hay began to rise and move, and a dark sleeve and trouser leg appeared. A man came wiggling out, spitting blades of hay and pawing at his eyes to clear them.

Dovie stood back astonished. He held his hands up before him in a pleading gesture. "I won't hurt no one. I'm just here for the race tomorrow."

"You're early. They fire the gun at noon tomorrow. If they catch you here inside the boundary…"

"Please, ma'am, don't turn me in. I'm desperate. I've got a wife and three children back in St. Louis, and they're probably hungry right now. They're counting on me to make a new start here. I promised Della I'd get some land for us to live on."

"What happened?"

"I have to admit I gambled everything away. I'm sorry now. I feel like killing myself. I can't face them, a failure."

Dovie jabbed up some hay with her pitchfork. The man jumped aside.

Her face was frowning but she said, "Anyone can have trou-bles." She thought a minute and added, "And I know what it is to want a home. You had better hide yourself in case one of my sons comes out here. They might not be sympathetic. They'd call you a Sooner."

"Beg pardon, what's that, ma'am?"

"A Sooner is what they're calling the ones that don't wait for the starting gun."

"I hate to mention it, but do you have any spare food? I'm mighty hungry." He twisted his hat in his hand.

"I'll bring you something when it gets dark. Listen for me to walk by whistling."

"Thank you. Just some bread would be so appreciated."

"Cornbread, sausage, and buttermilk. That's our dinner and you'll have it, too."

He groaned and rubbed his stomach. Then he began to burrow his way back into the hay. The last Dovie saw of him was the back of his suit coat with dried grass sticking to the dark cloth.

For days the road in front of her place had been crowded from sunrise to sunset with a stream of humanity. Some stopped to buy vegetables and milk. Scholar, farmer, man of all trades, they had all said they wanted to win land to build a home of their own. They traveled in every sort of conveyance, from beautiful horses pulling fine carriages to burros packed to the limit of their strength. She had seen men pulling a two-wheeled cart with all they owned inside.

Watching them roll past, Dovie mulled something over in her mind. She could sense people waiting, breathless with hope, on the borders of the territory. She walked rapidly through the fields with the tall prairie grass brushing her skirt. At the hired man's cottage she arranged for him to see to the grinding of the wheat tomorrow. Dovie went home to make her preparations; she, too, had caught the land fever that was in the air.

The next day, September 16, 1893, was a bright fall day. She saw Rusty as he started off for the Land Run. He was riding the white mule and his red hair was shining in the sun as he went to join the throng of people, to race for land and stake it out. Dovie hoped that in the mad rush no tragedies would occur.

She would ride with Sylvester. They had a light wagon and two good horses, Red and Drake. Sylvester had two registrations for town lots in the name of Thompson and Dovie would use the one meant for another son. The feather mattress was her idea and Sylvester shook his head but agreed. He would wrap her in it just before the gun and was to kick it out of the wagon at the bend in the stream and keep going to get his parcel of land. That way they could both get land. Each had a pack with stakes, hammer, tarpaulin and provisions.

"I worry about your safety, Ma, maybe you shouldn't...." Dovie brought out of her shirtwaist a mean-looking, black revolver. She flourished it and light glinted off the long barrel. Her son acquiesced.

They started off and soon left the road to cut across Bob Nighthawk's field; they were in a hurry to get to the starting line. The wagon scared up some pheasants which rose and flew a short way before they took cover again.

"Ordinarily, I would be interested in those birds; I like a pheasant stew," Sylvester commented.

Mr. Nighthawk came out on his porch to see who was on his place.

"He's very particular about strangers on his land," Dovie said and waved and yelled hello. She suddenly clapped herself on the forehead. "Oh, no! The Sooner! I forgot his food!"

But Sylvester's thoughts were elsewhere. "I'm thinking about where to position ourselves for the race."

The field of yellow mustard was so bright that Mr. Nighthawk didn't recognize his neighbors at first, but then he did and waved them on. After that it was silent with only the wind making any sound.

They went up and over several hills. It was still over an hour before noon, but the heat was like a weight on Dovie's head with sweat running down in her eyes. Then, she saw a cloud of dust ahead, and in a while began to hear a buzz, noise from a crowd milling around. Pretty soon she was near enough to see horses, wagons, and people. Everyone was pressing in close together to try for a good place in the lineup. There were mounted soldiers, well armed, two pistols in the holsters and a rifle on the side. They patrolled the border, forcing people back who came in too far. Sylvester stood up in the wagon and looked in all directions for a sight of his brother but couldn't find him.

It was blazing hot and near time for the signal gun to be fired. Some of the runners checked their ammunition and the fit of their gun belts in case they needed them to enforce their claim. Others tended to their mounts, tightening harness straps and watering the animals. Everyone, man and beast, was restless and moved constantly like water about to boil.

Sylvester saw a fellow on a horse, but the saddle wasn't cinched right and it was already sliding to the side. He said to him, "Hey, mister, your saddle ain't gonna hold."

He looked back, very surly, and said, "You ride your horse and I'll ride mine."

"Can you believe it? No use trying to be helpful to some people," Dovie said.

Everyone was edgy. Stories went around about the Run of 1889. Those who rode in at the signal found that Federal marshals had already laid out the town of Guthrie and taken the best lots. It was illegal, but the marshals were there in possession and fully armed. No one knew what was ahead of them today. Dovie could taste the fear—around her but in her own mouth, too.

One man, calm and deliberate, peeled and cut up an apple and ate it slice by slice as though he were alone in his own wheat field. Then he wiped his knife on his pants leg and fitted the blade in a scabbard. Sylvester pulled the wagon up next to him. It was the only still place in the whole stamping, whinnying, cursing mess.

It was time. Mother and son got out the rope and the feather mattress and holding her pack Dovie got trussed up in the mattress. She had closed her eyes and taken a deep breath when she heard a shot. She jerked her head up out of the covering to see. It had to be a false start, and Sylvester held Red and Drake back. All the horses surged but most people reined them in. One rider started off racing; he never looked back to see that he was alone. The soldiers started after him yelling, "Halt," but he was pounding along with his shoulders hunched around his neck, riding full speed. The soldiers chased him, firing over his head, and then one bullet took him off his horse. He spun around once, twice in the air, and seemed to hang in the sky until he dropped. Dovie strained and lifted her head to look. What had been a man the minute before was only a little, dark smudge on the prairie. Way off, his horse, feeling no rider on its back, slowed its stride. Like a wind in a wheat field the shock ran over the crowd.

"'He won't be celebrating tonight,' someone said.

"'That's one less to run against,' another said without turning his grim face away from the start line.

The official rifle shots were fired. Their wagon jerked into motion, Sylvester yelling from pure excitement. Whips cracked so near Dovie, she felt the breeze lift her hair. In a wagon swaying from side to side, a man screamed, 'Nellie, Nellie,' over and over. He whipped his horse and passed their wagon though it was streaking over the ground.

Dovie had put her sights on a particular piece of land just where the stream turned. She had ridden there many times. When they came over the rise it was already staked. A wagon and horses were tethered there and two people pulling on tent ropes.

Without stopping to argue over how they got there so awfully quick, Sylvester followed the stream and found a clear spot. "Everything's going to be all right!" he said and with one boot pushed the bundle holding his mother off the wagon. It was a jolt when she thudded to the ground. The mattress rolled over and over until it came to a stop against a bump. Dovie lay there feeling dizzy. Then, shaking her head to clear it, she wriggled her way out of the feather bed and saw that Sylvester had raced on.

In one motion she opened her pack and grabbed the stakes and hammer. She planted her banner and drove a stake in one corner of the plot. Wobbly on her feet, she walked off the distance to the next corner and worked like a locomotive until she had all four corners staked.

She hung the pack on a tree and began to make a home. The same tree with the tarpaulin tied to it and staked into the ground on one side almost completed it. Dovie dragged the feather bed over, shook it out and put it in. She gathered kindling, laid wood for a small fire and ringed it with stones. Then, she sat with her back against the tree and rested.

Supper was water from the steam which she drank from her cupped hands. With it, she chewed on some hard biscuits and dried beef. When it began to get dark, she lit the fire for company and watched the flames. She slept fitfully with the gun beside her on the feather mattress.

Something woke her, some sixth sense, and she saw, across the low-burning fire, a gray wolf. It stood on the edge of some undergrowth and its shaggy coat was lit up by the firelight. For a long moment, she stared at the wolf and the wolf stared at the fire, flames reflected in its eyes. Her hand felt for the gun; if needed, she could fire a shot in the air and scare it away. She bent over her gun, and when she looked up the animal had melted away into the trees.

She stood up. There were campfires dotted over the slopes as far as she could see. Coyotes yipped and she sensed deer and possums moving in the dark, looking for their lost roaming grounds.

✵ ✵ ✵

It was several days later that Dovie dished up potatoes and gravy onto Rusty's plate. "I'm not sorry I did it," she said. "Sylvester went to the Land Office and registered both our claims. I put it in your Father's name. We've got a pretty piece of land!"

Rusty had just returned from the land run. He was washing his face and head at the pump when she looked out the window and saw him. She met him at the door with a towel. With her son sitting down at the table, she fixed him a pork chop dinner. He ate his way through the pile of food. Dovie was quiet a moment as she poured Rusty a cup of coffee. "Here, drink your coffee. You might as well take the afternoon off."

Once all the crops were in, the older two boys accompanied Dovie and the others back to Mt. Vernon. Sylvester and Rusty had plans to return and develop the land. They wanted to get in on the excitement and work of the new towns that were springing up almost overnight in Indian Territory. Jack, at thirteen, wanted to go with his brothers, but Dovie decreed that he had a few more years at home before he could be on his own.

That January 1894, Joe turned over the office of sheriff to his successor. He had been sheriff for eight years and seemed restless now that he was just a farmer again working the land at Solitude. The family was used to living in the house in town and continued there. As Dovie went around Mt. Vernon shopping, several ladies dropped remarks to her about how she was missed; Sheriff Joe seemed lonely while she was in Indian Territory, but Widow Clayton had tried to cheer him up some.

Then, Joe mentioned a property case in court concerning Louisa Clayton. Dovie noticed that he'd called her Louisa but said nothing. There was already talk around town. She felt unknown forces at work but didn't know what to do; she tried to ignore it.

For a distraction from her worries, Dovie bought Mildred a parrot, green with yellow and red wings. It sat on a stand in the parlor and could imitate Dovie's voice.

"Joe, Joe," it squawked and made Dovie and the children laugh.

That winter, Sheriff Joe spoke often of Louisa, her inheritance, and what a large sum of money she would realize from the sale of her farm.

"You can't seem to quit talking about her," Dovie said sharply to him one day. He became very silent and then seemed to avoid the house until mealtimes or after. Dovie had seen the widow Clayton in town occasionally and struggled to remember her. She had only an impression of an oval face with large, brown eyes in the shade of a lace parasol.

The next time Dovie visited the general store, a parasol of cream-colored lace caught her eye, and on an impulse she bought it. As soon as she got home she regretted her purchase and dropped it on the hall table. Before she had the pins out of her hat she had decided to return it.

That evening as Dovie heard Joe open the front gate she remembered the parasol. She didn't want him to see it and started from the kitchen, but Joe was already in the hall. As Dovie watched through the door, he picked up the parasol and touched it to his cheek for a long moment.

Dovie turned and hurried back to the kitchen, and was stirring the soup when she heard Mildred call out, "Father's home."

✳ ✳ ✳

On the evening of March 12, 1894, Sheriff Joe bid his family good-bye as he left on a business trip.

"Now, don't go and lose your key ring like you did last time," were Dovie's parting words to him.

J. Noble, who had recently taken an interest in the fact that he had been named for his father, who went by Joseph N., lamented, "But you won't be here for my twelfth birthday!"

Sheriff Joe seemed not to hear and hurried out the door.

"And we are both named Joseph Noble Thompson," the boy said as the door closed on a gust of chilly air.

Only later did Dovie hear the story. At the station, Joe boarded the train for Topeka, Kansas, and the stationmaster waved the train out of the station. Sheriff Joe only went as far as Elliott Station, where he got off and was met by a wagon. The driver returned him to a farm on the outskirts of Mt. Vernon. The driver, a Mr. Willis, later said he loaded several of a lady's trunks on the wagon and took Mr. Thompson and Mrs. Louisa Clayton to Everton that night where they took the first train for Springfield.

He had deserted his wife. The scandal was told all over town. Dovie heard it, too, and had the uncomfortable knowledge that people were gossiping about her because of her husband's prolonged absence. She had heard nothing from him and did not know where he was. C.E. had gone to Springfield looking for him.

A reporter from the newspaper knocked on her door and told her that a letter from Topeka said that Sheriff Joe had not been seen there.

"Do you have any comment, ma'am?" he asked.

She stared at him, but his eyes were darting past her trying to see into the house. She shut the door without a word. After that she peered out through the curtain to see who was there and would only open the door to her children.

Dovie began to feel like a prisoner in her own house, looking out from behind the curtain, afraid to go out and face people. *What if they ask me, "Where is your husband," what will I say?*

In a moment of defiance, she put on her bonnet and went to the general store. She was waiting for her parcels to be wrapped when she overheard her name.

"Poor lady. I do feel sorry for Mrs. Thompson."

"I saw it with my own eyes. Sheriff Joe and Widow Clayton together around town—well, a bit too often," Mrs. Livery Stable said as she talked with her friend outside the blacksmith's shop.

"I never thought, no one thought, that it would lead to this. Desertion of a faithful wife and family? The lies! The deception! And him, responsible for law and order! I can't believe it," Beryl replied.

"Sheriff Joe's never been the same since he had to hang that boy; he's been unsettled-like," the blacksmith said.

Dovie hurried home with her head down. All she could think of was to reach her door and close it on these voices everywhere discussing her and her business.

She had an appointment with a photographer for her twenty-eighth wedding anniversary, but when the day came, Joe had not returned and she didn't know where he was. Rumors were swirling about his continued absence. Dovie was up most of the night alternately making excuses for him—*he's had an accident and is in a hospital somewhere*—and blaming him—*how long has he hidden this and made a fool of me in front of everyone?*

She prepared to walk to the studio on the square just a few doors down from the jail. Dovie usually didn't bother with the curling iron, but this time she curled the front fringe of her hair around her pale face. Sensitive about possible comparisons with the hated Widow Clayton, she had dressed in a rustling taffeta dress with the gold medal around her neck.

She held her round-cheeked little girl by the hand and strode slowly along the square. People whispered behind their hands or nudged each other as she passed. A man with a chaw of tobacco in his cheek turned to stare and squirt a stream of tobacco juice on the pavement. Dovie lifted her skirts aside and walked on.

Dovie and Mildred entered the shop and sat to pose for their photograph. The photographer was businesslike as he set up his equipment. Dovie was serious, her mouth just a straight line in her youthful face. Her clear-eyed gaze regarded the camera steadily. *I am forty-five years old, I have seen a lot, but I can hardly believe that my world is falling apart.* Mildred held onto her mother and rested her face against Dovie's cheek. The child's hand and arm stretched protectively across her mother's chest, and her soft, baby face turned to the photographer in an angry pout. *She knows someone or something has hurt me but she isn't sure what it is.* Their images recorded, they returned home just nodding to the townsfolk who spoke to them.

That evening C.E. and Gus, her two married sons, came to Dovie's house with bad news for her. It had emerged that Mr. Thompson was short in his accounts as sheriff. He'd surrendered the office and his accounts to his successor January 1, 1894. After the time of his disappearance in March, the shortage of $3300 dollars was found. Dovie was in shock when she heard this.

"There's more," C.E. said grimly. "He's been charged and has surrendered everything he possessed to secure his bondsmen. He gave a mortgage on this house and the farm at Solitude. He also turned over the land and teams and growing crops in the Territory."

"My stake of land—gone?" Dovie's voice was harsh.

Gus took up the story when C.E. choked up. "He has left you and six children with no home and in destitute circumstances. The man has lost his senses. Everyone in town is sympathetic to you, Mother."

"He has thrown away honor, friends, and family. I can't understand it." C.E. shook his head with tears in his eyes.

"I will fight this to the bitter end," Dovie said. "Get me a lawyer."

As they went out the door, the parrot began to call out, "Joe, Joe," mimicking Dovie's voice.

They all stopped and stared at the parrot. It cocked its head and watched with a shiny black eye as Dovie gave a strange sound like a whimper.

"Joe, Joe!" it called until C.E. pulled the cover over its cage.

✢ ✢ ✢

In May 1894, Dovie sued Mrs. Louisa Clayton for alienation of the affections of her husband and asked two thousand dollars in damages. The suit said that beginning in January of 1894, the said widow did seduce and debauch and carnally know Joseph Thompson, Dovie's husband. Mrs. Clayton's property was about to be attached, and unless she appeared before August 1894, a judgment would be rendered against her and her property sold to satisfy this two-thousand-dollar claim.

That August, after waiting for the last possible moment, Mrs. Clayton asked for a change of venue. She had returned to Mt. Vernon very briefly to attend to the matter of her property and collateral that had been attached by Mrs. Gwendolyn Thompson. When Mrs. Clayton went to do some banking, she encountered such a hostile questioning from the banker's wife, Jane, that she fled the town.

"Mrs. Clayton insisted that she had not seen Mr. Thompson since leaving Mt. Vernon," Jane told Dovie and added, "She refused to reveal where she was residing."

In November, ex-sheriff Joe was indicted for embezzlement and Dovie was called in to testify. In the courtroom, she heard the clerk say, "Geraldine Thompson." She felt a flush of anger; they didn't even get her name right. She glared at the clerk.

Dovie's lawyer rose and called for a correction: "The name is Gwendolyn Thompson."

The clerk scribbled and then read the corrected version.

Dovie had not laid eyes on Joe since the night in March when he bid the family good-bye and went out the door as though he would return from a business trip in a few days. The chance to look him in the eye and make him ashamed of what he had done gave her the strength to appear in court today.

Across the courtroom, Dovie saw Joe; he sat at the table beside his lawyer but kept his forehead leaning against his hand. Only a glimpse of beard and shoulder were visible. She wanted to tear his hand away to make him look her in the face. He had hidden from her again.

She took a deep breath and stared straight ahead as she answered in a clear voice, "Yes, I am his wife. He left our family destitute. I have six children at home, the youngest only five."

The State vs. Joseph Thompson was declared wholly or partly ended because Joe had surrendered everything he possessed to make bond for the missing money. He might subsequently have to pay more.

His former colleague, the mayor, had been called as a witness for the prosecution. Afterwards, outside the courthouse, Dovie heard the mayor comment to his friends, "He says he was only careless in his bookkeeping and meant to make good on the money. Sheriff Joe was like a tree in a flood when all this happened; the waters were just too strong for him. He lost his footing and was swept away."

People will find excuses for him, Dovie thought, *but that's no help to me and the six children I've got to take care of*.

In March 1895, a year after he had left, ex-sheriff Joe filed suit for divorce from Dovie.

When Dovie read him the legal paper, C.E. went rigid with anger.

"I'm calling a meeting. I'll get Sylvester, Gus, and Rusty, we're the oldest sons. I've located where he's living."

"You know where he is? Why didn't you tell me?"

"He's with the widow Clayton; I didn't know how to tell you. We'll demand a meeting. The four of us, we're going to tell him."

"Tell him what?" Dovie asked.

C.E. nodded grimly but didn't answer.

* * *

Later, Dovie heard the whole thing from C.E. When he put his plan before them, the younger brothers felt queasy about it.

"I have never allowed the boys to be anything but respectful and obedient to their father," Dovie commented.

C.E. nodded and continued his story. "I looked each one in the face until they made a vow to take up for their mother and younger brothers and sisters."

The day of the confrontation, the four grown but young men gathered nervous and sweating in the front parlor of C.E.'s house. No one sat down in the stiff velvet chairs. Just as the front doorbell rang, C.E. strode over to the wall where the framed portraits of his mother and father hung side by side. He turned the picture of Sheriff Joe's face to the wall.

Joe entered the room to find four young men, his sons, standing in a row. He tried to stare them down, but his eyes faltered and he looked away.

C.E. stepped forward and said, "We won't stand for it. You are not to leave our mother for this—this woman, or we will shut you out of the family. No one of us will ever see you again. We are united in this."

He turned to the others and they nodded with strained faces.

Joe's eyes fell on the portraits with his turned to the wall. He flinched as though he had been struck.

"You will never see any member of your family again, not children, not grandchildren," C.E. continued. "If you do this to our mother, none of us will ever even speak your name. It will be forgotten."

"Even little Pete? He wouldn't forget me," Joe said.

"Pete will be guided by us if he has no proper father."

At this Joe turned away. "I—I have to think. I haven't thought clearly in a while. Tomorrow, I'll send my answer tomorrow."

He left abruptly, and through the window they could see his tall, thin form rushing away down the street. Rusty found a balled up handkerchief in his pocket and wiped his forehead. The brothers stared at each other. C.E. shook each one's hand as they filed out.

"Now what will happen?" Dovie asked. She paced around the room in her distress.

The next the brothers heard was a letter from their father. He had left the widow Clayton and broken off the suit for divorce from Dovie. He was leaving for Ft. Smith, Arkansas, where he was to be trained and sworn in as a United States marshal with jurisdiction in Indian Territory. Beyond that, he did not know his plans.

Indian Territory

The family couldn't stay in Turnback County, they all felt that. Dovie regretted leaving the town that had become home with its big houses, sloping lawns, and shade trees. Her solid, red brick church was a presence in her life. The women's circle exchanged recipes and with them she had made watermelon pickle or apple butter when the crop of apples came in every fall. The literary club that she had started would have to be left behind. *Who will visit Floy's grave now*, she thought, *or put flowers there on Decoration Day?*

Dovie decided that they could get a new start in the Territory. Turnback County represented civilization, and she would have to leave it to go to a muddy, raw place. She would try to make a new home—not knowing if her husband would join her or if she wanted him. She had been lied to and humiliated. Others in town had known or guessed the truth about Joe and the widow. She avoided the ladies in Bible study and swore to herself that she was finished with anything but the plain, unvarnished truth.

She prepared to sell most of their belongings to raise some cash. To avoid having the townspeople come in and pick over her things, she called in an agent from Joplin.

He went through the house and she followed him. Her skirts brushed against the tables and chairs that had been part of their daily lives. She hesitated next to the needlepoint-covered stool. Oleva had labored over every flower and leaf. Dovie whisked it into a closet and closed the door firmly. "Not this."

The buyer made notations in his book. He looked at the battered breakfast table and scratched down some figures.

"Worth very little," he said. He repeated it often.

Dovie felt worse and worse. At the end he toted up his columns and offered her sixty dollars for the lot. "Remember, I have the expense of carting it all away," he said.

She needed more to make the move to the Territory. Dovie brought out her gold school medal. "What will you give me for this?"

He held out his hand for it and she handed it over. He examined it.

"Pure gold," she said.

"Engraved with a name—that detracts from its value. No one wants someone else's name on anything. Two dollars and fifty cents." He was watching her face. She shook her head. "Well, I could go to three—three dollars and that's my limit."

Dovie took it from his hand. "No. I won't part with it. Settle up for the rest and you can go."

Soon after that, she left town. All that was certain was that she would have most of her children around her and try to get a fresh start. Dovie had kept back a cow from the sale and walked most of the way leading it so her children would have milk. At night on the journey, Dovie's legs hurt her so that she sent Rusty to find water and fill two pails. She soaked her feet and legs, trying to get some relief from the pain. Rusty made johnnycakes, a thin gruel of cornmeal and water cooked on a broad knife blade over the open fire. They ate it hungrily with salt pork and apples.

Their new home in the Territory was near Black Jack Grove. When Dovie saw the rented place, her eyes ticked off the details. A small, unpainted board house stood amid ragged trees and stumps. The door hung crooked. She pushed it open and went in. The ceilings were low but had two lofts with a bed each. With six children, they would be crowded. She sat down on a bench and rubbed her forehead. She felt a draft on her neck and looked up. There was foot-long chink in the wall. The children were running in and out the door.

Noble stood in front of her and said, "Ma, where will I sleep?"

"There aren't enough beds," Pete chimed in.

Dovie sat up. "Rusty, I'll need you to fill that open place in the wall." He looked at a loss. "Get mud and grass. Noble, everyone will have a place to sleep. Now, you do your part to unload the wagon." It had rained recently and they had to struggle to get the horse and wagon near the door. That night at bedtime, Dovie tucked the children in to sleep two lengthwise in each bed and one across the foot. She and Rusty each had a pallet on the floor.

Dovie had to get used to being poor again. Shelagh's children, now grown and established in their own lives, helped her with rent money. She settled in as best she could. Months went by and they had no word from Joe, but she would not allow her sons to speak ill of their father.

And Lily! Dovie brooded over her, married at twenty to a good-for-nothing. She was such a beauty, tall and graceful with blue eyes and a queenly air. She could have had anyone, but instead chose Wade Francis. He'd caught her eye back in Mt. Vernon when he came around with his guitar and easy manner and she never could see anyone else after that. While Sheriff Joe was still at home, he ran him off once with a shotgun and told him to leave Lily alone. Lily had taken advantage of her father's absence to marry the fellow when he followed them to Indian Territory.

Now, Oleva, eighteen, was keeping company with a young sheriff of the Tulsa district, Lon Lewis. Dovie noticed their interest in each other from the first time they met in the new place. Dovie was out by the barn when the two came to tell her they planned to marry. Oleva was embarrassed to see that Dovie had tied knots in the four corners of a handkerchief and had it on her head.

"Oh, Mother," Oleva said and removed it.

"It keeps the sun off," Dovie said and shrugged.

Oleva seemed to be making a good choice, but Dovie thought of marriage as a leap in the dark and could only hope her daughter would land safely. The couple was still talking of all their plans and their future as they left her.

Dovie stood looking out over the field of golden wheat waving in the wind. She, too, had once had a plan of how her life would be. She picked up the rake and went on working. The sound of crows cawing loudly behind her back seemed to mock her.

☆ ☆ ☆

Sheriff Joe showed up the day of the wedding between Oleva and Lon Lewis. He had a knapsack with him and set it down at the threshold of the cabin. He didn't enter the door but held out his arms, and his favorite son, Pete, ran into them.

Kneeling and holding Pete close, Joe spoke to Dovie. "I hope you will accept me back."

The last time she had seen him was over a year ago across a crowded courtroom. He had hidden his face from her. She looked at him and saw his eyes above the beard. He was paler and thinner, kneeling but not penitent. She felt a wave of anger.

However, this was what she had wanted, for him to come back to her. It meant that she had won her battle with the widow Clayton. In her mind she saw the dark, twisting oaks at Solitude and felt the loss of her home.

"You will have to cut off your beard," she said.

His hand went up and stroked his long beard. "Here?" he bargained, indicating halfway.

"No, clean-shaven, or you don't enter this door." She spoke and turned her back on him.

He took his knapsack and walked into the yard, where he propped his shaving mirror up on the limb of a tree. Pete ran eagerly to get him some water in a tin cup. Sheriff Joe mixed up some lather and started work with the razor. Clumps of dark hair tinged with gray began to fall on the ground to reveal pale skin on his jaw and neck.

He returned and stood in the doorway with his face bare. It was the first time anyone in his family had seen him without the cover of a beard, and his children stared but didn't dare speak. Dovie looked him over. His white chin and long, skinny neck showed red nicks of the razor. She nodded. He stepped over the threshold and into the house.

Some of the older boys were still angry and barely spoke to their father. He went around to each one and offered his hand instead of an apology. They did shake his hand, but grudgingly.

* * *

At the wedding that afternoon, the guests talked about the Jennings brothers and their latest escapade, a bank robbery in Ponca City.

"The Al Jennings gang, they are now," one of the men, Mr. Simpson, said, "but I knew them as boys."

"And I know the father, Judge Jennings over in Woodward. There were four brothers, all lawyers before they went wrong," Sheriff Joe added.

"How did they get to be the Al Jennings gang?" Pete asked.

"It all started when Ed Jennings and Temple Houston, the lawyer son of Sam Houston, had a dispute in court. Tempers flared pretty bad, and they all left in anger. Later that night Ed was shot to death in a saloon. Well, no one was charged." Mr. Simpson took a breath and settled back to continue his story.

"That's when Al and Frank Jennings started out to avenge their brother's death and got into robbing stores and banks in the towns around here."

"They joined with some other outlaws and began robbing trains." Sheriff Joe said. "When they stole money shipments and passengers' valuables the marshals went looking for them. We'll get them sooner or later."

"It has got so if you are on a train and have a gold watch you can hardly get out of the Territory with it," Mrs. Simpson added.

A few months later, in November of 1897, Joe got word that the Jennings gang was holed up at the Spike S Ranch, about four miles south of Bixby. He began to gather a posse to go after them. The first ones he called on were his son, Gus, and his new son-in-law, Lon Lewis, also a U.S. marshal. Two other marshals joined them, bringing warrants and two more men. The seven men gathered at Joe's house during the night. They left quietly before dawn, with only a creaking of leather saddles and the soft whinnying of horses, to set out for the Spike S Ranch.

When their dust trail had about settled, a big mare exited the Thompson's gate with two boys on its back.

"Pete, close that, the cows will get out and we'll get a whipping."

"Keep the horse still. Ma'll whip us anyway if she finds out," Pete whispered but leaned back and latched the gate.

Noble kicked Big Bessie's sides with his bare feet and the horse moved on. Noble and Pete followed the plume of dust that rose over the distant riders but always kept their distance.

In the still darkness the marshals surrounded the ranch house. The two boys kept inside the forest, leading Bessie. Noble and Pete looked for a likely hiding place when a figure on a horse loomed up beside them. It was their mother who put her finger to her lips and frowned. She motioned them over to a ravine and the two frightened boys stepped down. The place was overgrown with scrub trees and vines but they stood by the little creek there and looked between branches for a view of the farmhouse and barn.

Lon crept up on the lookout who was sprawled on a hay bale, sleeping. The marshal tied him up and stuffed a bandanna in his mouth so he couldn't make a noise. The three hidden onlookers strained to see what was happening.

As sunrise began to lighten the horizon, the ranch house door opened and a man, rubbing his eyes, came out to feed the stock. Noble tensed with excitement and elbowed Pete to look. They watched their big brother, Gus, wait for the man at the barn door and capture him.

As the sky became a pale gray, a bird rustled in the bushes next to the boys and they jumped. Dovie petted Big Bessie's neck and whispered to her, afraid she would whinny and give them away.

The ranch house was still just a dark shape when a light winked on in one window. Soon a woman, pulling a shawl around her, came out the door calling for the man who hadn't returned. Lon grabbed her as she came into the barn, showed her his badge, gave her orders and sent her back to the house.

"The gang won't come out, they won't surrender," Dovie whispered when two women and a child were put outside and the door closed behind them. Those three ran from the house to the barn.

Shots were fired from the barn and answered from the house. Bullets began to fly thick and fast, then zinged a tree branch and it fell, just missing Pete. Noble saw his brother's face drain of color and become as white as the mist hanging over the creek. They heard shouting and saw figures run across the open in the smoke-filled air. Pete and Noble crouched low, afraid to breathe.

Three bandits bolted out the back of the house. Dovie and the boys saw that one was wounded and limping, but the others managed to tug him onto a horse. It was a terrible moment for the observers. If they yelled a warning they knew the first reaction of the posse probably would be to fire in their direction. The boys watched the gang's horses disappear in dust before the posse knew they were gone. When their shots weren't returned, the lawmen ran to the house. "Empty," they heard Gus howl. Yelling to each other, they got on their horses and chased after the bandits.

The two boys looked at each other. Without a word, Dovie mounted her horse and turned toward home. The boys followed.

They rode in silence a good way. Pete spoke first, "Ham, hot biscuits and red eye gravy." The sun was climbing in the sky and he had eaten nothing for many hours.

Dovie whirled on them. "You not only endangered yourselves, you put the whole capture at risk. The minute I heard the posse leave, I heard you two going after them. I can't believe I have two sons who are so reckless."

Noble and Pete hung their heads and shifted around on the horse as the worst of her tirade came down on them. When she finished, Dovie saw that they looked hungry and ashamed. "And no bragging about seeing the gunfight and the gang— absolutely none." She rode on toward home with the boys trailing behind her.

Later that night, the lawmen, tired but jubilant, returned to the house and told their story. At first, the gang eluded them. Lon Lewis knew that there was only one place to cross Cane Creek and get away. He led the group of marshals there and they set to work to fell a large tree so that it blocked the road. There, they laid in wait and ambushed the gang when they rode up.

The capture at Cane Creek Crossing was talked about all over the territory. The Al Jennings Gang that had plagued the area surrendered and went to jail. Dovie and her two sons kept quiet about their part until well after the excitement had died down.

✲ ✲ ✲

With Joe's return to the marriage, the family resumed life; and things might have seemed normal, but Dovie could remember when she had felt close and confided in her husband. That was no longer true. *I don't know why he left me or why he came back so I am always wary of him.*

One day, Mildred, seven years old now, looked closely at the oil painting of the wolf. It had been salvaged by Dovie from the breakup of the house on Cherry Street and now hung on the wall under the low ceiling. Mildred got up from her chair and stood on tiptoe to look more closely. The plump, fair child studied the scene. A wolf stood alone in snow at the edge of an icy stream, his head thrown back in a howl.

"Why do you have that picture on the wall?" Mildred turned and asked her mother. "I don't like it."

"It reminds me of the bad times," Dovie said and thought a minute, "and that I've come through them one way or another."

✲ ✲ ✲

It was a remote place where they lived with no other house anywhere in sight. Dovie was out in the yard where she had a fire under a big tub and was boiling water to do the washing. Three men rode up.

Dovie looked up and saw their unshaven faces and bleary eyes. She saw their boots and trousers stiffened with mud and the horses' legs, mud-spattered.

228

"We want food," one of them demanded.

There was no one else on the place; all the family was gone. Dovie heard the extreme quiet in the clearing; even in the woods there seemed to be no sound. The place had never seemed lonelier.

"Wash up there at the pump," Dovie said and went in the house. She heated up beans, corn, and spoon bread and poured milk to wash it down. As they crowded into her kitchen, she picked up her Bible and held it like a shield in her arms as they sat down at her table. She dished up the food and began to quote scripture at them. "And the Lord saith..." She never let up until they swallowed the last bite, got up hastily, and left.

When Mildred got home from school that day, Dovie had mopped the kitchen floor clean of the dirt the men had tracked in and was resting with her feet propped up on a footstool. When she was alone, Dovie liked to put her legs up and smoke a pipe near the open window. It gave her a pleasant sense of lassitude and temporarily eased the pain in her legs. She hadn't even mentioned the visitors yet when Mildred got a horrified look on her face. She had caught sight of the knotted and protruding varicose veins in her mother's legs. Mildred went straight to her room to check that her legs were still smooth and white.

When C.E. heard the story of the rough guys' visit and how Dovie had handled them, he shook his head in admiration and said, "Wouldn't you know, Ma Bibled them over."

✳ ✳ ✳

As a deputy U.S. marshal for the eastern district, Joe was gone much of the time. He did not get a salary, but got paid for jobs such as transporting prisoners and testifying in court. He and Dovie quarreled a lot now; their underlying anger bubbled up to the surface over any little thing. Money matters or the children could cause a fuss. Only Noble, Pete, and Mildred were at home now. Rusty was married and on his own, and Jack was off working alongside Sylvester.

The first week of March 1898, an army officer was on the town square in Muskogee recruiting men for the Spanish-American War and, more particularly, for Teddy Roosevelt's volunteer cavalry. Roosevelt had a commission to form a unit, and he wanted the kind of men he had seen on his trips to the West—rugged and tough. One of those who stepped forward to join up that day in Muskogee was a ruddy, brown-haired, blue-eyed cowboy, Sylvester Thompson.

When the family heard that Sylvester had signed up, Joe said. "They're trying to kick Spain out of Cuba so American business can go in."

"Why does Sylvester want to go and get himself killed for that?" Noble asked.

Dovie said, "That one step forward," she held her head in her hands. "How many men have taken that step? And now, my son goes into war and danger."

Sylvester wrote home. *The volunteers are eager, one walked sixty miles just to join up. Right away I met a Pawnee Indian and a Baptist preacher. We have every kind of guy in this outfit.*

I joined up just after a little guy with a handlebar moustache named MacNulty. I asked him how a little guy like him got in the regiment. He said my other name is Bronco Buster and spat tobacco juice. Just missed my boot.

Sylvester wrote home often and gave a running account of his new experiences which Dovie read avidly. *We ride, shoot, and drill every day. If you read about the Rough Riders, then you are reading about your son because I am one of them.*

I will never forget my first sight of Teddy Roosevelt. He had on leather riding gloves with cuffs to his elbows and a wide hat brim swooped up on one side. I wish every one of you could have seen Colonel Roosevelt up on his horse, Little Texas. He was like a monument standing on the flat desert, and I was proud that he was our leader.

My buddy, MacNulty, was up close to Colonel Roosevelt, but all he talked about was the funny spectacles on Roosevelt's nose and his big, toothy grin.

In his last letter from the training camp, Sylvester wrote, *There's a horse called The Bucker in camp, and every man had a bet on his favorite to ride it. Naturally, I bet on MacNulty and he didn't disappoint me. I saw him earn his name, Bronco Buster, by hanging on to the back of the Bucker for four minutes. Minutes seemed like hours while he was tossed around but he won a nice pile of money for himself.*

MacNulty paid two bucks for a photograph of the two of us, which I have enclosed. The photographer said, "Show your weapons," so we drew our pistols. Training is over and tomorrow we ship out.

Dovie studied the photograph. Her son's eyes shone in his tanned face as he leaned forward in unison with MacNulty and held a big pistol in front of his chest. *He's having a good time, going to war,* she thought. *That can't last.*

In his next letter, Sylvester told how once they got to Florida the men were sat down in a field and a chaplain preached to them: *But in the hot sun and with only tall, thin trees that gave no shade, I hardly heard a word he said—sorry, Ma. When we sailed for Cuba, some men climbed the rigging of the ship for a last look at home.*

In Cuba, the heat and damp are unbelievable. Wading across rivers with a full pack on my back and hacking a path on land is no fun. We will attack the Spanish when and where we find them.

When the newspapers arrived on July 2, Dovie read that the day before Teddy Roosevelt led the Rough Riders and others up Kettle Hill and captured it. Roosevelt, on foot after losing his horse, rallied his men and they charged down Kettle Hill, across the valley, and up San Juan Heights.

When Sylvester's next letter came he told the family, *Roosevelt called our charge his "crowded hour," and it certainly was full of bullets whizzing by. One bullet knocked his glasses off, but he had several spares in his pocket. A bullet grazed my arm and felt like a hot poker on my skin, but I kept on following the colonel. Bodies were falling all around me in the tall grass.*

At the top of the hill, two Spaniards were left; the rest had run away. But those two shot at Roosevelt, who fired two times, missed the first man and killed the second. We captured the heights, and who do I see but MacNulty. We were hugging and yelling, glad we had survived. When we looked down on

*Santiago, I knew the war was just about over. Only then did I
see that my leg was bleeding and had been shot.*

Dovie read the newspapers for every bit of news looking for
clues about how her son was faring. There were high casualties and then tropical diseases began to kill even more soldiers
with dysentery, yellow fever, and malaria. *What kind of care
is Sylvester getting? The doctors probed his leg wound but
couldn't remove the bullet. They said he would have to live with
it. I'm worried and I never get enough information.*

The Secretary of State called it "a splendid little war." Dovie
threw the paper down with a cry of anger when she read that.
Roosevelt and others called for the Americans to be shipped
home quickly to save lives.

Sylvester wrote that he *"looked around him at the American
soldiers killed, wounded or down with disease. One out of every
three the reports said. I wonder how I survived when Roosevelt's
outfit had the highest casualty rate of any American unit in the
war."*

Sylvester was excited to return home, a Rough Rider, a hero.
He swaggered with importance; the U.S.A. was now a power
in the world, and he had played a part in that. The United
States made a treaty with Spain that allowed them to occupy
Cuba and take over the Philippines, Guam, and Puerto Rico
as well.

When Sylvester was due to arrive home, some friends met
him at the depot with a band. As he stepped into a carriage
decorated with "Old Glory," he waved and lifted his bandaged
arm. He walked stiffly on his wounded leg.

Dovie and Joe were waiting in front of the house when
the carriage brought him home. His mother looked for the first
sight of her son's face. She saw the same bright-eyed look that
she knew but then her eyes went to the wounded arm. Anger
flooded over her. *They've hurt his arm,* she thought. Pete ran
forward to carry his rucksack.

"Be careful of that." Sylvester tapped the canvas.
"Champagne. Two bottles. I want to celebrate once I see the
faces of my family around me at the table."

"Well, I had a good night of hunting and we got four possums in brine and ready to roast," Pete replied.

Dovie led Sylvester to the best chair and saw that his stiff leg was propped on a footstool. His family sat around him on lesser chairs and admired the bronze medal of his regiment as he showed it to every visitor. He told over and over of the charge up San Juan Hill and said, "I shot a hundred rounds, and the Spaniards fired enough shots to kill all the people in the United States if they had hit them."

Each new listener gave him rapt attention, but the younger brothers became restless on the third or fourth telling. Rusty whispered a plan to slip out of the room one at a time. Noble was on his feet when a rap of Dovie's cane stopped him and he slunk back to his seat. A stern look from their mother fixed the other two in their places. Rusty, behind the cover of a chair, took out a knife and pared his fingernails. Pete fidgeted the long afternoon away, bored by talk of heroism.

When the aroma of roasting meat filled the house, they said good-bye to the last of the visitors and finally sat down, just the family, to a dinner of possum and champagne.

✳ ✳ ✳

While Sylvester was away at war, Joe made an effort to restore the family finances. He rented some land nearby in Creek County and moved there to farm it. He lived in a room in a boardinghouse during the week and was sometimes lonely; he had no one even to quarrel with. After a year passed, he had a chance at a job as jailer at the county jail in Sapulpa. He would be provided housing back of the jail. He rode over and asked Dovie to move there with him. On the grounds that the school there would be better for the three children still at home, she agreed.

Rusty, Noble, and Pete wanted to try cattle ranching and persuaded their father to try it. They pooled their money and leased land for the new venture.

Joe had always been a farmer and grown crops. He could deal with one mule for plowing, but Dovie knew he had no patience with "dumb animals," as he called them. Now, as a rancher he had a new horse, Tony, a saddle horse, black with a star on his forehead and two white socks.

Pete, now sixteen, was good with livestock. He told Joe, "Tony is the hardest horse to put a saddle and bridle on, but he's a wise animal and independent. He's different from the plow horses you know, Dad."

Dovie rode out to see their first roundup and was just in time to see Sheriff Joe get impatient with the dust and confusion and turn angry. Pete heard him cursing and turned to see Joe slash Tony across the head and ears with his reins. Pete opened his mouth to protest just as Tony pointed his ears forward and started off running. Dovie put her hand over her mouth as the horse went straight to a big sycamore tree where he scraped Joe off his back. Joe landed in a heap on the ground.

"They have a mind of their own," Pete tried to tell his dad as he helped him to his feet.

Sheriff Joe set his mouth in a grim line and didn't look Dovie's way even though she called out, "Are you all right?" He climbed on Tony's back once again.

Dovie heard Elvin, the ranch hand, say in a low tone, "The slower you go, the quicker you get through." Dovie saw that he knew better than to try to tell his boss how to do a roundup. Elvin had learned patience the hard way. He had only one finger left on his right hand; the rest he had lost in an accident. She knew he had practiced until he could rope with the best of them.

Back on Tony, Sheriff Joe could only herd the cattle by driving them along the fence. Dovie shook her head; she turned her horse and headed back to the house. She had cooked hot biscuits with pork chops and gravy for everyone's breakfast. She had done her part to make the roundup a success; now it was up to the men to do the hot and exasperating work all afternoon.

She turned back for a last look and saw that a couple of cows just wouldn't be driven. In frustration, Joe gored Tony with his spurs and cursed him. Tony ran right into the cattle that had been rounded up and scattered them. Then he brought his rider alongside a fence post and dumped him again in the dirt.

✵ ✵ ✵

That fall there were terrific rains, and the creek on their ranch was swollen to a muddy torrent. Dovie riding her horse, Brownie, saw that three cows were stranded on ground that had become an island surrounded by rushing water. She brought Joe, on Tony, and Pete, on Lassie, there to save the animals.

The cows were bleating and rolling their eyes. The rain had plastered their hair into rough swirls. Pete coiled a rope and went out into the swift water. His horse stepped sideways, not liking the situation, but Pete urged her on. He tugged and pulled and got the three cows in a line with rope around their necks. They voiced deep distress as they were pulled into the stream and led towards Joe on the bank. Pete on his horse and the three cows were all slipping and sliding.

One cow managed to get halfway up the bank. Dovie ventured out into the water and tugged on the rope. Joe was behind her pulling and got one, then two to solid ground. As he was hauling up the third one, Dovie's horse stepped in a hole and staggered. Joe turned just in time to see Dovie swing sideways and fall underwater. Brownie struggled on with an empty saddle. Joe froze to the spot for a moment before he kicked Tony's sides. He kept his eyes riveted to the spot where he saw Dovie's head go under. He urged Tony forward but they floundered in the mud. Seconds seemed like years.

Joe screamed, "Dovie, Dovie!" Pete turned toward them. At the spot, Joe leaned down and searched with his arm under the brown surface. He made a wider sweep, combing with his fingers. He turned and reached deeper. Fingers touched and grabbed his fingers. The two cupped their fingers in a grip. Joe pulled, leaning low out of the saddle. Tony staggered but then bowed his neck and planted his hooves supporting Joe. Dovie's head broke the surface, and Joe tugged her hand. Bit by bit, with Tony hesitating and then stepping, horse and man dragged Dovie up on the bank. Pete was yelling and trying to move through the water.

Dovie lay in the mud, gasping and coughing, half turned so water could run from her mouth. She had mud and saliva on her chin and her sodden skirts were twisted around her legs. Her husband laid his hand on her and then sank to the ground. Pete reached them and Joe looked up, seeming dazed. "You saved her, you saved her life!" Pete said as he pulled his mother into a sitting position. She sat, propped up in a puddle of water, and her eyes met Joe's before she closed them and slumped. The cows bawled and Tony and Brownie rubbed necks.

Later, when Dovie told her family about the accident, she said, "I can't get the taste of creek mud out of my mouth. I can't forget my skirts like a weight dragging me down." She held up Joe's hand and said, "This hand grabbed mine, I knew it was my only chance."

"Well, Tony helped a lot. Without that horse," Sheriff Joe shook his head. "He understood as well as any human what needed to be done and did it."

* * *

C.E. and his wife, Minta, and their three children left Mt. Vernon and moved to Beggs, Indian Territory in 1901. C.E. had a loan to build his long-dreamed-of drugstore on Main Street. All the family was settling in Beggs or on ranches nearby. Rusty, Noble, and Pete pooled their money and bought land outside of town, which they divided into three cattle ranches. Dovie lived in Sapulpa and had her family all within an easy distance. She felt happy again when she saw them prospering and settling on their own land. There were now seven grandchildren.

One of them, Melville, was from Rusty's first marriage to a wife who had died. He was kept by C.E. and Minta until he was eight years old and Rusty had remarried. Then Rusty came to get Melville and brought a horse for him to ride back home. When they rode up to Dovie's house, the boy was a hundred yards behind his father.

"He's done that the whole trip," Rusty complained.

"Now, son," Dovie told Rusty, "remember the boy's had to leave all that was familiar." It seemed like an echo of her own experience when she left her home in Wales. "To him, you are practically a stranger. Give him time to know you as his father."

* * *

Oil was discovered near Beggs. It came in with a rush that sounded like an explosion and sprayed oil over the top of the derrick. The land was an allotment to a woman who was one-eighth Creek Indian. The Glen Pool, named after her husband, Mr. Glen, turned out to be a very big find of oil. It was 1905, and as word of it got out the rush was on.

Even though there was not a paved road in the territory, people flocked there from all over the country and the big companies moved in to explore. Not too many years before, Tulsa had been a town of only three stores and about four hundred people. Now, the railroad brought people rushing to the oil fields. They, in turn, needed supplies, and Tulsa boomed. Texaco Company leased and drilled the three Thompson brothers' ranches and found oil. It seemed that the black gold was under all the land there.

One day Rusty, with Melville in the buggy, came by to get Dovie. "Come on, Ma, come with us over to Pawhuska. I'm going to show you two the 'Million-dollar Elm.'"

"How long are we going to be? I've got bread rising," Dovie asked, but she put her bonnet on and hurried out.

After traveling lanes in open countryside where their dust trail was all the company they had, the buggy entered a narrow spot hemmed in by vines. Dovie saw wild blackberries, but Rusty wouldn't stop.

"No, I got to get to the auction," he said.

Soon they began to see others heading the same direction they were going, three men on horseback, then a wagon full of Indians and two buggies off in the distance.

Their buggy passed several little wooden houses, and then in the shade of a large, leafy tree they saw a milling crowd and the auctioneer, who stood on an overturned crate with a sheaf of papers in his hand. He adjusted his spectacles, read silently, and then cleared his throat to call out, "Lot number twelve, offered by Mr. Jim Porter, near the town of Sperry, never drilled."

A big oil company representative bid against a speculator. The representative puffed furiously on his pipe as the price shot up. In the time it took Dovie to dismount from the buggy and join the crowd, thousands of dollars had been pledged. She looked from one man to the other, hearing a shout of forty thousand. She saw a puff of pipe smoke and heard fifty thousand. *Dollars*, she reminded herself. Jim Porter was a farmer with a creased leathery face under his cap. He looked like he had never held more than ten dollars in his hand before that day, no different than most of the people in the shade of the elm. "Sold," the auctioneer called, and the victorious oil company man knocked his pipe against his shoe to empty it.

By the time they left, Rusty was satisfied that he and his brothers could do well here another day. They went home through Red Heart, named by the Indians there. Oil was discovered right in the street downtown, and the owners drilled and put a rig pumping there. Rusty started to complain when they had to drive around it in their buggy but stopped and laughed at this unique sign of the new prosperity.

Dovie looked around her and saw the oil frenzy disrupting the Indian way of life even further. She knew they held land, sea, and air sacred. Land was the center of the universe and to be used and tended by everyone. A person who set himself up as an owner of private lands was seen as greedy and acting against nature. But she had as strong a drive as any of the whites to have her own place and manage it and keep it for herself and her family.

Land the government thought was worthless had been given to the Indians. Dovie saw that those who had head rights, which meant that they were on the tribal rolls as having Indian blood, owned much of the now-valuable oil lands.

Dovie was indignant over the story of an Osage Indian man, Jim Runningwolf. First, he became very wealthy and drove around in his new, fancy car. She saw his children abandon Indian-style clothing and wear the suits, dresses, and hairstyles of the Americans. But then, Runningwolf got into a rigged card game, lost his land, and ended up working for the white man who had cheated him. The man cheated him again by paying him only a pittance for his labor.

Sometimes the Indians were on top in this shifting world. Dovie's son, Jack, lived in Red Heart, where his brothers had found him jobs maintaining oil rigs so he could support his family. Money was a problem for his family, and his son, Bobby, had to sweep up the theater for tickets when the traveling shows came to town. A full-blooded Creek boy, Tom Two Moons, whose family had head rights money, sat in the theater eating popcorn and candy. He had bought his own tickets and walked in right past Bobby wielding his broom and being "careful of the corners" as the manager had instructed him.

Gus and his wife, Minnie, found oil on their cattle ranch. When the first royalty check came in, Dovie asked them what they were going to do with it. "Nothing, just bank it," Gus replied.

When the second check came in, Gus told her, "I want none of this buying and overspending that others are doing."

Minnie wanted to see Europe and all its wonders. She confided this to Dovie but said nothing at first to her husband.

Along about the sixth or seventh large check, when Gus saw that they were pulling this money out of the ground regularly, he went to downtown Tulsa and bought the biggest car they had, a Curved Dash Olds. He sat up high and drove, scattering the chickens out of the road with liberal use of the horn, a bulb he squeezed to make an *ugga-ugga* sound.

Minnie felt put out. Dovie advised her to broach the subject with Gus. Minnie began hinting mightily and Gus never got his plate of chicken and dumplings without hearing the words *Paris* and *London*. But Gus had a hankering to see the mountains of Montana, so they took their children on a long trip out West.

Back at home Minnie told Dovie about the lavish trip into the wilds by horseback and carriage. All the fine baggage they took was strung out over a long, winding trail, carried by hired helpers. They stayed in a lodge in the mountains where they saw bears and eagles. "Once we saw a herd of gazelles leaping and running but I vowed that I would see the Eiffel Tower and Versailles."

"Your trouble is that you were brought up to think that women should let men do all the talking. You tell Gus to take you to Europe," Dovie advised her.

Minnie continued talking of France and England to Dovie and the maid who was mopping the floors in the log ranch house. That very day, Minnie confided, a white horse grazing in the field had looked up at her. Her listeners nodded, for this was a well-known sign. "Good luck coming," the maid said.

The next day Minnie was able to tell Dovie how that afternoon Minnie let one thing and another get in the way and when Gus came in from the horse barn there was no dinner on the table. He went and washed up and sat down at the empty table. After a minute he bawled, "Minnie!"

She appeared around the corner of the kitchen door. "Gus?"

He took a deep breath. "You know, Minnie, that about the only thing I ask of you is dinner ready and on the table at six o'clock."

Minnie rearranged the salt-and-pepper shakers on the sideboard, carefully putting the salt on the left of the pepper. She sighed deeply. "Yes, Gus, that's true ..." She moved the salt back to its original position and looked at it.

"Gus has dealt with many a balky animal in his time," Dovie commented.

"He agreed that evening to take the family to Europe," Minnie ended triumphantly.

Minnie divided Europe in half, and they went two weeks to the first half. Dovie welcomed them when they came home to Tulsa. Minnie kissed her and said, "We're going to rest a month and go back for three weeks to do the second half."

"How did you like France, Gus?" Dovie asked.

"That Eiffel Tower," he shook his head in wonder, "if they'd put sides on it, it would hold a lot of hay."

* * *

Pete got himself a car and learned to drive it. Then he began to work on Rusty to get one, too. Rusty took Pete with him to the car dealer. "Heck, I don't even know how to drive the thing home," Rusty said. Pete gave him a lesson, explaining over and over the crank, the steering wheel, and the horn.

The next morning Rusty started out to drive his new car, got her cranked up, and got in. Dovie was doing her errands on the town square when a new automobile veered dangerously near the sidewalk. She moved away from this conveyance only to look up and see Rusty leaning out to tip his hat to her as he narrowly avoided a horse and wagon.

"Keep your hat on and steer," she advised him and entered the bank with the bullet holes all around the door, still there from the robbery by the Al Jennings gang. As they ran out with the money, Al had turned and shot a spray of bullets to keep anyone from chasing them.

When Dovie emerged there was Rusty in his automobile circling again. "Can't you stop that thing?" she called out. He hunched over the wheel looking desperate. He went another round and then saw a friend. "Hey, call Pete Thompson to stop this thing!" he yelled. On the next circle he began to call out to everyone, "Call Pete Thompson!" Someone found Pete, who came running and managed to jump aboard and put on the brakes. The two brothers climbed from the car and sat on the curb laughing. Dovie exited the square at a dignified pace but when she turned on the side street, she was laughing too.

✧ ✧ ✧

The Indian Territories became a state under the name Oklahoma in 1907. Sheriff Joe heard that President Theodore Roosevelt was due to drive right past his ranch on a visit to the new state.

"This calls for something big. We are going to greet the president Oklahoma style."

Every person and horse on the ranch turned out fixed up to look their best when the president drove by. Elvin Graves rode Little Jim, a round, short horse, and his wife, Leota, was on a Shetland. Dovie wore a new Stetson hat and the three Thompson boys had on their best shirts with bandannas around their necks. Whistles and praise greeted each one who rode up to join the group.

Rusty carried the brand new flag of Oklahoma. Sheriff Joe held the stars and stripes, furled and balanced in front of the saddle horn. Tony, his handsome black-and-white horse, was looking particularly good with a red blanket under the saddle.

At first they talked excitedly; then time passed and they let the horses mosey around a little just to relax them.

"Maybe they aren't coming," Pete said.

Dovie lit two lanterns to light the group up as evening was falling and the president had not yet come.

Then out of the dusk came a motorcar full of uniformed men, then a large, shiny, black car with a flag whipping in the wind. Rusty held up the Oklahoma flag. Sheriff Joe unfurled the United States flag. Elvin twirled his lasso high above his head, the one-fingered hand as nimble as ever. The others swept off their hats until the procession passed by.

"I'm afraid he didn't see us," Dovie wailed. "I waved the lantern up high to show Elvin's lasso."

"They went by so fast," Pete mourned. Their exhilaration now drained away and disappointment crept in.

"No," Noble piped up, "I saw President Roosevelt. He turned and waved out the back window."

✵ ✵ ✵

It had been peaceful between Joe and Dovie since he rescued her from drowning. Then, an old argument between them, that she spoiled Mildred, came up again.

"An automobile! She's too young and irresponsible for such a machine," Joe argued.

"She is fifteen, almost sixteen," Dovie said. "Nonsense, she wants a car and I can give it so she will have it. Thank you for your advice."

A week later, when Dovie opened the door and saw the minister all in black and the police officer on the porch, she slammed the door in their faces. She knew what news they were bringing. Mildred had left in her new car only an hour before. When they stepped inside, there in the little hallway, the minister told her that her daughter was already dead, smashed up against a tree.

Mildred's parting words were, "I am riding to glory," as her little cousins watched her drive away. Dovie's hands trembled so that she could not close the door when the two men left.

When C.E. came to comfort his mother, he saw that her stare was vacant.

Dovie said, "I am already dead. I still walk, but this has killed me."

Then the next April, C.E. died at forty years of age. He had been working on his accounts at the drugstore one night, and a kerosene lamp overturned and started a fire. He tried to put out the flames and was so badly burned that he died. He left Minta a widow with four children. The youngest, Avadna, was five years old.

The day of his funeral, Dovie watched her daughter-in-law walk down the church aisle. Her taffeta skirt rustled and she wore a gold watch on a chain, but her face was suddenly sunken and frightened. The three little girls clung to her skirts when she took a seat.

Dovie stood across the open grave from the new widow and her children. She saw Avadna with a scared look on her face. When the coffin was lowered into the ground, the child began to weep.

"Are you going to let them put Poppa in that dark, cold place?" Avadna said tugging on her mother's skirt. Minta patted her youngest on the back but was speaking with Brother Lindsay, the preacher. Dovie went to Avadna and picked her up.

"He's not here anymore. He's gone away."

"Well, I want to see my Poppa."

Dovie struggled for something to say that would soothe her. "Your Poppa's in heaven now. He's safe and happy with the angels," she told the child. She felt that she was repeating what people had always told the grief stricken, a pretty story to try to make them happy.

C.E.'s widow and four children needed her help. It was deeply painful for Dovie to stir herself out of her grief over Mildred and now C.E. She had outlived her youngest daughter and her oldest son. To begin to think and feel again was like trying to make the first weak movements of an arm that had been broken. She had to come back to life to help her family. It was the only thing that could even get her attention, lost in despairing thoughts as she was.

C.E.'s oldest child, Raymond, had to quit school at twelve to help support the family. Dovie saw that he got a job on Rusty's ranch. The drugstore business could be sold or leased to provide some income. Dovie took charge.

How can I grieve for these two that I loved so much? she asked herself. *I don't know how to go on without seeing them every day. If only I could talk to Mildred.*

She found a pencil and paper and sat down at her table. Dovie rearranged the slant of the paper several times and then wrote, *Today is warm and I see the first thin asparagus spears on our plants. I broke one off and ate it right there in the garden. I think spring is here.*

Dovie rummaged through her cabinets and found a nice box, which had held tea. She placed her note inside it and made a special place for it on her bureau.

Then a few days later, she saw C.E.'s oldest daughter with her hair out of braids for the first time. She sat down and wrote to him.

I saw Opal today. She is not wearing braids anymore. With her smooth face and shiny hair, I could see how she will look as a young woman.

Soon the box, in its place of honor, was filling up with notes.

✷ ✷ ✷

When Tony was old and dying, Joe stood over the suffering horse but couldn't fire the bullet that would kill him. Joe paid a horse doctor twenty dollars to come out in an ice storm and put him down. Tony was given his own grave, marked with a stone carved with his name. And then, only months later, Joe died while being operated on for appendicitis.

At Joe's coffin, Dovie bowed her head and whispered, "All the mistakes we made."

Once his funeral was over and the mourners had left, Dovie sat down. There was a bulging envelope on the table.

One by one, she unfolded the rustling papers of varying sizes.

"Two black horses to pull the hearse. Thirty dollars, paid in full."

"One suit of clothes, twenty-five dollars." *He'll wear that for eternity*, she thought.

"Casket with hearse from Reed Bros, Pianos, Organs, Furniture, Carpets and Undertaking, $60."

The estate was listed: shovel; iron pitchfork, bent; one black mare, seventeen years old; one brown mare, ditto; twelve head of hogs; one red cow and calf; one spotted cow, dehorned; mule cart, black; one-half interest in twenty-four acres corn in field; five tons of hay; one old mower and rake; one old hay frame. Cash on hand $50.00

She called Oleva in and told her, "When I go, my rocking chair goes to you. Give my Bible to Lily. She needs religion with that husband who can't seem to keep a job."

"Of course, Mother, I'll do whatever you want, but don't talk of this now."

"Nonsense, Oleva. Open that bottom bureau drawer."

Oleva bent down and pulled open the drawer.

"I want to be buried in my good, gray dress," Dovie continued.

Oleva saw the gray wool neatly folded and slammed the drawer shut.

Dovie looked down at her feet. "I guess these shoes will do. Bury me with the pictures of Mildred and C.E. in my coffin."

"Oh, Mother! I'll do as you wish but..." Oleva broke into tears.

✳ ✳ ✳

In her old age, Dovie had a bank account that her sons had given her. Behind her back, the town gossips said she gave her money to anyone with a hard-luck story.

"Excuse me, Ma'am, I know I look dirty but I got no place to wash at. I am hungry and thirsty,"

Dovie turned and, first of all, saw the girl's feet. She wore high top shoes with the laces tied up in many knots where they had broken and been repaired. Then Dovie's eyes traveled up to the dress, a kind of lifeless and wrinkled cloth of an indifferent color.

"I ain't had nothin' to eat since yesterday," the girl whined.

It was then Dovie looked at her face, young, with scraggly hair tied back wilth an unraveling ribbon. "Have I seen you before?"

"Well, I work at the Bumble Bee Café but I'm in back. I wash and clean."

"What's your name?"

"Josie!" a man's voice yelled through the window of the café. "Go on, you don't work here anymore."

"Who's he?" Dovie asked as the girl followed her on the walk home.

"That's Mr. Beale, the owner. He wouldn't open the door."

They walked a minute, the girl following. "Why not?" Dovie turned to face her.

"Late, just a little bit. It's not *my* fault. My landlady is supposed to wake me up and she forgot and now I got no job." Josie twisted her foot in the dirt. "And I'm hungry."

"Not your fault? I see. You need some food," Dovie said and started for her backdoor and the girl rushed along with her. "Wait here," Dovie told her.

Josie stopped in her tracks. "I'm too dirty to come in your nice kitchen. I know it."

At those words, Dovie stopped and looked closely at her. *This is how dirty life gets you. Miz Presley said it and then I repeated it and now–.* Dovie handed the girl soap and a towel off a shelf. "Be washing up at the pump." *You can wash clean and live a good life.*

Dovie came out of the house a few minutes later. "Do you have any relatives, Josie?"

"Maybe, back in St. Louis." Josie was gobbling a biscuit and ham. "I had a Aunt Versa."

"Josie, I want you to go find your Aunt Versa. You need your family."

"You mean I can get out of here?" Josie left with folding money in one hand and still gnawing on a piece of ham in the other.

The next day Josie boarded the train wearing a fancy red dress. Dovie, passing by, saw that it was the train going west not east for St. Louis. Josie leaned out to wave the town of Beggs goodbye. Dovie waved her white hanky. "It's up to her now."

When he heard of this, Noble chastised Dovie, saying, "Ma, you are giving away money my brothers and I meant for you."

Dovie drew herself up and said, "You must stay out of my business." She rapped her cane at him and he said no more.

Her sons had built Dovie a house right where she wanted it overlooking the fields and open country in Beggs. She felt very satisfied with her frame house at the top of a green meadow. Her daughter Oleva was widowed and came to live with her mother there.

Pete, Rusty and Noble were partners in business. They had built a very fine office building on the prime corner of downtown Tulsa. The Thompson Building had ten floors. The polished granite foyer was lined with shining brass cuspidors, and there were not one, but two elevators.

If she was shopping in downtown Tulsa about four in the afternoon, Oleva often saw a man with a creased, tanned face and merry eyes under the brim of his beat-up fedora. He would be leaning against the granite front of the Thompson Building. Later at dinner she would tell Dovie, "I saw Rusty today. He had gravy spots on his tie and scuffed shoes," and they would both smile.

Rusty's second wife, Louise, was in despair over his habits because this was not some fellow down on his luck but co-owner of the building, awaiting his chauffeur to pick him up in a big Packard car.

"Louise told me she goes though his closet periodically and has everything sent to charity," Oleva said.

Tulsa continued to be such an oil-boom town that the brothers were soon adding on five floors and a penthouse to the Thompson Building. Pete told Dovie he would like to live in the penthouse up high where he could see all the way to the Arkansas River and the bridge their partnership was building across it at Twenty-first Street.

Dovie went to see Rusty's grand, new house in Tulsa. It had been a long time being built and was now finished. She stood in the columned entrance. With her eyes a pale blue that seemed to reflect far skies and waters, Dovie looked out over the gardens, but she thought of Wales, once her home and now so distant. She wished Shelagh were here with her. Who else would understand? *This is what we dreamed of—going west and finding riches.*

She could hear the mourning doves calling, one long sigh and three short moans. They still lived here, remaining through all the changes from wild field to pasture and now to formal garden.

There were over two acres of gardens and paths. New vines were trained around the aisle of stone pillars leading up to a large, solid house of three stories. Under her feet were marble floors inlaid in patterns of pink diamonds inside white circles divided by richly veined gray marble strips.

She stepped with her plain shoe in the center of a circle. She had dressed carefully for the visit with the gold medal, her school prize long ago, on its chain around her neck. At the last moment, she had picked a bunch of wildflowers in back of her house as a present. In the time it took to travel from country to town, the petals had already shriveled and the daisies drooped on their stems. Dovie paused with the wilted bouquet in her hand and listened. It was so quiet that water falling from the fountain made a loud sound. Oil brought from deep in the earth had made this airy, fanciful place. She left the wilted bouquet on the rim of the fountain; Louise wouldn't like such common flowers anyway.

She didn't bother to knock; this was her son's house and she went on in. This was where the guests in their silks and satins would enter for the ball the family anticipated. Dovie looked up. Animal horns, thickly mounted, bristled overhead. She saw the long, slender antlers of elk, curved horns of mountain goat, branched deer antlers, and the dainty horns of antelope. The chandelier was of moose horns like great ragged wings hanging over her head. It was reported that Louise was upset—"a nightmare to dust," she complained. Rusty had insisted and there they were. "Let the maids do the dusting," he had told her.

Dovie started up. The stairs were covered in flowered carpet. At the first landing was a chair, corded and tasseled, a table, a lamp, and a vase of dried grasses and peacock feathers, even an embroidered footstool. She went on, but after a few more stairs she returned and sat in the chair to get her breath.

She had hoped to avoid the elevator. She felt nervous about closing herself in a metal box hung on wires. Now, with a push of the button, she summoned the elevator and stepped in to the contraption. She wanted to see the ballroom on the third floor. There was endless speculation about when the first ball would be given, and it was rumored that the governor had promised to attend.

When the elevator door opened on the top floor, she saw long rows of windows curtained in maroon velvet and tied back with gold, tasseled cords. Gilt chairs were spaced along the walls. As she stepped in, the floorboards creaked under her feet. She walked to the center of the enormous room. It was hot up there under the roof, and she could hear the gurgling of pigeons in the eaves. Maroon and gilt and emptiness—she turned and left.

Downstairs again, she seated herself on the gallery. If she wanted tea, Roy, the butler, would serve it; she had only to ring.

Louise, who was perfecting her refined ways, had admonished her, "We ring, we do not shout, for the butler."

Dovie's wiry wrists were tough as cord, and her white hair was wound around her head in a crown of braids. One hand held the worn knob of her cane, ready to hoist herself up. She rapped her cane. Once her legs stopped aching, she would be up and getting home. She had lots to do; there was never an end to it.

The End

Made in the USA
Charleston, SC
17 March 2013